Wiz

Duos

Book 2

Wiz Duos

Book 2

Juliet Kemp & E.M. Faulds

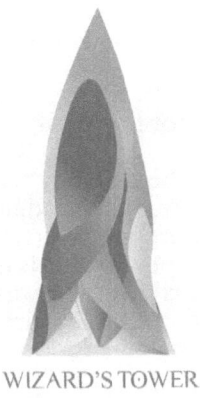

WIZARD'S TOWER

Wizard's Tower Press

Rhydaman, Cymru

Wiz Duos

Book 2

Stories by Juliet Kemp & E.M. Faulds

Edited by Roz Clarke & Joanne Hall

Text © 2025 by Juliet Kemp, E.M. Faulds, Roz Clarke & Joanne Hall

Cover art by Roz Clarke
Cover design by Ben Baldwin

Book design by Cheryl Morgan

First published by Wizard's Tower Press,
May 2025

ISBN: 978-1-913892-98-2

http://wizardstowerpress.com/

Contents

FOREWORD

By
Roz Clarke & Joanne Hall

Both of us have always loved the novella as a story form: long enough to open out and permit the author to explore a well-rounded tale in a fleshed out world, yet keep that story sharp and concise. It is a real delight to share these stories with you.

Here we present two works that could both be described as highly original transformation stories, with characters growing and coming into their own, but they are very different in terms of setting and tone.

Juliet Kemp's 'Song, Stone, Scale, Bone' is an entertaining adventure, following the quest that Cade, a knight from an order of pathfinders and protectors, finds herself on after she loses her confidence and taste of adventure due to the death of her companion Graf. It touches on many of the themes you might expect – there are rival political factions, an ailing king, bone-mages, dragons, ghosts and knights at arms. But nothing about this story is predictable. It is funny, fast-paced and action packed, yet also thoughtful and moving.

Juliet carries the reader along with effortless ease, and delivers a satisfying ending at the end of the dragon-flight.

E.M. Faulds' story, by contrast, is SF, set in a near-future world in which space colonies are draining human talent from an Earth ravaged by environmental disaster. Two sisters on opposite sides of the world are facing their separate crises. Selen is in that rebellious teenage phase, and in her efforts to impress her peers she gets a piercing with a difference – elagite, a spacetech alloy, knits with human DNA and can unlock your latent talents. Selen is trying to fix the holes in her life – her lack of identity, the absence of her sister, the contempt of her boyfriend – by putting a literal hole through herself.

In Australia, her sister Phoebe is sent by the government on an undercover mission to infiltrate a cultish group of environmental activists. This is a far more dangerous situation than Phoebe is equipped to handle.

In this tense and compelling story, Faulds explores the challenges of making meaningful social connections when you aren't sure who you can trust, coping with threats from both outside and inside yourself, and personal transformation. When a hole has a point of connection at either end it becomes a tunnel, and tunnels can be travelled through – journeys that can change individual lives and sometimes the world.

Song, Stone, Scale, Bone

Juliet Kemp

SONG, STONE, SCALE, BONE

1.

This was all wrong.

The duty-spot felt familiar. The bench was as comfortable as ever, the blue-grey tiles as smooth under my boots. The road out in front of the chapterhouse looked exactly as it always had.

But it shouldn't. It should be different.

And I shouldn't, for my preference, be here at all. But Sir Belaran had finally decided I'd spent enough time helping him—"hiding in the archives" were his exact words, screw him—and put me back on the duty roster. So here I was, watching the spring sun make shadow-patterns through the leaves, waiting to see if anyone needed a guide today.

It was quiet. The wind rustled the trees, and a lark sang somewhere high in the clear blue sky. I glanced over at the rough grey stone of the Archive, the oldest part of the chapterhouse. In there, Belaran would be at his ceaseless humming: rehearsing old guide-songs; creating new ones from information delivered by my knight-siblings; teaching them to whoever came by for updates. One of the reasons Belaran had refused to let me become under-archivist, when I gave up waiting for him to say something and asked flat out, was that my memory might be good enough, and I could cart boxes around with the best of them, but I was no teacher. I'd argued with him—I *could* do it if I just tried harder, and I so badly wanted just to stay here and let everyone else go off out, though I didn't say that part—but he just smiled understandingly at me, the bastard, and said the thing about hiding. That was that.

An hour more until my shift ended, then after lunch I was due in the kitchen gardens out back of the chapterhouse. I shifted my stiff leather breastplate on my shoulders. If I was lucky...

I wasn't going to be lucky. There, coming through the gap in the hedge that led to the red-brick building housing the saal, was the Archon, still upright in her grey robe despite her advancing years, accompanying someone towards my duty-spot. I stood and straightened to attention, hand on my sword-hilt, as they drew near.

"Daughter," the Archon said, bowing to me. "Your service is required."

Bugger. "I serve at the will of Siremos," I said.

The Archon turned to the woman with her, and gestured towards me. "This is Sir Cade, Knight of Siremos. She will guide you on your path. Sir Cade, Lady Arel of the Family Xeria requires your assistance."

"I serve at the will of Siremos," I said again, a statement you can't go far wrong with as one of our order; and took a good look at Lady Arel.

Her dark hair was tied up in complicated braids that I presumed were this year's aristocratic trend, and her pale skin looked like she never set foot outside her family's compound. Rather unlike my own sun-baked look. It would be a lie to say that knights aren't bothered about their appearance—we can be as vain as you like in the right circumstances—but fashionably pale isn't really an option when you make your living riding around guiding people and waving your sword about as necessary.

But then there was the very practical shirt and trousers she was wearing. In my previous experience of guiding aristos, *practical* wasn't a feature.

"What is my lady's will?" I prompted her. If I had to do this, I might as well get on with it.

"I wish to visit the catacombs," she said.

Which was unusual; we trained down there, but there weren't many visitors, and hardly ever aristos.

But of course that was where she wanted to go, because it was precisely the place I absolutely, categorically, did not want to go, ever again.

However. I was still in the Order, and an oath was an oath.

"Very well, my lady," I said, and ignored the way my stomach turned.

"A brief visit, then," the Archon said comfortably. The catacombs were a bare couple of miles from the chapterhouse.

"I wish to go to the mausoleums," Lady Arel said.

The Archon looked as surprised as I did.

"Ah," I said. I looked sideways at the Archon, but this was my responsibility now. "I am sorry, my lady. The route collapsed six months ago." I didn't let myself think about that. "We no longer have a guide-song past that point." The Archon nodded in regretful agreement.

Lady Arel's chin went up. "You are the Knights of Siremos, no?"

"...Yes?"

"You are obliged to guide."

That was, technically, true.

"Our visitors rarely wish to put themselves in the danger of having no guide-song," the Archon said gently.

"And yet," Lady Arel said, "in this case, I do. Are you refusing to take me?"

The Archon looked at me.

I could get out of it, if I wanted to, without dishonour. There was no guide-song. The Archon would find someone more comfortable with that risk. But.

I'd taken an oath. I hadn't *wanted* to be standing back out here again. I hadn't wanted to leave the quiet safety of the archives. But here I was, standing in this familiar spot as I had so many times before; and I was a Knight of Siremos, sworn to guide.

"As you will, my lady," I said. "But I do not know the way. No one does."

"Then we will find out," she said. "And you will have a guide-song for the next person."

She smiled at me, but it didn't reach her eyes. Those were determined, and... worried?

Huh. What did she want down there, anyway?

"We will equip you correctly," the Archon said, which ought to go without saying, but I read it as the Archon reminding me she had my back, and it warmed me.

"Then let us away," Lady Arel said, and led us briskly back towards the saal and the stores. I trailed behind, wishing I wasn't there at all.

I could have done with it taking longer to get kitted up, but we didn't need much. We wouldn't be out overnight, even if we made it past the collapsed part; the catacombs were potentially dangerous, but they weren't large. I'd expected to have to sort Lady Arel out with more or less everything; aristos don't usually think about this stuff. But no: she had knife, flint and steel, a water-bottle, some wrapped bread, and a thin blanket, all tucked into a neat haversack. I took a little more—rope, for starters, and more in the way of weaponry—but then I was supposed to be the one doing the carrying. We both bowed our heads for the Archon to bless us, and set off down the path towards the catacombs' entrance. She was striding out swiftly, like she was in a hurry, shoulders back, not slumping under the weight of her bag. I eyed her sideways. All in all, I was curious about Lady Arel. Her clothes were good quality, but practical; she'd packed a perfectly sensible kitbag; and she wanted to go poke around the catacombs, which wasn't a customary aristocratic sport. It interested me, despite myself. Foolish. It doesn't do to get too interested in clients. Do what you're told, stick your sword in whatever needs a sword stuck in it, get out. That's what Graf always reckoned.

She caught me looking, and gave me a brief quarter-smile. "Sir Cade," she said.

"Lady Arel," I said. I *wanted* to ask what was so important that she didn't care there wasn't a guide-song, but that wasn't my business. Our oath covers guiding, not judging the value of the trip.

Doesn't stop you being curious.

"Have you been to the catacombs before?" she asked.

I snorted. "Course. We all have. We train down there. I mean, it's convenient, right?"

"Train to navigate?"

"First song any of us learn," I said. "Half a song, now. And it's good combat practice."

"Combat practice?" I glanced over again. Her eyes were wide.

I rolled mine. "Did you think we'd just happily skip through there with nothing to bother us? Why do you think I have this bloody big sword?" I've taken an oath to *guide* people, not to be polite to them. Which is handy, because I'm all right at guiding but not much good at being polite.

"You are a knight," she said stiffly. "Of course you would have a sword."

"Fair. Well. I might need it. Minitaurs, caroths..."

13

"You have encountered them before?"

"First time I went down I was a novice," I said. "They send a few proper knights down with you in case anyone gets stuck on the song, and to whack the beasties if need be. My— Graf," I hoped she'd missed the hiccup, "was determined we wouldn't need any help. We did pretty well, to start with. Saw off a swarm of minitaurs." I saw Graf's exultant face in my mind's eye. He'd barely been old enough to shave. "Graf wanted to find a caroth. I figured I would just as soon not. We were arguing about it when the biggest spider I've ever seen dropped straight down onto his nose. Never heard anyone scream like it. He belted straight back the way we'd come, and I scrambled after him because we'd been told to stick together no matter what. Every proper knight in the place heard him and came running too, and they all clattered into each other at a crossroads like something out of a farce-play." I grinned. "He got latrine-duty for a month, and I got it with him because—" because he was my sword-brother, but I couldn't get that out, "apparently I should have stopped him. Dunno how, he was twice the size of me back then. I got my growth spurt late, and Graf was always a big lad."

Lady Arel was smiling, properly this time. "I hope you made him pay for it."

"Been a joke between us ever since," I said. Had been.

And there was the entrance. I gestured. "Here we are. Onwards, my lady."

2.

The catacombs are much like you'd expect: stone; dark; slight smell of damp; strong tendency to moss and algae around the edges. They were the city once, before the city sank, somewhat dramatically according to all the songs, a few centuries back. It sank (and the residents who hadn't had things fall on their heads all upped sticks and moved a couple of miles south to a nice solid hill), but it didn't, mostly, fall apart. The earth just kind of...grew over it. Or rather, trees grew and tangled together into a sort of roof. It would all have become root bound, except the Knights of Siremos took on the job of keeping the streets passable. Maintaining our history, according to Belaran. He knows a lot of old and often contradictory songs and poems about it, but the gist is that we took it on for love of the city.

The Court families are very into their history. I ought to be, but in all honesty, I joined more for the bit where you get to guide people all over the world. Turned out more of it is close to home than I expected, but there you go. We all make decisions we don't fully understand the implications of in our youth, don't we?

Anyway. It's damp down here, and only a little light comes through the tree roots. I turned my hands over one another, muttering the rhyme, and my guide-light appeared.

"This way, my lady." I started along the main road. The cobbles were moss-slick underfoot, and buildings in various states of ruin loomed in the shadows to either side. Grey stone, mostly, like the oldest chapterhouse buildings.

Lady Arel, beside me, was looking around her, but still moving fast. "I have never before been down here," she said, in the tone of one making conversation.

I couldn't *ask*, but I could... suggest that I was interested. And it genuinely might be useful to know. "If I knew your purpose here, my lady, I might be better able to help."

She was silent for a moment, before she sighed. "Well. I suppose there is no reason for you not to know, and it might help. I am my family's archivist. You know what that is?"

"You can recite all your ancestors," I said. "Something like that." Like Sir Belaran, but for stuff the Court cared about. As I understood it, not that I'd ever been that interested, family history and associated matters was the foundation of both law and entertainment for Court families.

"Well, yes, but not *only* that. I know the stories of my family, and our history. I can *tell* them, well and truly. And I keep the archives." She hesitated, glancing at me.

"The oath binds me to confidence, if that helps," I said. I was really curious now.

Her lips tightened, then she jerked her head in a sharp nod. "The foundational bone of our family has... gone missing. And Court formally convenes tomorrow."

"Gone missing?" Didn't sound like particularly good archiving to me.

"Stolen," she said, in a voice that could have cut diamond, and marched faster, head up and back straight, right past me. "So I must go to the graves of my ancestors."

"Look. If you want me to keep you safe in here, you need to stay *behind* me." I pushed firmly ahead of her, ignoring her huff.

The mausoleums were beyond the roof-fall, right enough. I considered what she'd said. There're bones in our archives, too, but we don't use them the way the families do. We don't need to prove who we are; we just have to keep the oath. "You need a new foundational bone."

"Without the bone, we cannot prove we are entitled to be at Court. Without the bone-ritual, there *is* no family. Of course, in theory," now she sounded sarcastic, "I might not be challenged tomorrow. It happens rarely, and usually it is," she waved a hand, "political jockeying. An insult, of sorts. Causing trouble for one's enemies. Except I most certainly will be challenged, because someone *stole* my bone."

"You're certain you didn't just lose it?"

"I *assume* that you do not intend insult."

"Uh. No. Sorry." I glanced over my shoulder. "Honestly, my lady, I didn't mean to, um, impugn your honour."

"Very well. I accept your apology. I assure you, I know my job, and my responsibility." I believed her. Or at least, I wouldn't dare contradict her. She wasn't that big, but she was looking pretty scary.

"Right. Course." I considered the matter. "Have you considered stealing it back? Rather than, for example, traipsing through badly lit caverns?" We'd reached a junction marked by the remains of a statue, water dripping on it from the earth above. I hummed the next bars of the guide-song, and turned right, into a narrower passage. The houses here had been wooden, and had mostly rotted away.

"I did consider it," she said, to my surprise. "I know who has it. But I do not know where, and in any case they most likely destroyed it."

"Harsh."

"It's *Court*," she said, as though that explained everything.

Well, she was dedicated, and determined, I'd give her that. And she'd gotten ahead of me *again*. I bit back a growl, and took a couple of brisk steps to catch up.

"I must insist you let me lead, my lady. Since I am the one with the sword. That being why you hired me."

She made a dismissive noise. "Surely it cannot be dangerous so close to the entrance."

That was when the minitaurs charged us.

Minitaurs aren't large, but there's a lot of them in a pack and their horns are sharp. Lady Arel tried to smack at them with her knapsack, which was the opposite of helpful. I hip-checked her into a corner and laid about me with the flat of my sword. They're pests, minitaurs; you'd feel an idiot massacring them when you only need to scare them off, but you can't just ignore them.

Eventually, I upset enough of them that the rest decided we weren't worth bothering with and fled, shrieking. I checked around for any other movement before I went over to Lady Arel.

"My lady? Are you injured?"

"If I were," she said ominously, "it would be because you *pushed* me into a *wall*."

"My lady. I have a sword. I am trained to protect you. I cannot do that if you are *in my way*."

"Hmmph. What were those, anyway?"

"Minitaurs," I said. "Not seriously dangerous, but they can rip your ankles up something shocking, and if you fall over they're suddenly a whole lot worse." I'd seen someone once—a dead someone—who'd been swarmed by minitaurs. Their hooves were just as sharp as their horns.

"Minitaurs," she repeated. "And you mentioned caroths. Right. Our nanny used to tell us stories about dragons. And eralin. I suppose that's just something to scare children with, though."

My stomach clenched. "No dragons down here these days," I said. "But eralin, nope, not just stories." I did my best to fake a smile. "Rare, though. Very unlikely we'll run into one."

"Have you, ever?"

I pretended I hadn't heard her. "Come on. Let's get going."

She didn't ask again, but I didn't miss her assessing look. Didn't matter. My oath holds me to the truth when I speak, but it doesn't oblige me to speak. I didn't owe her that story, or any other.

We covered a fair amount of ground in silence before we rounded a corner and I came face to face with a caroth.

Bugger.

Caroths really are dangerous, and you're not going to convince one to lay off you without a proper fight. On the other hand, any Knight of Siremos, or indeed of anyone else, would be ashamed not to be able to see off a caroth; and Lady Arel had the sense to stay back this time.

Once you're in a fight with one you need to finish it: they won't stop tracking you, and if they contact another of their nest, you've got two of the things on your trail. Thankfully they're too single-minded to take advantage of that and deliberately run for help; that or they don't realise they're losing until it's too late.

But they do know how to put out a guidelight. After I'd got the first blow in, and seen the shine of blood, it reached up, caught the guidelight in one giant furry paw, and squeezed it out.

Don't try that at home. It doesn't work for humans. Either we're not furry enough, or caroths have a different sort of magic than we do.

I was expecting Lady Arel to shriek, but all I heard was an indrawn breath. "Stay where you are," I called. "Don't want to run into you by accident."

Caroth magic might be different from ours, but it's still magic, and in the dark, with nothing else to confuse me, I could tell where it was. Lady Arel I couldn't, other than by knowing where I'd left her and where *I* was. I was counting on my ability to remember both things and keep track of the caroth at the same time. No time to recite the light-rhyme; no point when the caroth would just put it out again.

There was a limit to how long I could manage in the dark, but thankfully the rest of the fight was short. I dodged a couple of blows from the caroth's long paws, the second time by only the barest of margins, feeling fur brush past my cheek; then got it through the heart. The caroth-magic flickered out as I heard its body slump to the floor. I stood for a moment, breathing hard, before I could manage the light-rhyme.

"Ugh," Lady Arel said, succinctly, as my guidelight flickered back to life.

The caroth wasn't a pretty sight. I'd gotten away with a couple of small scratches.

"Do you need help with that?" Lady Arel asked, nodding at the wound on my arm.

"Nah," I said, and began the wound-song. "*Once there was skin, whole and entire, sing it together, together again. Here there is blood, to knit it together, to remember and knit it together again. Once there was skin, whole and entire, sing it together, together again...*" and it was done. It had been kind of her to ask, though.

Lady Arel's eyebrows were high.

"You must have seen healing magic before, my lady."

"They do it silently at court."

I shrugged. "Quicker this way. And the magicians in court are likely better. We're a bit rough-and-ready."

"Bone-magic is sung aloud. Though I suppose with that you must."

"Songs are rituals are truth," I recited, thinking of Belaran.

She prodded at the caroth with a toe, then looked up. "Well. How much further?"

20

I shrugged. "Another mile or so to the roof-fall. After that I don't know."

"Are there likely to be any more caroths?"

"Maybe," I said. "But that's what I'm here for." The fight had cheered me up. Probably something about getting the blood pumping.

"I would *slightly* rather you need not prove your valour all over again," Lady Arel said tartly. "Let us go."

She tried to take the lead again, but this time when I stepped in front of her she didn't huff. Instead she muttered something that might even have been 'sorry'.

3.

I hadn't been looking forward to this bit. I'd been hoping, in all honesty, that we'd have to tap out earlier. But the minitaurs were just a nuisance, and while the caroth was more than that, obviously I wasn't about to be defeated by one, and I couldn't quite countenance faking it. Also, if I'd faked it, it might actually have killed me.

But I really hadn't wanted to get here.

We stood on the edge of a bloody great chasm. Just beyond it was an equally large pile of rocks where the houses on either side had come down when the hole opened up.

I remembered it well, thank you.

It was dark. The trees overhead had grown in thoroughly, the earth had caught on their roots, and undergrowth had established itself into the earth-and-root matrix. Together it created a full roof.

Lady Arel looked perturbed. I bit back "told you so", because it would be poor form and I was supposed to be a knight and all that.

"That is... a very large hole," she said, eventually.

"Told you so."

Her chin went up. "How do we get across it?"

"For my money, we don't," I said. I didn't want to be here, and it was her fault I was.

She didn't look at me, but her shoulders tightened. "I will go on. If you are unwilling to go further, I am happy to release you from your duty."

Which wouldn't help, as it happened. She wasn't at the end of her journey, and she wasn't safe. By the terms of my oath, she was still my client. I couldn't just leave her here.

I did consider it, just for a fraction of a second. Then I saw, in my mind's eye, across the chasm from me, Graf. His tawny hair pulled back into an untidy queue, his arms folded across his broad chest, leaning against the wall behind him with one boot propping him up. Just the way I'd seen him last.

Well. Not quite last. But I wasn't going to think about that.

Imaginary-Graf looked at me and raised an eyebrow.

Fine. So I wasn't going to abandon my client.

"I'm coming with you," I said, tightly.

"I admit that is a relief," she said, shoulders easing as she turned to throw me a quick smile. "You know more about this place than I."

"That's my job," I said, instead of 'didn't help much last time'.

I stepped forwards, gesturing Lady Arel back when she tried to join me, and peered down into the pit.

My guidelight bobbed downwards. Yeah. Still a bloody deep hole. You could get to the bottom, if you were motivated, and even back up again, but I doubted Lady Arel would manage the climb and I wasn't keen to repeat the experience.

I've got magic, but it's not the sort of magic that builds invisible bridges across chasms. Which left us with rope and a grappling hook. The classics are the best.

I sent the guidelight to the side. Better than I'd thought; there were enough bits of broken stone sticking out that I could climb across. Wasn't keen on Lady Arel trying that, though.

"Well?" she asked eagerly.

"Shush," I said. "Right. I need you to stay *well* back from the edge until I tell you otherwise, yeah?" I glared at her until she nodded.

On my third try, the grappling hook held on the other side of the chasm. I was all too aware of how badly this could go wrong. I yanked on the rope as hard as I could, throwing my whole weight against it. Nothing shifted. I did it again, just in case; then tied the rope tightly around my waist and started the climb across.

It was easy enough, despite the fear coiled low and slippery in my stomach. (Despite the memories I wasn't thinking about.) I was waiting to miss my footing, the whole way—nearly did, once, but only nearly. Then I was over the other side, and unwinding the rope from my waist.

"You want me to do that?" Lady Arel asked, a betraying squeak in her voice.

"Not especially."

I untied the grappling hook and tied the rope to a bit of house wall, then the rest of that end around my waist, in case the wall went. "Right. I'm going to throw this to you, then you're going to loop it around that pillar," it was bloody lucky, that pillar, perfectly placed, "and throw it back to me." Practical. Concentrate. Don't think beyond what's happening right now. My hands were steady. I was doing my job.

Once she'd done that, we had two strands together, which still wasn't much but it wasn't like she had to walk across it. I got out another rope, tied that one round my waist too, and threw the end to her. "Around your waist," I directed her. "Good and tight, please." Should have done that myself before I went over, shouldn't I? But I watched her carefully, looked over the lines of the knot once it was finished, and she'd done a decent job. "Right. Now, you're going to sit astride those two ropes there, and you're going to pull yourself along on your arse. You understand? One leg each side. Nice low centre of gravity, hard to fall, and I'm on this rope," I gave it a tug, "if anything goes wrong."

Give her credit, she didn't balk. She swallowed, hard enough I could hear it all the way over the other side of the bloody great pit, and then she sat down gingerly on the edge, and slid along the ropes, just like I'd told her to. Slow but steady.

My heart was in my mouth, and that fear was still there, squatting cold at the base of my stomach. My breath echoed oddly in my ears. I could feel Graf hovering over my shoulder. Graf never even had a chance to get hold of a rope. Graf...

Lady Arel was nearly at the other side, nearly within arms-reach, when she slipped. She scrabbled at the ropes, nearly righted herself, then her weight shifted again and she went over.

She didn't scream.

I did.

I screamed, and I saw—but the knots held, and she smacked into the wall of the chasm. I heard a shower of tiny stones tumbling downwards, and then I heard her saying, breathlessly, that she was fine, she was fine, just bruised.

She was fine. It hadn't happened again. I couldn't let myself think. I had to—I hauled her up, my hands shaking. She scrambled over the edge of the chasm, panting, and began to say something, then looked at me and stopped. She took my shoulder, and led me gently away from the edge. Pushed at me until I sat down. I put my head in my hands, and sat there, shaking, while Lady Arel undid the knots and pulled the ropes back to our side.

She didn't ask. I didn't say. I couldn't. I couldn't risk letting any of it out, not here and now.

After a few minutes, I looked up to find her making a total pig's ear of coiling the rope, and my hands were steady enough to take over.

After all of that, scrambling over the rockfall was easy.

4.

I was fine. I was absolutely fine. It was just strange not to have a song to guide me, that was all. I'd hoped maybe once we were past the rockfall the old song would still work; but there was another, more comprehensive, pile of rocks just beyond that, several houses tumbled into one another, which definitively blocked off the song-route.

"Ugh," I said. Lady Arel looked over. She still hadn't asked about what happened at the pit, for which I was deeply grateful. "We're definitely out of guidance now, my lady."

"You can drop the 'my lady'. Arel will do. You just saved me from falling to my death." I couldn't quite repress the flinch. "I think we can be on first-name terms."

"It's my job," I muttered. "But all right. Arel. We're still out of guidance, whatever I call you."

"Then I suppose we must find our own way." She looked around. "Is anything from your song still useful?"

I considered the next few lines. "Trouble is, it's not left or right, it's 'follow the tree sigil' or 'the path downwards' or whatever."

"The path downwards!" she said. "Look. That way is uphill. That is down. Which way does the song tend?"

"Downhill. Deeper."

"Well then." She marched off briskly. I caught up and took the lead again; she had the grace to look ever so slightly abashed.

We came across a passage with a feather sigil, which was a later line in the song, and after some debate about whether it was useful if it was probably in the wrong place, took it anyway. I was trying to make up a new guide-song on the fly, partly to take back to Belaran, and partly in case we needed to retrace our footsteps. It hadn't a tune yet, and the words would need a polish, but it had rhythm enough to stick. Once or twice we ran into more rockfalls and had to go back and try again. I was beginning to feel uncomfortable about the amount of fallen rock down here, but it wasn't like Arel would listen if I said anything. I'd never had a client quite this determined. I could respect that, even while I wished she'd been easier to put off.

Anyway, just because there were rockfalls everywhere, that didn't mean one was likely right now. These catacombs had been here a long time. By those standards, there really weren't all that many rockfalls at all. One could, in fact, argue that if you'd been unfortunate enough to be caught in one already in your life, you surely weren't due for another one ever.

That wasn't as reassuring as it could have been.

But we didn't get caught in a rockfall. Not even nearly. We made it, in fact, to the edge of the square that Arel was looking for, with the mausoleums. We stopped just shy of it, in an alleyway.

"There they are," Arel said. "My ancestors' tombs. Exactly as the square is in the history-song."

I squatted on my haunches, staring across the square. "I'm guessing the song doesn't mention the dragon."

The dragon was sprawled across the middle of the square. So much for what I'd told Arel earlier.

Although we'd been going steadily deeper, here the 'roof' was high above us, and there were holes in it—places where more rocks had fallen in, maybe, given the piles of rocks and dirt scattered around the square. Faint shafts of light pierced through the cracks up there, highlighting beautiful carvings on the facades of some of the buildings, where they hadn't been knocked off by falling rocks or smoothed by dripping water.

The dragon was illuminated by those same shafts of light, its scales shining blue. It was maybe the size of a couple of horses together. It was beautiful, if you cared to see it that way.

"Dragons never *come* this far south any more," Arel said, in the face of the evidence. "My tutor said even in the northern mountains they are nearly extinct."

"Fine, it's a bloody big lizard just *looks* like a dragon." I supposed... well, it was a cave, and dragons liked caves, and obviously one of them had come back from the mountains, for whatever reason. How long had it been here?

"And you said..." Arel continued.

"Because I thought it was true!"

"I can hear you, you know," the dragon rumbled. "Come out of there, or I'll flambé you, sight unseen."

We gazed at one another for a horrified moment.

"Stay there," I mouthed fiercely at Arel, and stepped out into the cavern.

"And the other one."

"I am her knight, on oath, and I will protect her," I said, and did my best to sound like I meant it. I mean, I did mean it. You know what I mean.

"Knights," the dragon said petulantly. "Knights are dull. I'll fry you both if she doesn't come out too. I might fry you anyway."

I was trying to think of an argument when Arel—of course—came out too. I didn't know why I'd thought she'd start doing what she was told all of a sudden.

"I don't care what your *oath* says," she hissed at me. "I will not stand around while you get roasted alive."

"Oh, an argument." The dragon sounded more cheerful.

"How, oh Great Dragon," Arel said, stepping forward and bowing her head, "can we persuade you not to harm us?"

"Flattery is unnecessary," the dragon said severely, but it shuffled its wings. "Trial by combat is traditional, but boring. I want something interesting. Tell me a story."

"I've got a lot of guide-songs," I said, doubtfully. I ought to have more of the archive-stories by heart, but... well, I'd been moping around too much.

"Guide-songs are not stories," Arel said. "*I* have a story."

She stepped forwards again, and I barely suppressed the urge to drag her back. Instead, I stepped forwards too, to stand at her shoulder, and glared fiercely at the side of her head. The dragon made a noise that might have been a laugh. Bloody lizard.

"I am Lady Arel of the Family Xeria, and I will sing of our history," she said, in formal tones, and began.

It was, obviously, a very practised story. Practised; beautiful; formal. Tales of ancestors and their deeds and valour and craftiness. All the edges smoothed off.

It was a bit boring, to be honest.

The dragon thought so too. It politely let her finish, then it huffed a big plume of flame and smoke off to one side. (I'd like to claim I didn't flinch, but I totally did.) "Bor-ing. Pretty, I'll grant you, but no emotion. No interest. Ugh. Are you going to try again or shall I get on with the fire?"

"You want a story that has not been perfected by generations?" Arel demanded. "One that is not the pinnacle of the archivists' art?"

"Yep," the dragon said.

"Here, then. I will tell you why I am here. We—our country, Ralia—have been on the brink of war with Perren for years. My family's land runs along the border. In the event

29

of war, our people, our land, our villages, will be destroyed. We have been trying to persuade the Emperor to peace. He spent the whole of his youth creating peace, uniting the kingdom, his middle years enjoying that prosperity, surely... But all we have achieved is delay." She sounded sorrowful, and confused.

It was a while since I'd been to Perren. I knew tensions had been increasing, though not why. I hadn't realised it was that bad. I'd grown up near the border. Creeping dread coiled up my spine at the idea of war, spilling into the farms and valleys of my childhood.

"The Family Bethene," Arel continued, "have, as all know, been speculating on war. Seeking to profit, when and if it does. And then, of late, despite my—our—best efforts, war has come ever closer. Diplomatic missteps, outright challenge. We could not understand why, until I discovered that the Bethene have been manipulating things to that end. Not openly, publicly, as would be their right. Subtly. In secret. Perhaps even manipulating the Emperor."

Her chin went up, her posture shifting into determination. "Once I *knew* what they were doing; well, my family and I have our methods too. We have a treaty, that would protect the interests of both us and Perren. We have proposed it in Court before, and tomorrow is the bone-ceremony. But then our foundation-bone disappeared."

"Humans are full of bones. Bones and ghosts." The dragon flipped its wings.

"The bone-ceremony protects our place at court," Arel said. "And the Emperor surely must be there for it, and we can recite our treaty. We can persuade him. *If* we are there. If our bone is there. Even if I could *prove* theft, that alone would destroy our reputation. So I came to the Knights of Siremos, and Sir Cade," I inclined my head, "has escorted me, past minitaurs and caroths, across a great gash in the earth, through lost passageways. To this place, to reclaim a bone of my ancestors, and protect the future."

She stood there, head high, slender and upright. She looked like a hero, or a princess.

"Mmmm," the dragon rumbled. "Well, that was certainly better. Anger. Resentment. A suggestion of heroism towards the end. And yet, and yet. I still feel it lacks a certain... something." It waved a claw. "Not fully from the heart, perhaps? Well-spoken, though, I'll give you that."

Arel's shoulders were tense. She opened her mouth; then, in the corner of my eye, a few yards behind her, I saw again the shadow of Graf. He leant against the carvings of what had once been a fine house, arms folded, head tilted. Watching me.

I stepped forward before Arel could speak. "You want a story?" I said. Shadow-Graf's mouth quirked. "I'll give you a *story*."

5.

Arel was frowning at me. "Cade, I am not sure that the guide-songs…"

I ignored her, and took another step towards the dragon.

"Tell on," it rumbled. A puff of smoke escaped its mouth.

"First time I came down here was with my sword-brother Graf. Because we did nearly everything together, as apprentices. And the second time was with Graf too, because even after we were apprentices we worked together whenever we could. Graf saved me from a caroth that nearly got the jump on me, then we ran into its nest-mates and had to fight our way out, back-to-back, then right at the entrance a rock-serpent bit Graf and I had to put a tourniquet on him and drag him back to the chapterhouse before the poison reached his heart." I grinned, mirthlessly. "We thought we were invincible after that. Of course we did. We were seventeen. Who doesn't think they're invincible when they're seventeen?"

In the corner of my eye, Shadow-Graf grinned affectionately at me.

"We were knights. We were lovers, sometimes, but," I shrugged, "it wasn't that important, not compared to everything else we were to each other. We rode out together when we could; we told each other of our adventures after we'd gone out alone. We were Graf-and-Cade." I swallowed. The dragon wanted emotion, didn't it? Reality. Rawness. "I loved him. He loved me. Together, we were invincible. There's guide-songs due to the two of us, you know. Separately, neither of us was any slouch either."

I stopped. Shadow-Graf gestured encouragingly.

"Last year. We." My throat was dry. I forced myself on. "It wasn't supposed to be the catacombs, not originally. We took a client out to the deserts. Then on the way back, he—the client—wanted to detour through the catacombs' western edge. Neither of us were sure of the guide-song from that side, and we hadn't expected it, so we hadn't had it from the archivist before leaving. Graf wanted to go home above-ground, like we'd planned, then come back out again. The client was grumpy about the extra days, doing it that way. I." I winced, that cold place in my belly twisting. "I said, we could just do it and be done. We'd been down often enough before. We had *most* of the guide-song, between us, and we knew the catacombs, didn't we? Perhaps not that edge so well, but..." I shrugged. "Graf wasn't sure, but—well, the client was a bit of a shit. We both thought so, but I disliked him more, because it was me he condescended to, though Graf tried to make him stop. I said, don't make me spend any more days than I absolutely must with this fool. So Graf agreed. Against his better judgement."

And how many nights had I spent regretting that?

"We went down. We got lost. Then the eralin attacked, and we had to run for it." I saw again its shadowy form shiver over the rock, stalking, reaching out dark elongated fin-gers. "We shook it off, but it would find us eventually, if we couldn't find the exit, and we weren't sure where we were any more. We found somewhere defensible. Graf wanted to wait and fight it off from there." He'd shrugged and said it proba-bly wouldn't come anyway. He'd said we could just wait, find the route out once it had gone. But I'd been impatient. "I could hear it, a little way away, and I thought if Graf stayed with the client, I could go ambush the eralin. We argued, and I won, again, and I went off." I swallowed. "It ambushed me, instead. Graf heard, and came after me. And we defeated it, of course, because together we were always invincible. We defeated it, and we stood there and laughed." I wasn't seeing the square any more. I was seeing Graf, smiling at me, reach-ing a mailed hand out. "And then the earth opened up, and

Graf went straight down into it." Straight down, still reaching out to me.

In the far distance, Arel gasped.

"I forgot all about the client. I climbed down there, after Graf, just in case, in case..." I was swallowing over and again. "I found him. His body. I went back up with him on my back. I found the client. He was fine. Terrified, and convinced we were both dead, but fine. Guided him out. Nothing else came after us." I bared my teeth. "I wished it had. I really wished it had. Graf lies in the chapterhouse crypt, in stone, and I'm still here. I guess we weren't invulnerable after all."

Shadow-Graf appeared in front of me, more than just a shadow this time, hand held out towards me. "Hey, Cade."

"*Graf?*" No. I'd carried his body up that crack in the ground myself. I was imagining things. Really clear things. "You're a ghost." My voice cracked. "Or a figment of my imagination, or..."

"Right first time," he said.

"Cade?" Arel said, cautiously. "Are you all right?"

"There's a ghost," the dragon told Arel. "You can't see it?"

I hadn't seen a ghost before. I knew they existed, or at least, people said so, but I'd never met anyone who'd seen one. They said, usually there were only a couple of people could see any particular ghost.

Wasn't surprising I'd be the one could see ghost-Graf.

"It wasn't your fault, Cade," Graf said.

"Of course it was." My eyes were wet. This was Graf, but not-Graf, and everything was all wrong. "You didn't want to come down here. You didn't want me to ambush the eralin."

"Maybe not, but I agreed. You didn't overrule me. I decided you were right." He shrugged. "Guess we were both wrong."

"It's my fault. If I hadn't —"

34

"If, if, if. If I'd gotten a charm-knife into it. If either of us'd remembered the guide-song. If the client had been less of an arse. It is what it is, Cade love. Not your fault. I got unlucky. Two feet the other way and it'd've been you. Four feet and neither of us. Or both. A different fall and you'd have carried me up alive. You did everything you could, right?"

I couldn't accept that. If I'd acted differently it never would have happened. And now he was down here, and I hadn't even *known*. "If you're still here... Why didn't you come *find* me?"

"Couldn't." Graf shrugged. "Can't go that far."

"You've been on your own?" My throat was too tight. "I'll... I'll sort something out, all right? I'll..."

"Cade. Love. It's fine. Don't worry about it."

"It's *not* fine! You're stuck here!" Stuck down here on his own; and did that mean forever? Would he never be released, his self-stuff never go back to the Lake to dissolve and return again? Just down here in the dark, forever?

"Ghosts don't last that long." The dragon's nose was suddenly much closer to me and Graf, and I jumped backwards. "You'll fade eventually. I could eat you, if you liked?"

"*No*," Graf and I said. Fade? What did that mean?

"Hmph. Be that way." It sounded sulky. "Well. You," it waved a paw at Arel, "you can get your bone, if you still want to. I can't really complain about the denouement of *that* story, can I? Pathos, drama, all that stuff. Unpractised, yes, clearly, but the rawness, the rawness I liked. Off you go." It sighed, and put its head down on its paws, and I felt a pang of sympathy. It must be boring, alone down here.

Like Graf had been. My stomach clenched again.

Arel hesitated, glancing worriedly over at me, then began to skirt carefully around the dragon towards the mausoleums.

"Graf..." I started. "I'll stay, I..."

"Shuddup, Cade. You're on a job, remember? You have to take your client home." He rolled his eyes and slouched against a wall. A tiny bit of him sank into it.

He was right. I was on a job. I was under oath. I looked over as Arel came out of a mausoleum reverently holding a long thigh-bone, and an idea bloomed. I bent and picked up a stone. "Look! You're stuck here, right? But this is part of here. If I take it out..."

"Won't work," the dragon said. I ignored it.

"Huh. Worth a try," Graf allowed.

"Cade?" Arel asked. "Where now?"

It took me a moment to refocus. "I, um. We have to go back again." Right back across that pit.

Arel pointed towards the back of the square. "Could we not go up that way?"

The old guide-song described the square as a dead end; but where Arel was pointing the buildings had collapsed, forming a pile of tumbled stone that led upwards towards the roof of the cavern, joining an earthen slope at the top. A broad shaft of daylight lit the slope.

"It's perfectly safe," the dragon said, craning round to watch us. "I go up it all the time. I flattened it out a bit."

I wasn't sure, but it looked solid enough, if a bit of a scramble, and if I went first, I could test the footing. And I wanted, very badly, to be out.

It was a long scrambling way up those rocks, weighed down by Graf's stone in my pocket, but it was shorter than retracing our steps, and no monsters other than the dragon humming below. Graf kept pace at my shoulder.

To distract myself, I thought about Arel's story. "Your bone thing," I said, after a couple of minutes. "And this business of war. You've already proposed your solution to the Emperor? And he didn't go for it?"

"To the court," Arel corrected. "The Emperor has not been seen in Court for some time. Perhaps he hears. Perhaps he has considered it. But tomorrow, I am sure, he will be there—he must be—and we will persuade him. We cannot let war happen."

"Right. Can't say I'm keen, either."

Arel scowled. "I don't *understand*. My grandmother told me stories—she went with him and the Prince of Perren to broker the peace with the mountain people, when she was young. It was after that the towns of Western Ralia returned to the Empire and stopped their raids, and it was the Emperor's delegation that opened the route for both us and Perren to trade with the Islanders. Surely the Bethene cannot possibly have turned his mind so far as to welcome *war* with Perren, when we were once so close? And then, in whispering in the Emperor's ear this way they have surely put themselves out of the succession."

"Eh?" I glanced over at her and nearly stumbled as a stone shifted under my foot.

"The Emperor is old; everyone is considering the succession. The noble families make the choice, you know?" I didn't, but nodded anyway. "Of course everyone is thinking about it, but it is just not done to move in advance. Nico, and Nico alone, being so far in the Emperor's confidence, this close to the end of his reign? Far too obvious. No one will ever vote for him. I don't understand what... but that doesn't matter as much as peace."

The exit was in sight; above us, the rocks gave way to earth rising up into sunlight. Graf was still at my shoulder.

"Our lands run along the border," Arel said. "I am my family's archivist. I know the stories from the last war with Perren, long before this Emperor. The Bethene, who want the war? They sing stirring songs at Court evenings. Flashing swords and heroic deeds. That is not the truth of war. The archivists before me collected stories from those who lived on the border. The soldiers who survived. Their songs do not flash, and they are not heroic. That must not happen again. I will not permit it." Her voice was fierce.

"Good for you," I said. Her determination lifted my heart. Surely she'd manage this. Whatever this other family might be doing, no one could *want* war, could they? Not really. The Emperor must just... not be paying attention. Lost in stories of his past, perhaps, rather than looking to the present, the way old folk got sometimes? Arel just had to make him listen; and I could believe that she could, if anyone could.

There was earth under my feet now.

"Shit," Graf said, from behind me.

I turned to see him standing on the last of the rocks, pierced through by a single beam of sunlight.

"Not gonna work. Can't get any further."

"*Shit.*" I chewed at my lip. "Maybe... maybe it needs to be from where you actually..." I started back towards him.

"Cade. Stop."

"But you're stuck. Down here on your own. I can't..."

"You're on a *job*. C'mon, Cade, you're the sensible one."

Maybe I used to be the sensible one. That was when there were still two of us. But he was right. *Shit.* "I'll come back," I promised, my voice cracking. "Soon as I can."

Graf shrugged. "No hurry. I'll be here." He half-grinned. "I'll go have a chat with the dragon. I'd've done that before if I'd known it was there."

"If you need to help your friend," Arel said, hesitant, "I can walk back on my own."

"No, you can't. Under oath." I forced a smile. "Don't worry about it."

I looked back as we scrambled up the last of the earthen slope and out into the sunshine, but I couldn't see Graf.

Soft turf lay under our feet. Some kind of small pink flower with a sweet heavy scent spread under some bushes away to our right. The city was off to our left, with the squat shape of the chapterhouse outlined in front of it.

The sooner I got Arel there, the sooner I could get back to Graf, and fix this. Somehow. Whatever that meant.

6.

Arel was in enough of a hurry that she nearly outpaced me on the way back; at least out here I didn't have to keep telling her to stay back. As soon as we were through the chapterhouse gates, she bid me goodbye and was off towards the stables to retrieve her horse and head for the city.

I was in just as much of a hurry. Graf was stuck in the catacombs, and it was my fault. I had to get him out of there. The guilt of knowing he'd been on his own down there all this time was horrible. But—after that? What then? I racked my brains for everything I'd ever heard of ghosts.

Ghost-whisperers. I'd heard of ghost-whisperers, though I wasn't wholly sure what they did. Exorcised ghosts, in spooky stories, and I didn't want *that* happening to Graf. But I'd heard something else, too, something more helpful, in some other story or guide-song. I just couldn't think of the details right now. But the name said *ghost*, so surely they could help Graf, somehow. If I could find one.

Because I had to do *something*. The dragon had said Graf would fade. Losing him once had been bad enough. No way would I let that happen again. Sir Belaran would know about the ghost-whisperers, and he might even tell me without demanding to know why I was interested.

The supper bell rang. I had to get Graf out of there, but the gnawing feeling in my stomach suggested I should eat before going to muck around in the catacombs on my own. I'd been thinking, a rock from the side of that chasm, or the bottom of it—but it wouldn't help anyone if I went wobbly and smashed myself up too.

I was halfway to the hall, following the deeply savoury aroma drifting across the courtyard, when Graf blurred into existence in front of me. I nearly fell over my feet.

"What? You're here? We did it?" I was awash with relief. And confusion. I'd *seen* him, stuck back down there, unable to come any further. What had changed?

Another knight, also on their way to the hall, eyed me with worry. Perhaps stopping dead—not the best choice of words—in the middle of the courtyard and shouting at nothing was somewhat unusual behaviour. I gave them a reassuring nod, and diverted over to the left, where there were a couple of cherry trees, boughs laden with flowers, and I could lose my mind in peace. "You're out? But I thought you couldn't leave?"

"Yeah, me too." Was Graf slightly ragged around the edges? Had something gone wrong? Had this got *worse*?

"We have to talk to Sir Belaran."

"Cade."

"Or maybe the Archon." We had to save him. Someone must know how.

"*Cade.*"

"I was thinking..."

"Cade! This isn't the time! Lady Arel's in danger."

"What?" I blinked at him, snapped out of the whir of my thoughts. "Arel? What's happened? How do you know?" Could ghosts see the future?

"So I was thinking about distance, after you left, and I thought, if I can only go this far from the hole alongways, what about upwards? And, yeah, turned out I could go pretty high, which was cool. Then I saw this bunch of riders, coming out of the city in a hurry. With," he scowled. "I dunno. I can't see how I could know, but I was positive they'd nothing good on their minds. Only thing I could think of was to come warn you."

"But you couldn't leave, before?" I was still stuck on that part.

SONG, STONE, SCALE, BONE

Graf gave one of his massive shrugs. "And then I did. Kind of hurt a bit, though. Not the *point*, Cade. Come on, get with it."

"You think it was Lady Arel they were after, specifically?"

"Yeah. Can't tell you why," his broad face creased in irritation, "but—yeah. I know it sounds weird."

Something had just occurred to me, with freezing clarity. If Arel's court enemies had stolen her bone, wouldn't they know where she'd have to go for a new one? And wouldn't they take steps to prevent that? Like, for example, accosting her when she was on her way back home, out there with no one to see?

Shit. I swung round on my heel and headed for the stables, stomach still growling. When I turned back round, Graf had disappeared. My stomach dropped; but I couldn't deal with that now. I had to check on Arel.

I cut across country rather than follow the road, partly for speed, and partly because there was a bit of a rise which would give me a decent overview of the road back into the city. I reined Monty in towards the top—not right on the top, to silhouette myself for anyone who might be looking—and eyeballed the situation.

There was Arel, making decent time.

And there, halfway between her and the city, mostly hidden in a clump of trees by the road, a group of people and horses. Who, sure, could be perfectly innocent travellers. But by 'mostly hidden', I meant mostly hidden even to me, looking with trained eyes from above. You'd never see them from the road.

And I trusted Graf's judgement. Especially after what happened the last time I'd overruled him.

The road curved downwards and to the left just before the copse; Arel wouldn't be visible to them yet. I had just enough time to intercept her, if I kept on the far side of this hill and looped round towards the road.

It was a close-run thing, but I reined Monty in a few yards in front of Arel just before the crucial bend.

"Sir Cade? What on earth is the matter?"

"You're going to be attacked," I said bluntly.

"Attacked?" she repeated, voice awash with confusion. "By whom?"

"At a guess, by whoever nicked your bone," I said. "But I couldn't identify them from a distance." Bringing Graf into this right now would just be a distraction.

"They would not be so obvious," she said, but she didn't start moving.

I shrugged. "Well, someone's waiting in a copse around that corner—several someones—and given that you already know you've got enemies, I'm disinclined to give them the benefit of the doubt."

She'd lifted her chin again, like she did when she was being stubborn. "I must return to the city. *Quickly.*"

"Being stabbed won't improve the situation," I said. "Nor will losing that bone we went to all the trouble over."

"But this is the fastest way to the city."

"Not," I said, with heavy patience, "if you get stabbed."

"One of them's called Misha," Graf said, appearing behind Arel's shoulder. I didn't actually recoil and start swearing, but it was a close thing.

"Cade?" Arel asked.

"I'm. Fine. It's fine. Uh. One of them's called Misha, if that helps?"

"Misha," Arel breathed. "That little snake."

"You know them?"

"Xe is the youngest sibling of the Family Bethene. Once, we were..." She refocussed on me. "How do you know?"

"Uh. Did some reconnaissance," I said, eliding who exactly had done the reconnaissance. Graf and me were sword-brothers, it was close enough.

"Misha's in charge," Graf said helpfully.

I carried on. "Couldn't get close enough to tell what their plans are exactly—not like they were sitting around loudly discussing the matter for my benefit—but the Misha person was in charge."

"Right. Well." She scowled. "But I *must* get to the city."

"Go cross-country," I said. Behind Arel, Graf had vanished again. My heart clenched; but I had a job to do. "We'll have to avoid that copse, but we can do it, if you follow me and keep quiet."

"Let us go," Arel said, decisively, turning her horse, then hesitated. "Although—I thought you were keen to return to the catacombs?"

"Knight of Siremos, remember? Not going to leave a client," ex-client, technically, but still, "in the lurch." Wasn't up for talking about the catacombs right now.

I led the way off the road and towards the paths and field-edges that would lead us round to a different city gate.

"Told you so," Graf said, behind me.

I nearly fell off. I turned to see him perched on Monty's rump. Monty didn't seem to notice anything; Arel was a few paces behind, scowling in thought.

"She was in danger. *Told* you so."

"For all I know," I hissed, "we're carefully avoiding some innocent travellers. Misha or no Misha."

But I didn't believe that, and Graf knew I didn't. He grinned at me, and I stuck the tip of my tongue out at him and turned forwards again. Something warm and comforting swelled under my breastbone as Graf began a tuneless whistling I recognised all too well from a great many other rides together. I still didn't know why or how he was here, and not still in the catacombs, but he was.

Now I just had to make that stick.

7.

We made reasonable time back to the city. I'd have liked to detour to check out that copse, but getting Arel back safely was more important. The guards at the side gate nodded and let us pass; and as we joined the main road towards the centre of the city, Arel took the lead. I go to the city from time to time—mostly the bits with things like pubs and music-halls—and I know the guide-songs, but it was her home turf. This time I was going to see her all the way home before I turned back.

"So this thing tomorrow at court," I said. "You're seeing the Emperor?"

"Hmm?" Arel looked over at me. "Oh. Well. Surely. I hope. No one has seen him in person for some time now. He reports his wishes through his household." She sighed. "It is frustrating. At least the household are known to be relia-ble—a lifetime service, you understand. But tomorrow, for the bone-ceremony, he *must* be there."

"So, what, you all stand around waving your bones at each other?"

"It is rare, to demand the bone-magicians. But it is per-mitted and, well. Someone stole the bone, and they had a reason for it. But that no longer matters. Afterwards," her expression firmed resolutely, "each family may beg hearing of the Emperor. I am to recite the peace treaty."

"Good luck," I said. The idea of the border peace shat-tered, of the fields and villages of my childhood churned under boots and bodies and blood... But Arel was going to sort it out. I had faith in her.

The noble family houses were all close to the river (but not too close, due to the summer smells), and as we rode in that direction, the buildings became larger and more impressive, the street-stalls fewer, and the bustle more sub-dued.

A few more minutes and we reached the courtyard of Arel's family compound. The huge main building was built from the same grey stone as the rest of the city, quarried at the foothills of the mountains and brought downriver by barge. The intricately carved pillars and the lintel over the door had recently been repainted in bright blues and greens.

Arel slid off her horse and handed the reins to a servant who'd appeared out of nowhere to take them. She slung her bag over her shoulder, gesturing away another servant, and turned to me.

"Uh," I said, shifting uncomfortably on Monty's back. "I guess I should be getting back, then. Now you're safely home."

Arel looked at me reprovingly. "It is very late in the day, Sir Cade. Surely you must stay to dinner."

My stomach growled loudly, and Arel's mouth quirked sideways. I tried to ignore it. Yes, I had missed supper back home, but I'd be able to raid the kitchens. "Honestly," I said. "I should be getting back."

"Will they miss you?"

They wouldn't; the stable-hand knew I'd taken Monty out and gone off towards the city. They'd assume I could take care of myself until proven otherwise; that is, until someone showed up with my body or a report thereof.

The oath precludes *lying*, but I can evade the truth with the best of them. "I ought to get back," I repeated.

"I know you have commitments, Sir Cade," I really ought to tell her about Graf being out, "but you cannot possibly do them justice on an empty stomach. I must insist you let me thank you for your assistance by inviting you to dine with us."

"I've never eaten at a lord's house," Graf put in. I must have been getting used to that; I didn't jump or shriek or anything. I wanted to glare at him, but he was standing behind Arel, and she'd think I was glaring at her.

"I'm not even slightly dressed for it," I tried.

"I can lend you something," she said. "And we have a steam-pool for bathing."

I considered feeling insulted, but we'd been down to the catacombs and back today, and I'd fought a caroth and faced down a dragon. I needed a bath. Arel did too, come to think of it.

She stood there looking aristocratic at me until I gave in and slid down off Monty.

"Not too many oats," I said to the stable-hand who took the reins. "She's had plenty today."

Arel swept across the green-paved courtyard towards the huge doors of the main building, and I trailed uncomfortably behind her.

"Don't you have to, like, do the thing," I asked, hurrying to catch up with her and gesturing at the bag she was still clutching.

She shooed off a servant who'd come up to offer to take it. "No thank you, but please bring robes to the steam-pool," she said, then turned to me. "Not immediately. It works best at night—specifically, at either moonset."

I supposed that made sense, what with moonset being dark, and bones being horrible and creepy.

Inside, the main hall was floored with beautiful engraved tiles of a sort I'd seen once when I guided a trading party over the sea. They must have been shipped through Perren, on the estuary. Trading relationships might also be part of Arel's family's desire to maintain peace.

Arel took us rapidly through a maze of passages, which I automatically tallied in my head; part of the training, you understand. We came out in front of double doors that led into a white-tiled room with a sunken pool in it. Steam rose from the water.

I'd been to a chapterhouse in Dennoth, on the other side of the mountains, which had one of these, but at our place, we just had bathing-rooms with pitchers. Does the job, but rather less luxurious. To be fair, this was probably unjustifiably expensive and exactly the sort of thing that leads to people complaining about aristocrats, but, as I got out of my clothes, I didn't feel like getting on my high horse about it.

A servant appeared to leave grey robes on hooks for us, and started to gather up my clothes.

"For laundering," Arel said over my protests.

"What about my sword?"

"It will be taken to my room."

I had a moment of worry; but I was in a lord's house, and it wasn't like I'd need to hit anyone in here, was it?

The steam-pool was bloody lovely. Unfortunately we didn't have nearly as much time to soak as I'd have liked before Arel was chivvying me out, into the grey robes, through more corridors and upstairs towards, I assumed, her room and some spare clothes. At least I sincerely hoped I wasn't about to go into dinner in a robe and bare feet.

Arel halted in front of a beautifully decorated door, and went to push it open. Graf appeared at her shoulder, wide-eyed and urgent.

"Cade! Behind the door!"

Graf and I fought together a long time. My back-brain reacted before he was done warning me. I shouldered past Arel, slammed the door open, and cast my eyes desperately over the room in search of a weapon (I'd *left* my *sword*, what kind of an idiot bloody knight was I?). The best I saw was a big metal candlestick to my right. No one there between me and the wall.

I lunged in, grabbed the candlestick, swung round the edge of the door towards whoever it was...

...and nearly wrenched a muscle pulling my blow when it turned out the person behind the door was a cringing teenage kid. I stopped the candlestick a hair's breadth from their skull, and opened my mouth to demand what the fuck they were doing, but Arel beat me to it.

"*What* are you doing in my *rooms* unannounced?" she demanded, doing an impressive job of being Lady Arel despite the whole robe-and-bare-feet situation.

"Sorry," Graf said, apologetically, hovering behind the kid. "Only knew there was someone there, not who."

I glared at him, and the teenager, standing between me and Graf, caught the glare and cringed further.

"I was sent by the Emperor," they said in a tiny voice.

"Unannounced?" Arel demanded in a voice ringing with disbelief. "How?"

"I was told not to betray my presence." Their eyes darted to the door. "Please, if you could... quietly..."

Arel glanced over at me. I nodded, and she shut the door. Even if the teenage kid turned out to be secretly some kind of finely-trained operative in cunning disguise, I reckoned I could take them. They were very weedy, and I am pretty good.

Also, I'd just spotted my sword, propped up in a corner. I edged over there, without taking my eyes off the kid, and swapped it for the candlestick with a sigh of relief. The kid looked at me and gulped.

"Prove it," Arel challenged.

Slowly, glancing over at me, they reached into a pocket and pulled out some kind of seal, which they offered to Arel. Arel looked over it suspiciously, then her eyes widened, and she nodded. "That is the Emperor's seal," she said. "Stand down, Sir Cade."

I wasn't at all sure about *standing down*, plus I don't actually take orders from clients, but I compromised by *looking* less ready to run the kid through whilst not in fact impeding my ability to act at all.

"You broke in?" Arel demanded of the kid.

They nodded. "I was authorised. By the Emperor."

"How—no matter. What do you want?"

I was quite interested in how they'd got in, and I was absolutely positive that Lady Arel's family's security staff would be, but fine, that was probably lower priority than finding out what was going on here.

"The Emperor has a message for you," the kid said. They stood straighter now, focussed on Arel. "A directive. The Emperor wishes peace with Perren. You are to make this happen."

"What?" Arel's brows were creased. "You say this here, secretly, in my rooms, rather than the Emperor announcing it in court?"

"It must not be known," the kid said. "There are too many who oppose it. But the Emperor wishes his last legacy to be neither the start of a war, nor open battle in court. You must go to Harin, now, and arrange a treaty before it can be prevented. Then it can be public." Harin was the capital of Perren; a couple of days from here by carriage along the river-road. I'd been there, once, years ago.

Arel bit her lip. What the kid was saying did fit with what she'd been telling me; and with whoever'd stolen her bone and tried to catch her on the road back. "But why me?" She sounded suddenly plaintive, almost vulnerable.

"You are the archivist," the kid said, with a minuscule shrug. "You have recited in court the treaty drafted by your family, seeking the Emperor's ear. And you are known, Lady Arel, as one of integrity and resolution."

That smacked to me slightly of flattery, but Arel's back straightened and her tone grew more certain. "The Emperor wishes our suggested treaty? What if the Perren prince wants changes? Am I authorised to negotiate?"

"You will have the seal," the kid said. "You are the Emperor's presence. You must seal the treaty."

Arel's eyes widened nervously. "I must—but I need more guidance than that."

"The Emperor said, your conscience should be your guide. Your conscience, and the good of the kingdom. Your Emperor puts his trust in you, Lady Arel." The kid showed her the seal again, in a formal kind of way, with a sort of flourish. It was yellow-white, deeply carved with a symbol, and I realised it was bone. "Do you accept?"

The breath she took in hitched, but she had the same determined expression I'd seen in the catacombs. "As the Emperor wills, so I will perform."

The kid grabbed her hand—I flinched, but Arel didn't—flipped the seal over, and revealed a hidden pin. They jabbed it into Arel's finger, and squeezed two drops of blood onto the seal. There was a very low hum for half a breath, before it vanished without so much as a stain. Ew. Bone-magic.

The kid let go of Arel's hand—she pressed her thumb to her finger to slow the blood—and tucked the seal into a little bag which they handed to Arel.

"This must be *wholly* secret," the kid said, and looked sideways at me.

"Knight of Siremos," I said. "We don't go round flapping our lips about things." If someone asked me directly, I couldn't lie, but I didn't have to answer.

That seemed to satisfy the kid. Getting a better look at them now, I suspected they might have given me more trouble than I'd initially thought. Still, best not to smack fifteen-year-olds in the head with candlesticks without direct provocation, especially ones bringing Imperial messages. I grinned cheerfully at them. They didn't smile back.

"You must leave immediately," they said.

"After the bone-ceremony tomorrow," Arel agreed.

The kid shook their head. "Tomorrow morning at the latest."

"But—what could I say to my family?" Arel looked horrified. "The bone-ceremony, and I must present the treaty. They will think —"

The kid shrugged. "As it happens, the bone-ceremony will be delayed. You must hurry. Trouble may be on your tail."

"But —"

"At the Emperor's will." The kid bowed formally, then moved in a rush. I had a moment of abject horror and leapt in front of Arel—I'd have been in time, just—but the kid wasn't going for her. They were going for the window, and they were out of it almost before I could blink.

Yeah. I'd definitely underestimated them.

Arel, like a bloody idiot, went over to the window and was about to stick her head out before I yanked her back and cautiously peered over myself. The kid had reached the ground already—and there wasn't any handy ivy or anything, it was a good blank stone wall, kid was like a gecko—and was away into the bushes before we could blink.

"There's guards on the walls." Arel frowned out into the twilight.

"They got in. Pretty sure they can get out again."

A bell rang.

"Oh shit," Arel said. "Dinner."

8.

Dinner was long, and formal. At least the food was good. I was sat halfway down the long table, while Arel was at the top; but we wouldn't have been able to talk about anything important here anyway. So I ate as much as I politely could, made conversation when I couldn't politely avoid it, and waited for the end.

Halfway through, I realised what had been nagging at me about Arel's Emperor-assigned task: the ghost-whisperers had a temple in Harin. The Harin guide-song mentioned it.

And hard on the heels of remembering that, as if jolted free by the thought of the temple, I remembered the other thing I'd heard of the ghost-whisperers, in a story from when I was a kid.

The thing was. Graf was here, sort of, and it felt *so good* to see him; but none of this was right. He shouldn't be a ghost. He should still be alive, and it was my fault that he wasn't.

And the story I'd remembered was that the ghost-whisperers didn't only exorcise ghosts. Sometimes, just sometimes, they brought them back. Really back. Bodies and all.

Rumours and stories aren't reliable. And fine, perhaps that particular story was, in the matter of bodies, pretty gruesome. (Graf's body was six months buried; that wouldn't work.) But just maybe, if there was a grain of truth lurking in there...

I swallowed hard against the lump in my throat, and re-applied myself to my potatoes. I couldn't think about this right now.

But I didn't need to think about it, did I? I was going to Harin, because I was responsible for Arel, and I was responsible for Graf. I was going to Harin, and I was going to find the ghost-whisperers, and I was going to do everything I possibly could to save Graf. That was all there was to it.

Dinner went on far too long. Once everyone finally began to leave, I hung back to catch Arel.

"Do excuse me," she said graciously to her companion. "I must speak to my friend Sir Cade."

I wasn't about to start shooting my mouth off in public, so I stayed quiet as we walked away from the dining room. The corridors were panelled with beautifully carved wood, and the candles in the wall-sconces—good quality wax, burning bright and sweet-smelling with little smoke—must have cost a fortune. We weren't headed back towards Arel's room, at least not by the way we'd come down here.

Likely she wouldn't want to leave until the morning. Even if the bone-ceremony was delayed, there was her night-time foundation bone thing. And we'd be less obvious leaving openly in the morning for some pretended destination than we would be sneaking out overnight.

"Your clothing should be dry by the morning," Arel said. "And I will give you a donation to take back to the chapter-house."

"Hang on," I said, and stopped in the middle of the cor-ridor. The people behind us made disapproving noises, and I waited for them to pass. "You think I'm going back to the chapterhouse in the morning."

"Yes?"

"You think you're going on your own."

The corridor was empty now, but Arel still lowered her voice. "The message was for me. And it may be dangerous. I will take a guard, of course."

"You're seriously telling me that you're going to guide *yourself* to Harin?" Yeah, no way was I going to let that hap-pen. No Court family guard was going to be capable of getting her there safely cross-country. I couldn't let this happen.

Also, I was not about to let go of the opportunity that had fallen into my lap.

Arel scowled, and her chin went up ominously. "Everyone knows the road to Harin. It is hardly *difficult*." The river ran from here to there. You could hop a boat from the docks, or if you didn't care for water, hire a carriage to rattle down the well-kept road, and be there in a couple of days.

"Right," I agreed. "Nor is it *secret*."

She blinked, and I managed not to roll my eyes. "Oh." She regrouped. "But you have—your friend, in the catacombs."

"Not in the catacombs any more," I admitted. "It was him warned me about the ambush, earlier."

Arel frowned, distracted. "I thought he could not leave the catacombs?"

"Yes, well, so did I. So did he. No idea what happened, I'm not a ghost expert. We're getting side-tracked. The point is, you need a guide. And a guard. Your plan was to tell some random sword-swinger about this? That doesn't sound secret to me."

"My family's guards are very reliable."

"Shut up, I'm coming."

She scowled, then threw her hands up in frustration. "Oh very well. I suppose you are correct. The fewer people who know about this the better, and perhaps I cannot take the obvious route." It was pretty obvious that Arel didn't like to admit to being wrong, but she wasn't, thankfully, completely pig-headed.

"So." I started along the corridor again. "You have your—thing—tonight. I can go to the city chapterhouse this evening for supplies, and send a message to the Archon so they won't miss me at home."

"The servants can find you a guest room when you return. But if we are to leave tomorrow —"

"Things to discuss," I agreed. "I'll find your room once I'm back and wait for you."

"Will you be able to?" Arel asked. "The house can be confusing."

"Knight of Siremos, remember? Way-finding is kind of my speciality."

We came into the main hall, with the big entrance doors. People stood around in conversational knots. Arel's expression shifted back into the formal one I'd seen in the dining hall.

"Thank you for your hospitality, Lady Arel," I said, loudly. "I will gratefully accept your offer to stay tonight, but I fear before I can rest, I must pray with my siblings-in-arms." I probably would do a quick prayer, at that, while I was there.

Arel picked up the cue without even blinking, bless her. "Of course, Sir Cade," she said, also louder than necessary. "When you return, have the servants conduct you to a guest room. I look forward to seeing you at breakfast."

I bowed to her, and marched myself out of the doors.

"Nicely done," Graf said admiringly, from just behind my shoulder.

By the time I'd gone to the chapterhouse, shaken them down for supplies whilst fobbing off any questions about where I was going, performatively Gone To Bed and snuck out again, and spent half the night discussing our plans with Arel; I didn't get much sleep.

Our cover story had Arel visiting a friend over the mountains in Dennoth (the opposite direction from the Perren border), and me guiding her. It was an easy enough journey that she wouldn't usually need a guide, and we spent a while thinking up excuses; then decided that if I looked like I'd snuck into Arel's room at night, people would draw their own gossipy conclusions, and that would solve the matter. It wouldn't imply *great* things for my sense of duty, but *I* knew that my sense of duty was getting along just fine, and so did the Archon, so I didn't much care what a bunch of nobles thought.

Arel's main concern had been how irresponsible she would look, leaving before the bone-ceremony.

"It is not that I *have* to be there, but it will look bad."

"That messenger said it wouldn't happen."

"But everyone believes it will. And this is our opportunity to present the treaty."

"The treaty you're taking to Perren, right? So it doesn't actually matter if you don't present it."

"That is not the point. It is the look of the thing." She had on her dedication-to-family face.

Eventually we decided Arel would announce her departure at the last possible moment, in the hope the bone-ceremony would be cancelled first. To set things up for it, I got a few hours sleep on the floor, then ostentatiously 'snuck out' first thing. I ran into two servants in the corridor and made a whole production of looking flustered (helped or not helped by Graf standing behind them pulling faces, *thanks*). I was certain the matter would be around the household in no time flat.

Halfway through breakfast, an Emperor's messenger rushed into the hall to speak to the people at the top table, and about three heartbeats after that it was all over the hall: no bone-ceremony until next week, for some complicated (and presumably imaginary) political-magic reason I didn't get.

After breakfast, Arel loudly suggested to me that we leave for our trip immediately. We got a lot of knowing glances; the gossip mill had done its thing already. Shortly after that we were on our way, me on Monty and Arel on a different but equally well-set-up horse to the day before. Not that Monty was anything to sneeze at; a journeying order prioritises decent horseflesh.

Halfway through the city, someone pulled their horse directly in front of us. We reined in in a hurry, and I was about to say something extremely rude, when I spotted Arel's expression. Also, Graf sitting on the back of the other person's horse making large and dramatic gestures.

"Misha," Arel said, in a voice that was superficially pleasant but made me want to hide under something.

Oh.

"This is the one I saw yesterday!" Graf hissed.

"Arel," Misha said, with a very similar tone to Arel's. Xyr hands, tight on xyr reins, were covered in blue tattoos, echoing the lines of the bones under the skin. "Leaving the city again?"

Arel's eyes narrowed. "Social visit," she said.

"I do hope it goes well," Misha said unconvincingly.

"You must go out sometime yourself as well," Arel said sweetly. "It is bad for one to be continually cooped within walls. A pleasant ride up the road is always worthwhile."

Misha twitched xyr lips in a poor approximation of a smile. Xyr expression was confirmation enough both that it had indeed been xem out on the road yesterday, and that Graf'd been right about xyr intentions. "I will take that under advisement. Personally, I find it best to stay close to my family. Who knows what might happen in my absence?"

"My family are secure."

"I am glad to hear your confidence." Misha bowed, and rode away without waiting for Arel to bow in return.

"Shit," she said under her breath as we rode on.

"Hmm?"

"That was a threat. Xe is the Bethene's bone-magician. But the new bone resonates now," she'd said last night that the bone-thing had worked, and I hadn't asked for details, "and my cousin stands in my place in case of need, and I cannot..." She looked unhappy.

"You can't turn down this particular trip?"

"I am hardly the only one guarding my family. Misha wished only to upset me."

"Right," I agreed heartily, because she didn't have any option but to do as the Emperor asked, and worrying about her family wouldn't help her get it done, would it? "Good job you foiled the whole bone thing yesterday, then, right?" I considered what she'd just said. "If xe's a bone-magician, what was xe doing yesterday trying to ambush you?"

Arel shrugged. "Xe does a lot of things. Bone magician is xyr job, not necessarily the defining centre of xyr life."

As someone whose job was the defining centre of her life, I kept quiet.

"Xe did always want to be a bone magician," she added, almost to herself. "We thought, once..." She shook her head, almost violently, and stopped.

"You... used to know each other?" I hazarded.

"As children. We were friends, back then. Misha—chose to follow xyr brother, in the end." Her voice was tight. "It doesn't matter."

I wasn't about to push any further. All the same. The whole situation bothered me, and if all of this hadn't been secret, I'd have been seriously concerned for our safety. As it was, I spent a lot of that day looking over my shoulder, as we rode out in the wrong direction and then looped round after dark to the correct one—it would be more like four days than two, going this route—before I was satisfied we weren't being followed.

60

9.

We rode a fair way that night, my guidelight bobbing in front of us, before we eventually stopped a couple of hours after crossing the river upstream of Jiral.

"How far have we come?" Arel asked, as we dealt with the horses.

"We're near the catacombs."

"After being on the road all day?" She sounded grumpy.

"We came out the wrong way," I said, patiently, "and we had to loop around. We'll do better tomorrow."

"How far to Harin?"

I ran through the relevant bits of the guide-songs in my head. We wouldn't take the main roads, but there were plenty of back-lanes. I could do it by dead reckoning if I had to. "Day and a half to the border. Which I guess is mostly your land, so you ought to know it well enough. Two days after that to Harin itself."

I turned round and saw, in the moonlight, Graf lying stretched out on the ground with his hands behind his head. "I've just realised the advantage of being a ghost is not having to do chores."

"As if you ever did," I said, automatically. It wasn't true; Graf always cooked, and he was good at it.

"What?" Arel asked, and I startled.

"Uh. Just Graf. Don't worry." When I looked back, Graf had disappeared. I tried not to miss him.

The ghost-whisperers would help. They had to.

I didn't sleep well that night. But that was no excuse for letting myself be surprised by a sodding ambush halfway through the next day.

We were massively outnumbered, and we should have been in serious trouble; except I could tell from the start they were fighting to overwhelm, not to kill. Which, annoyingly, meant I couldn't fight to kill either. Arel, wielding a nasty looking dagger, obviously wasn't facing the same scruples, but neither was she much use as a swordswoman. Someone had disarmed her by the next time I looked around. Graf was trying to help but, well. Ghost.

They had scarves wrapped over their faces, but when one got close, I recognised Misha.

"Misha, you *shit*!" Arel screamed.

One of them had Arel's hands behind her back. I was still fighting, but there was no way we were getting out of this. Even if I started fighting to kill, there were more of them than I could take on. We were screwed. Misha closed on me, and xe was a decent swordsperson. I could see others moving in. Whatever Misha was after—but surely xe couldn't know about the seal?—xe was going to get it.

Something large swooped straight over our heads, and a tree beside the road caught fire. There was, suddenly, a lot of shrieking. Misha faltered, eyes upwards. I glanced up too.

The dragon. From the catacombs.

Shit.

It was diving straight for us, and neither of us even thought to move. Its talons were outstretched, its jaws open, and I waited almost fatalistically for the flame. At the last second, when I could have counted its teeth, it veered away. I recovered very slightly faster than Misha, and with a great deal of satisfaction, swiped xem straight out of xyr saddle with the flat of my sword. Xe hit the floor with a nasty crash.

The dragon swooped again. Arel jerked her head back and the person holding her hands went flying backwards with their hands clasped to their nose. Most of Misha's troops were scattering to hide under the trees.

"This way!" I shoved my sword into its scabbard, hauled Arel up behind me, and headed off down the road as fast as Monty could gallop.

What the fuck. Why had it suddenly decided to come after us? It had let us *go*. And however long it had been down there, it couldn't have been out in daylight before, or everyone would have known about it. Why now?

Eventually I let Monty slow to an exhausted walk, and turned to look over my shoulder. I couldn't see any of Misha's lot, but I could see —

"It's coming after us," Arel said, her voice somewhere between terrified and deadened. I felt about the same. Monty wouldn't be able to outrun a dragon even at the best of times.

But running in the road behind us—or sort of running, his legs were getting a bit confused with the road—was Graf, waving his arms and shouting, "It's okay! Don't worry! It's fine!"

Graf had lost his ghostly mind, then. Good to know.

The dragon landed in front of us. I dropped the reins, Monty put her head down, and I jumped off over her neck, leaving Arel still up there. I unsheathed my sword again and prepared to get roasted alive.

"Put it *away*!" Graf shouted. "Look! Honestly, open your eyes and *look*, Cade, you bloody idiot!"

The habit of trusting Graf kicked in. I didn't actually resheath my sword, but I squinted at the dragon.

Mouth shut. No further sign of flame. No bunched muscles, no preparation to leap at me.

"We meet again!" said the dragon happily.

"Um," I said, intelligently. "Hello?"

"Do you intend to eat us?" Arel demanded.

Well, that was one way to handle things.

"I didn't bother the other day. Why would I now?"

"Did you eat anyone back there?"

"No." The dragon opened its mouth as if to say more, hesitated, then closed it again.

"Pity," Arel muttered, but her shoulders relaxed a little. She'd moved properly onto Monty's saddle, and was sitting there, reins in hand, back straight, like she was at court.

I had a more pressing question. Well, two more pressing questions. "Are they coming after us?"

"Indeed not." I thought that was a draconic smile. "Running for home. Apart from the ones still on the ground. I followed them a little way before I came after you. I, ah, was hoping to ask a few questions of my own, as it happens, but they scattered off the path, and trees just don't keep burning at this time of year."

Hopefully that meant it hadn't started a forest fire. Slightly reluctantly, I sheathed my sword. "Next question. What are you doing here?"

"Oh, I smelt you," it said, with a draconic shrug. "Coming past the big hole in the ground."

"The catacombs?" Arel asked.

"Is that what you call it? Where I met you before. I smelt the ghost."

"And you came out?"

"I have been *so* bored. No visitors at *all* for years, no ghost-company for even longer." It sighed. "Maybe I should have eaten one of them after all. So! My name is Theo. Well, it's longer than that, but the long bit is dull."

"Nice to, um, meet you again, Theo. I'm Sir Cade. You remember Lady Arel."

"A pleasure," Theo said. "Where are you going?"

"You can't come," I said, and at the same time realised what I'd missed down in the catacombs: if Theo had been down there for decades, how come no one had seen them before?

Theo blew smoke at me. It wasn't fire, but it was hotter than I liked. Graf reappeared next to Theo and stuck his arm right into Theo's ear, and I do mean *right* in. Theo jerked in surprise and the smoke stopped. "I can come wherever I like. Are *you* going to stop me, with that flimsy piece of steel?"

"You. Can't. Come," I said again, because Theo might have a point, but there was no way Arel could show up in Harin and negotiate a treaty with a dragon hanging over her shoulder.

Well. Perhaps the dragon might help in *some* ways, but overall, I felt it would send the wrong message.

"Why not?" Arel asked, which I thought was wildly unhelpful.

"We can't feed them," I said.

"I prefer him," Theo said primly.

"Sorry. We can't feed him." We were going to have trouble feeding ourselves, in fact. Half of our supplies had been on Arel's horse, which was presumably either lost in the forest or halfway back home.

"I can feed myself."

"Yes, because Lady Arel taking a dragon across her family's lands and allowing it to eat half the cattle is going to go down *ever* so well."

"They *are* my lands," Arel said.

"And isn't that just like the bloody aristocracy," I snapped. "That only works if you're going to buy the cattle back and even then it's hardly fair."

"We can find a solution." Arel had her obstinate face on. "We must resupply anyway. You only have one person's rations and blankets in that bag, and we need another horse. If we find a farm, we can buy all that we need and food for Theo."

"Your money wasn't on the horse, then?" I asked. I was clearly going to lose this argument, but at least I could make sure it was well thought out.

Arel patted her belt. "The seal is also here."

I hadn't even thought about that. My stomach swooped sickly as I realised just how badly this might have gone.

"One cow will suffice for several days," Theo put in. "Also, I hate to point this out, but I'm coming with you anyway. You might as well make the best of it."

"Fine!" I threw my hands in the air. "Fine. A dragon is coming to Harin with us. *Fine.*"

"If Misha even thinks about ambushing us again, xe will think twice," Arel said fiercely, which, yeah, was a good point.

"So," Theo said cheerfully. "You mentioned a farm? And a cow? That was all rather hungry-making."

I looked around. I'd lost track of the guide-song while we were running, but this road went to the border. We'd taken a wrong turning at one point which we'd have to resolve, but I knew roughly where we were, and there was bound to be a farmhouse somewhere. Over to my right, not too far out of our way, I spotted the top of a chimney behind some trees with a curl of smoke coming from it.

"Come on, then," I said, and led our merry party onwards.

A noble, a knight, a dragon, and a ghost. What could possibly go wrong?

10.

I convinced an irritated Theo to stay well away from the farmhouse, and took Monty and Arel up to it. Food and a blanket I was sure we'd manage; I wasn't nearly as optimistic as Arel about our chances of finding a suitable horse, and I didn't know what we'd do instead. Monty couldn't keep carrying two, and we'd be a long time on the road if I had to walk.

But we were in luck. The farmers looked at one another, and the man sighed.

"We can't keep her forever," his partner said gently, and turned to me. "Daisy was his grandad's. Brought her home from the fair a few years back, said he'd got her cheap. We never did quite get to the bottom of that. She's a good horse, he shouldn't have got the bargain he claimed."

I'd place good money—ha—he'd won her gambling, and thought he'd be given into trouble for it.

"Old fool. Takin' up riding, his time o'life," the first farmer grumbled affectionately.

"Ah, it kept him young. But he died last winter. We've no time for riding, and Daisy won't pull anything."

"I dunno, I was thinking..." the first farmer started.

His partner rolled her eyes. "You've *tried*. It's not working. She'll be happier with something to do." In other words, she didn't want to be feeding a horse they couldn't use. "You said you'd take her to the fair come autumn. Wouldn't this be better?"

"I promise she will be well looked after," Arel said, in her most aristocratic tones. "My family's grooms know their trade."

The first farmer looked relieved. The second one looked like Arel's accent had significantly bumped up her financial expectations. We all went off to take a look at Daisy, a perfectly adequate horse who would do the job, but wouldn't in any other circumstances have made the cut for either Arel's or the Order's stables. While Arel was given extensive instructions about taking care of Grandad's Daisy, I undertook brisk negotiations with the harder-headed farmer. I did all right in the end, and she agreed to throw in food for us and Daisy, plus her tack and a couple of battered saddle-bags unearthed from a barn. The sheep for Theo were awkward; the farmers were baffled as to why we might want to drag two live sheep along with us, or indeed how we might manage that, and offered first cured meat instead, then to handle the slaughtering. Eventually I'd handed enough money over that they decided to humour us. They even offered to put us up for the night, but I wanted to get on; and I wasn't sure how long Theo would stay put.

We made reasonable time after that. (Theo, politely, waited to eat the sheep until we'd started off, then caught us up.) I wasn't sure if Misha definitely had given up, so I stuck to back-paths through the woods. I grew up round here; I knew all the local guide-rhymes as well as the Order's ones. We'd be slower than on the minor roads I'd planned for, but it was worth the trade-off.

Eventually the sun went down, and I called a halt and served out supper. Cold, mostly, but I'd got potatoes from the farmhouse to bake in the side of the fire, and I boiled water for tea.

After supper, Arel brought out a set of knucklebones from a pocket and beat me handily.

She shrugged at my surprise. "I spent a while on a barge, when I was small, visiting Gliance with my parents. The bargees played in the evenings and let me join in. They all cheated terribly."

"Which, obviously, you don't?"

Arel beamed sunnily at me. If she was cheating, I couldn't catch her at it. While we played, she told me and Theo some of the stories she'd heard from the bargees. She was a grand storyteller, whatever Theo might have said about her efforts in the catacombs; I saw his eyes lidded in contentment. We tried to get him playing knucklebones too, but they didn't work with his claws. It was comfortable, sitting around the fire like this. Familiar.

I really missed Graf.

"Do you think Misha'll be after us again?" I asked Arel.

"It sounded as if Theo chased xem off quite thoroughly. Xe would need to regroup, sort his soldiers out, and so on."

"So, maybe." I grimaced.

"Xe cannot bring many soldiers over the border," Arel pointed out. "We will be safer once we are in Perren."

"Mm." I didn't share her confidence.

"In all honesty, I am surprised at how hard Misha is pushing," Arel said. The firelight shone off the side of her frown. "Even though xe chose xyr brother, I would never have expected xem to follow him into war. They were always so unalike. I have barely spoken to Misha in years but when I see xem with Nico in court, there is no love lost between them." She shook her head. "I am surprised."

"Maybe xe is under more pressure than you know," Theo said, sleepily.

"Perhaps." Arel leant back on her hands. Above her, the first moon was low over the horizon, a curl of woodsmoke wisping up in front of it. "Is Graf here?"

I shook my head. "He isn't always."

"I imagine you plan to visit the ghost-whisperers at Harin?"

I looked over at her, and she shrugged. "My mother took me to visit their temple, when I was there as a child. I had forgotten it until earlier today."

"I thought they might be able to help, yes."

"Ensure he can go to a proper rest?"

I grunted non-committally and poked at the fire.

Arel, unfortunately, had wised up to the whole 'cannot lie' situation. She leant forward and tried to look me in the face. "Cade?"

"He shouldn't *be* a ghost," I burst out. "It was my fault. It shouldn't have happened that way. And they said, I've heard stories..."

"You wish to find him a *body*?" Arel asked incredulously. She was annoyingly smart.

I made another, grumpier, noise.

"Cade." Arel's voice was gentle. "I think that likely is just stories, you know. They help ghosts, certainly, but —"

I didn't want to have this conversation. "Oh, hey there Graf," I said loudly.

I wasn't sure if it actually fooled Arel, but she did shut up, so, that was a win. Fairly soon after that she yawned, and rolled herself up in her blankets to sleep. I ought to sleep, too; we'd need to be on the road pretty much as soon as the sun was up. But I sat a little longer, staring into the fire, and thinking about Graf. Arel, after a few minutes, began to snore, a quiet, gentle sort of snore. It was soothing. Quieter than Graf used to be. My heart clenched.

"Hey there love."

I looked up to see Graf between me and the fire. I couldn't exactly see it through him, but almost, like Graf was a sort of thick fog.

"Hey."

"You oughtta be asleep." He shifted to sit next to me, where he'd always sat when we were on the road. I wanted to lean into him, same as always, and I couldn't, and it hurt.

"Suppose." I stared into the fire for a bit. "Graf?"

"Yep."

"Where are you when I can't see you?"

Graf hummed. "I dunno. I think I'm sort of here, but not exactly. Like sleeping, maybe. Not paying attention."

"And then when you are here?"

"I kind of," he shrugged, "pull myself together."

"You said, before, you couldn't come to the chapterhouse. After." If only I'd gone back down there at the time. Those horrible days after he'd died, knowing I'd never see him again. I needn't have had those.

"Yeah," Graf agreed. "I tried, cos the catacombs were pretty boring. Got as far as the gate nearest the chapterhouse, and then I kind of got pulled back, I guess."

"Like you were tied to your..."

"To my death site, yeah," Graf said. The words didn't seem to bother him the way they did me. "Gonna be honest, didn't bother thinking about it, once I'd found it out. Didn't seem to matter much why." That was Graf all over. Practical. I'd been the one to do the speculating for the two of us.

"But now you can."

"Yeah," he agreed. "Dunno what's going on there."

I had a suspicion that I knew. "You said you were above the catacombs, when you saw Misha and Co."

"Yeah, that's right. Trying out the distance that way."

"And then you came to find me. Which you couldn't, before."

"Yeah." Graf thought about it for a bit. "I could see you, was the thing. Not see exactly, but I knew where you were.

You stood out. And it was really important. So I was kind of pulling and pulling towards you, and then it felt like something," he gestured, "kind of tore. Bit unpleasant." Graf had once described a near-fatal sword wound as 'a bit unpleasant'. "Then whoosh! Down to you at the chapterhouse." He nodded with satisfaction.

"Is it still uncomfortable?"

Graf sucked at his teeth. "Nah. I feel a bit fuzzy round the edges, but not that bad. And I'm not stuck in the catacombs, so, hey, that was a win." He gave me his old easy-going smile, and my chest clenched.

My suspicion was getting stronger. "Hey. Could you try something for me?"

"Sure."

"Could you find your way back to where we were attacked, earlier?"

"What? Right now?" Graf sounded bewildered.

"Humour me."

I was used to trusting Graf in battle. He was used to trusting me when I had an idea. "It's miles away, but sure, if you insist."

After a minute or so, I began to get a strange feeling in my stomach, something pulling at me from the inside. I rubbed at it, and it vanished, just as Graf reappeared, looking annoyed. "Can't get there. It was like the catacombs. Like something pulling me back. Got a bit of the way along the road, and then, nope. Nothing doing." He looked at me, and made a resigned noise.

"You've got a theory. Out with it."

"You were haunting the catacombs," I said. "Where by *haunting*, I mean, you were tied there. To where you," I took a breath, "died. That's why you couldn't leave. I mean, I know jack shit about ghosts, but in the stories, they're associated

72

with a place, right? You get the ghost-whisperers in to a place where a ghost is, you don't wrap the ghost up and take it to them." Mostly.

"Uh. Yeah." He frowned. "But I'm here now."

"Yeah. You're haunting me."

"Huh." He sank back down next to me, cross-legged. A wisp of woodsmoke twisted through him.

"I mean, I don't know. But it makes sense. You've been travelling with us, so it can't be that you started haunting the chapterhouse; and now we're stopped, you've got a limit to how far you can go from here. You said it was me you came back to warn. And it felt weird, when you tried to go too far." I rubbed at my stomach. "You're haunting me. Can't prove it, but. It fits the facts."

"Cool," Graf said, then paused. "Is it cool?"

"Do you mean, do I mind?" I sighed. "I can't *mind*, Graf. You're my sword-brother, and you died on my watch."

"It wasn't your fault," Graf said, fiercely. "At worst it was, like, shared responsibility. It wasn't your fault."

"And now you're back," I said. I still wasn't sure I believed him about the fault thing. "So. Of course I don't mind."

I didn't. I was glad he was back. It was still bloody weird.

"Still bloody weird," Graf said, and I grinned affectionately at him. "I guess I'll have to clear out of the way the next time you get laid."

"Oh, for pity's..." He laughed, and something relaxed in my chest. "I'd better go to sleep," I told him. "Early start tomorrow and all that."

"Night." Graf waved a cheerful hand at me. Once I'd rolled myself up in my blankets, I glanced over at him. He was still sitting by the fire, staring at it, sunk partway into the ground.

I was going to fix this.

11.

When I'd been a kid, travelling with the sheep to the annual market in Gethenet in Perren, you barely noticed the border. There'd been a sign either side and that was about it.

Now, when we crested the hill, I stopped short in dismay. There were soldiers, and a barrier across the road. They were questioning someone in a cart, and as we watched, they lifted the barrier, let them cross, and dropped it again.

"Didn't used to be like that," I said.

Arel's face was sad. "I know. Our country home is over the river, close to the border north-west of here. I remember crossing without even thinking about it." Her shoulders set. "This is why the treaty matters. It should be like that again. We already had one war here. I will not let it come to another one."

"Were you involved in the last war, then?" Theo asked. "To be so upset about it, I mean?"

"It was in my grandmother's time," Arel said. "In the early years of the Emperor's reign. But must you have been personally involved with something to care about it deeply? I need not have been in a war to know what it would mean. I need not have seen devastation to wish to avoid it."

"Well said." I squinted down at the border. "But getting back to the practicalities: we won't get Theo through that. And they're going to ask what we're doing." Not a problem for me, mind; even irritable soldiers don't hassle us.

"I am a lawyer," Arel declared, "going to a client in Gethenet." Gethenet, as well as being the nearest decent-sized town, was conveniently away from Harin. "We will change direction once we are out of sight."

"Theo?"

"I'll fly," Theo said. "I prefer flying, but it seemed more polite to walk with you, my new friends." He beamed at us. Dragon smiles were bloody unnerving. He'd strolled alongside us most of the morning, which I found a touch unsettling, Arel seemed completely fine with, and the horses didn't like at all. Monty only snorted and occasionally snatched at her bit, but it had taken us a while to convince Daisy she wasn't about to be eaten. I couldn't blame her; it wasn't as if Theo would turn down horse, in the general way of things. I hoped those sheep had filled him up.

"I'll find you on the other side," Theo said, and took off straight upwards. Monty snorted again, and Daisy shied and nearly had Arel off. Shading my eyes and looking up, I saw a tiny dot, way up in the sky. You'd assume he was a bird if you hadn't seen him on the ground.

The border wasn't as bad as I'd feared. They didn't shake us down for money, for starters, but the mere fact of its existence prickled the back of my neck with irritation. Arel did most of the talking; I drew on my extensive prior experience in standing around looking knightly.

We headed towards Gethenet, and once we were over the hill and out of sight, I hummed through the guide-song and checked the sun. I was halfway through calculating a cross-field route to get us back on course when a shadow fell over us, the horses spooked all over again, and Theo landed neatly in the middle of the empty road.

"You want the big city, don't you?" he asked, once everything was back under control. "Because you're going the wrong way."

"We did not wish the soldiers to know where we were going," Arel said. "Cade is working out our route now they can no longer see us."

"That way." Theo pointed a wing. "I saw it."

There was *some* advantage to having a dragon along.

We camped that night in a field, and I discovered another advantage to having a dragon along which we hadn't needed in the sheltered forest the night before: he was lovely and warm and made an excellent windbreak.

Settled in against his side, tending the fire I'd got him to curl around, I finally remembered to ask why no one had ever seen him down in the catacombs.

"Well," Theo said thoughtfully, "there was quite a long time where I was having a nap."

Further enquiry revealed that 'quite a long time' probably meant 'five to ten years'.

"But surely *someone* would have seen you and reported back," I said. "We go down there quite a lot."

Theo did something with his eyes which I was fairly certain was the equivalent of an eye-roll. "I'm not *stupid*. I had no desire to have a bunch of baby knights shrieking and waving swords at me. It was hardly difficult to avoid you. You're all very noisy, and even when you come as far as the square," which admittedly we didn't all that often, since there were plenty of training opportunities nearer the entrance, "none of you ever look in the mausoleums."

Well, that was a lowering realisation. We'd all been walking straight past a dragon for decades.

"I go out at night," Theo said, "and no one sees me then either." He sighed. "It's easier up in the mountains, but I wanted to get away from my family for a while."

Relatable. Judging by Arel's expression, she was thinking about the same.

"Why, then, did you come out and talk to us?" Arel asked, head tilted curiously.

Theo shrugged. "Bored. It's been so *long* since I had a proper conversation. And there were only two of you. I knew

I could always just—ahem." He coughed and examined a claw. 'Eat you', I filled in mentally. "And we had an interesting chat! With stories!" he finished brightly, looking back up. "So evidently it was a good decision."

"And if I go back and tell the Archon?" I asked.

Theo revealed his teeth. "I am sure you won't do any such thing."

I'd have to, though, wouldn't I? Maybe I could think of some mutually agreeable solution.

Arel glanced between the two of us. "What magic can you perform, Cade?" she asked, in an obvious bid to change the subject.

"I can make a guidelight, light a fire, and fix leather tack and minor-to-middling skin wounds, but not metal or cloth." Graf could do cloth. After the third time I stuck my tunic to my finger, I gave up and he did the mending for both of us. "I can put an edge on a sword or a knife, but not polish a nick out, and a whetstone's easier, really." That's true of most magic, save maybe the healing; if there's a non-magical alternative you're as well using that. I'd lit that evening's fire with flint and steel. A guide-light moves with you and leaves both your hands free, which is great in the field, but in the chapterhouse we use candles like everyone else.

Theo gave up glaring at me and put his head on his paws. "What about you?" he asked Arel.

Arel shook her head. "I was never taught. I doubt I even have any ability."

"Not everyone does," I allowed. And it's a skill like any other; learning takes time and effort. "I suppose you lot have people to do it for you."

"Every family has a bone-magician, but that is a very long time learning."

I found even the idea of bone-magic distinctly unnerving, so I let the conversation drop, and before long Arel and I were both wrapped in our blankets and asleep.

The next morning, we confronted the main disadvantage of having a dragon along: there was no way we could take him into Harin.

Theo lashed his tail. "But they *revere* dragons in Harin! I was there in my youth."

"And I was there five years ago," I said, "and there wasn't a single dragon in the place. When was your youth? Three hundred years ago or so, I'm guessing?"

Theo blew smoke at me, and Graf appeared and twisted his ear until he stopped. "It may have been some time, as you humans count it," he said, grudgingly. "I had a lovely chat with the ghost-whisperers."

"You'll cause far too much commotion. This is supposed to be a secret mission."

"It won't be that secret once you reach the palace," Theo pointed out, which to be fair, was true.

"We still won't be 'those people with the dragon.'" I ground my teeth in frustration. "Do you *want* never to be left alone again? Maybe we can find a compromise." I was struggling to think of anything.

"I want to see the palace," Theo said obstinately.

"I'll come back and get you tonight," I offered desperately. I had no idea how I'd manage that, but it had to be an improvement on walking through the gates with a dragon in broad daylight.

"If you don't, I'll come and find you," Theo warned, but Graf was talking urgently into his ear. After a moment he huffed smoke again and said, irritably, "Very well. I will stay here and you will come tonight."

"Late tonight," I clarified. There'd be some kind of dinner to attend first, I expected. "Between the moons." The first moon set late evening, and the second didn't rise until a couple of hours before dawn, this time of year.

Theo stomped away through the field, complaining under his breath, and I got moving before he could change his mind.

I was expecting Arel to announce herself at the gates, but she claimed to be a penitent come to visit the city's temples. I was Sir Cade, Knight of Siremos, as per usual. They touched their hearts and let us through. Not that I saw anyone being turned away.

"Can you navigate us to the palace?" Arel asked.

"That is literally what I am trained to do," I reminded her, and began to hum under my breath.

The grey mountain rock I was familiar with in Jiral was common here too—they were only a little further downstream from the mountain quarries—but there were also plenty of smaller houses built of bricks in a red clay that I guessed must be local. The palace, looming over the rest of the city from the top of a hill, was white marble, glowing in the sunshine. That would have come in by sea, but shipping it from the port, either overland or upriver, must have been quite the undertaking. Well; that was royalty for you.

Once I'd got us to the palace, it was Arel's turn. She asked one of the guards on the door to bring her a secretary, and showed them the Emperor's seal. There was a lot of quietly-conducted fuss and before long Arel and I were being ushered into a resplendent guest room. I'd visited the palace before, but I'd never been treated this well.

The room was huge. Two large beds barely took up a quarter of the floorspace. A fire was laid ready to light in the fireplace, the large windows all across one wall had proper glass, and there were beautiful rugs and wall-hangings. I put my hands behind my back. I was fairly sure I shouldn't touch anything, especially not before I'd washed.

Graf, of course, had lain straight down on one of the beds, although presumably ghosts didn't get dirty in any physical sense. Or, indeed, benefit from the softness of the mattresses.

"I wish to see the Prince as soon as I have bathed," Arel said to the flunky who'd shown us up here. She was being Lady Arel to the hilt. Bathwater appeared as if by magic.

"There is plenty of water still, Cade," Arel said as she emerged from behind the ornate blue-and-gold bath screen in a very fancy under-dress.

"I don't want to delay you further," I said.

Arel frowned at me. I frowned back at her.

"I'll be coming to guard you?" I said, accidentally making it a question.

"You will not," Arel said, chin up. "I will not be permitted to take an armed knight into the Prince's rooms, and there is no value in you wasting your time there if you are unarmed."

"I don't need to be armed to be dangerous."

"In which case they will refuse you entry altogether."

We carried on arguing while she got dressed, and eventually I won, and walked down to the Prince's rooms with her, through miles of corridors with marble floors and mosaic-tiled walls, trying not to act too triumphant.

Which was just as well, because once we reached the door and the very broad-shouldered guard that stood there, she was proved right: they didn't let me in. Arel smiled sweetly at me and vanished through the door before I could remonstrate or try to insist on her having personal protection.

Well. If the Prince stabbed her then it wouldn't be *my* fault, although it would be pretty much a disaster as far as making peace went. I scowled at the closed door.

"You're welcome to wait," the door-guard said politely.

I waited a few minutes in case Arel got booted straight out again; when she didn't, I went back to our rooms to take advantage of that bathwater.

After that, I hummed through all the guide-songs of Harin I knew until I found the right one, then strapped my armour back on.

If Arel was going to be busy negotiating peace, and I wished her all the luck in the world, then it was time to do what I'd come here for.

12.

Graf appeared at my shoulder as I walked through the palace gate, smiling politely at the guards. The late afternoon sunlight shone golden off the street's smooth flagstones. There were only a handful of people outside the palace, but as I turned left down the gentle slope of the road towards the main part of the city, the streets became busier, and the buildings changed from the large mansions around the palace to a mix of shops and smaller, less ornate, houses.

"Where're you going?" Graf asked.

"For a little walk."

He eyed me suspiciously. "I don't believe it. You never go off wandering just for fun. What are you after?"

"Maybe I've changed." I hummed more of the guide-song, and took a right. There should be an alleyway on my left— yes, there it was—which would open out into a square, and the ghost-whisperers were there.

I'd expected something dark and shadowed and gloomy. Instead, the small square outside the ghost-whisperers' house caught the sun far more than I would have expected in the middle of the city, and it was full of trees, all sorts of different trees, in glorious spring leaf. They were arranged in wedges pointing in towards the centre of the square, where there was an open area with a small formal garden. I walked towards it, hearing the hum of insects around the flowers. I'm not much on flowers, but the purples and yellows and oranges were cheering.

"Oh shit. No way," Graf said.

Someone in an unbleached robe knelt in the middle of the garden with a trowel. They looked up at our approach.

"No. Way. They're going to exorcise me!"

"I prefer xe," the person said mildly, standing and brushing off xyr knees. "And I assure you I will do no such thing."

"I'm not going to *exorcise* you, you idiot," I echoed, but Graf had already disappeared.

"Shit," I said, then looked at the ghost-whisperer apologetically. "Sorry. Language."

"Not at all. I am Emar. It is a pleasure to meet you."

"Sir Cade, of the Knights of Siremos," I said. "And I would introduce you to my sword-brother Sir Graf, but he appears to have taken his leave."

"*Cade.*" I turned around. Graf was skulking in the entrance of the alleyway. He never was any good at skulking. Too big. In theory being a ghost ought to make him better at it, but as the only two people around could both see him, it didn't help.

"Please excuse me," I said to Emar.

"Why the fuck are we at the ghost-whisperers?" Graf demanded.

"Not to exorcise you, you idiot. To see if they can help."

"What do you mean, *help*?"

I shrugged. "I don't know, do I? I'm not a ghost-whisperer. At the very least they can tell us whether you really are haunting me. Now, I'm going to go ask Emar there some questions. You can come with me, or you can stay here."

"*Fine.*"

"A pleasure to meet you, Sir Graf," Emar said, bowing to him. "If the two of you would follow me inside?"

In the same way as I'd expected the square to be grey and gloomy, I'd expected similar of the house. Grey stone, dark iron, gloomy corridors, all that sort of thing. Instead, Emar ushered us into a buttercup-stone building with huge windows. The large open hall had pale wood panels and rich stained glass in large sheets which threw the sunlight into pools of colour on the pale tiles of the floor.

"Some tea, perhaps?" Emar offered. "Come, sit."

Xe guided us to a smaller room off the main hall. It had the same light, airy feel, with more of those soothing colour-ed-glass patches of sunlight. Two couches sat at right angles to one another. I sat on one, and Emar took the other. Graf stood next to the door with his arms folded mutinously and his shoulders hunched, looking a lot like he had when we were teenagers in trouble. I tried to catch his eye, but he wasn't looking at me.

A kid in an unbleached robe like Emar's appeared with a tray of three cups and a pot, and bowed politely to Graf before edging round him and bowing to me and to Emar.

"Why three?" Graf demanded. "Not like I can drink any."

Emar smiled patiently, and poured tea from the pot into all three cups. Then xe held xyr hand open over one of the cups, and closed xyr eyes. Slowly, the cup emptied—or at least, to me it emptied. Graf, however, was watching it, frowning. Once it was all the way empty, Emar took xyr hand back and opened xyr eyes.

"If you please, Sir Graf," xe said, gesturing to the empty cup. "And Sir Cade, please take one of the others."

Graf came closer to the table. He lifted the cup, which was startling in itself, sipped with visible doubt, then looked delighted.

"Ghost tea?" I asked, incredulous.

"Wow. You have no idea how good it is to get a cuppa. Thank you, Emar." He bowed, finally. About time.

I sipped my own tea. It was a very nice brew but I didn't have quite as much reason for enthusiasm as Graf.

"So," Emar said. "How can I help?"

"We don't need help," Graf said. He'd relaxed a bit, with the tea, but he still hadn't sat down. I scowled at him. I hated it when he hovered like that, even when he was alive.

"Am I haunted?" I demanded.

"In general, or specifically?" Emar asked.

"Either. Both. I think Graf's haunting me in particular, but, hey, if there's anything else haunting me, please feel free to cover that too."

"You mean, are you the site of Sir Graf's attachment? Yes, yes, it's perfectly clear." Xe nodded to both of us. "How did this come about?"

"We're not sure," I said, "but it seems like Graf was haunting where he d-died, first."

Emar nodded encouragingly. "Yes, that is customary."

"And then he saw something he wanted to warn me about and he... moved."

Emar frowned. "Sir Graf?"

Graf shrugged. "I really wanted to tell Cade. So I just—yanked. A lot. And it kind of hurt, but then I could move, and I went to find Cade."

Emar's expression twitched in momentary surprise. "You moved your attachment to Sir Cade. Well. That is very unusual. Very unusual indeed."

"Is it a problem?" I demanded.

"His fading will likely be speedier," Emar said. "His substance was clearly damaged."

A lurching hole began to open in my stomach. "When... when you say fading, do you mean... He goes back to the Lake?"

"It depends," Emar said. "When I say *fading*, you could think of it as his substance falling away, piece by piece. When a ghost reaches the point of fading altogether, there is no longer enough of them to usefully think of that particular individual returning to the Lake. What happens, in due course, to the substance that has fallen away, that is one of the great mysteries."

Now I really felt sick. Graf, arms folded and wearing a truculent expression, was obviously bothered too.

"There's an alternative, right?" I demanded. There had to be.

"We can detach him now," Emar said, nodding. "Return him to the Lake whole." Xe pursed xyr lips. "Mostly whole. Sufficiently whole."

"Right." Better than fading away, I supposed. But not what I wanted. Not even slightly. "So, my next question is, how about *instead* of that, can we put him back into, like, a body." I gestured up and down mine, and then, for good measure, Emar's. "Because the stories say you lot can do that."

"The stories say they're scary monsters, too, Cade!" Graf protested. Which was rich coming from him, given how he'd first reacted to Emar.

I shrugged. "Yeah, fine, stories say lots of things. But I wondered, maybe..."

Emar was looking closely at me. Xe had wholly shed the cosy welcoming persona. "You wish Sir Graf to live again?"

"I am alive," Graf said testily. "I mean, obviously I'm not, I'm dead, but, you know, I'm right here bloody arguing with you, and there's literally no difference between that and when I was properly alive, so it hardly matters."

"But you'll *fade*," I said. "Or they'll send you back. Gone, either way." I turned back to stare down Emar. "Can you do it?"

"No," Emar said, but I heard the tiny hesitation.

"You can, but you don't want to." I folded my arms, and resisted the urge to put my hand on my sword-hilt. It wouldn't help. Probably.

Emar's expression of discomfort?—distaste?—didn't sit well on xyr calm wrinkle-free face. "You are correct that the stories have a kernel of truth. But the ritual requires a live body, and that is no longer considered ethical."

"Why not?"

"Because I'd bump out whoever was in it," Graf said. "Obviously."

"Oh." I thought about it. "You can't share?"

"One spirit per body is the rule." Emar looked sympathetically at me. I resisted the urge to punch xem. "I understand your concern for your sword-brother, and I regret this very deeply, but I am afraid that there is nothing we can do for him, beyond detaching him altogether."

"No," I said, without even thinking about it. Not yet. There had to be another answer.

Graf pulled a face. "Not just yet, thanks. I'm not that faded yet. And I'd like to see how all the..." I scowled ferociously at him and he stopped himself before mentioning Arel. I didn't expect the ghost-whisperers to be gossips, particularly, but there was no point in borrowing trouble. "Later," he said, instead. "I've got a while yet, right?"

"A few days," Emar said, bluntly. "No more, I fear. But yes, *later*, if you prefer."

Yeah, no. I wasn't accepting this. I wanted Graf *back*.

"What about me?" I asked.

"What?" Graf and Emar said together.

"You want a live body. What about mine. If I'm consenting, there isn't an ethical problem, right?" Ha. They couldn't object to that.

"*No*," Graf said, with great force. He was glaring daggers at me.

"I think not," Emar said. "Whilst I understand your point about the ethics of consent, I regret that I and my siblings will refuse to be involved in such an undertaking."

I tried to argue, but Emar just ignored everything else I said, and Graf wouldn't even look at me. But it *couldn't* be, I couldn't...

We finished our tea with Emar, and Graf, of all people, made the running in terms of appropriate polite conversation, whilst I swallowed tea past the painful lump in my throat, and desperately tried to think of another plan to save Graf. I came up with absolutely sod all.

"It was very nice to meet both of you," Emar said, once the tea was done. Xe stood up. "And I wish you both the very best of luck during Sir Graf's remaining stay in this sphere. Do come back to us once you are ready to depart, Sir Graf."

"Isn't there *anything* you can do?" I asked, despairing. "It was my fault, you know. Can't I...?"

"I am so sorry," Emar said, with gentle finality.

Out in the alleyway that led away from their beautiful garden square, I turned to Graf, and found him doing his level best to pin me to the wall; which is difficult when you're not a being of matter. He was so angry that I found myself taking a step backwards anyway.

"I thought you were done with all this guilt shit," he said, through his teeth. "I thought we went through this, down in the bloody catacombs on day one."

"I —"

"It was not your bloody fault. How many times have I said that now? It was my fault a bit, and fine, maybe your fault a bit, but it was mostly sheer bad luck."

"Just because you never took responsibility for anything —"

"Yeah, that's true, I'll cop to it, but it's just as true that you take far too bloody much. You don't get to push me into this. You don't get to fix everything, Cade. You *can't*. This is one of those things. And what *bullshit* were you on about, offering me to take over your body? As if I'd ever say yes to that, you utter fucking idiot."

"I miss you," I said, which wasn't quite what I'd meant to say. I'd meant to say something more irritated, and perhaps some swearwords. I'd meant to argue this out properly, get into the sort of shouting match Graf and I always got into, the sort I always won in the end. I couldn't fix everything, sure, whatever. But I could fix this. I could. I had to.

"I don't know why, 'cos I'm right here."

"But you *won't* be," I said, and hated that I could hear the tears threatening in my voice.

Graf rode straight over me. "Also, if I took over your body, I'd just be missing *you*," his voice was tight with emotion too, "so I don't see how that would help."

It would mean I didn't have to deal with any of it, because I wouldn't be there; but that argument might not go down well. But surely, surely...

Searching for something to say, I glanced to my left. Passing the alleyway, out on the street we were about to emerge onto once Graf stopped yelling at me, was a face I immediately recognised. "*Misha?*"

"What?" Graf's head whipped round, but xe'd gone already.

"Misha. I saw Misha. I'm sure of it."

Graf wisped away into air; then, before I had time to wonder what he was doing, wisped back again for just long enough to say, "It is. The shit. Come on."

13.

I'd have been completely screwed following Misha on my own. I'm a knight. I'm not good at blending in, with the surcoat and that. And Misha had seen me, at least twice, which wouldn't help. Graf always argued that the surcoat made you less recognisable, not more, because people see that and not the person, but I was never convinced.

Graf wouldn't have been any help either when he was alive; with his height, he was even more obvious than me. As a ghost, however, he blurred backwards and forwards, checking on Misha up ahead and then coming back to direct me. I'd no idea he had that much control over how he moved, but it was impressive.

We were heading back towards the palace. Which would have been less surprising if Misha were trailing the quantity of retinue I'd have expected, instead of being all on xyr own. Obviously Arel wasn't trailing servants either, but then Arel was supposed to be conducting a secret mission. What was Misha up to?

Eventually Misha went into a respectable inn just under the palace's walls. I hung around in the street trying and failing not to look conspicuous, while Graf wisped away inside.

"Xe's settled down in the taproom and ordered food," Graf reported back.

I leant against the wall and tried not to look like I was talking to thin air. "Why isn't xe up at the palace? Being all Court Families and that?"

"Xe's *hiding*, Cade."

"Yes, Graf, I got that. But why? Arel was here on the down-low until she got into the palace because the Emperor told her to get this done in secret so no one could scupper it. Misha's on the side that wants to do the scuppering."

"Oh, I get you. Why not just barge into the palace and scupper away? Huh. Maybe xe's here for something else."

"Too much coincidence." I sighed. "I can't think how xe would undermine things at this point."

"Killing Arel?"

I did not like that idea at all. "You couldn't just stab someone in the middle of the palace and get away with it."

"You could when they were on the way out," Graf said. He was flickering in and out as he thought about it, which was giving me a headache.

"But if xe's watching for her, why is xe sat on xyr arse inside a taproom?"

"Someone else watching on xyr behalf?"

That made sense. "Ugh. What do we do now, then?" I wasn't used to this political intrigue nonsense. I just guided people, and occasionally hit other people with my sword.

"I stay here and keep an eye on xem. You go in and warn Arel."

"Is it close enough? For you to stay here, I mean, if I go in. It's pretty big." We both looked up at the palace.

Graf shrugged. "Well, if it is too far, we'll find out when I'm pulled back."

"And you'll lose track of Misha."

"No, because you'll walk a few yards backwards and you'll be close enough again. I'll only be gone a few seconds. Go on. Shoo."

The guards at the palace gates greeted me by name, which was disconcerting but spoke well for their security. I was most of the way up to our rooms before I felt a weird tugging in my middle. I stopped and bent down to fiddle with my boot, waiting for Graf to appear beside me. He didn't, and the feeling faded. It reappeared once I got to the rooms; we must be close to our maximum distance. I sat on the window seat, where the tugging was least, and waited for Arel.

A huge pile of fancy dresses were arrayed carefully on the bed. Did palaces keep wardrobes full of spares for visiting guests who'd lost their baggage? Perhaps they did.

Eventually Arel breezed in looking satisfied.

"Is it all sorted, then?" I asked, mostly teasing. I was pretty sure these things took weeks.

"Nearly," she said, to my surprise. "They are as keen as I to resolve this. I recited the draft treaty to the prince. We have made some changes, and there is little disagreement left. The prince's reciters are going over the agreed parts now."

"So you're done?"

Arel shook her head. "This is a break. There is a semi-formal dinner in half an hour, and then we will finalise the last sections. I must, I suppose, keep a close eye on my wineglass." She really did look immoderately cheerful.

Which was a bugger, as I was going to have to un-cheer her. "That's great. Bad news. Misha's here."

Arel stopped dead and stared at me. "Misha? Why?"

"Well, I don't know, but given that xe's hanging around in a tavern by the palace, not barging in here dressed fancy and demanding to see the prince, I'm guessing it's not entirely on the level. Graf and me reckon xe's waiting for you to come out."

"That is a problem for another time," Arel declared, chin going up. "I am here, xe is not, and I have a treaty to negotiate." She waved a dismissive hand and turned to the pile of dresses. Which was aggravating.

"Lady Arel," I said. She turned, frowning, the formality catching her attention. "There is a known enemy of your family, who has attacked you three times in the last week, hiding in the city which you have reached *in secret*. I strongly recommend that you do not dismiss this. Something is going on, and you need to know what."

Arel's face screwed up. "That is all very well, but I am due at dinner in twenty minutes. As are you."

"What?"

"You must be at dinner," Arel said, impatiently. "As I said already."

"You did not," I said through gritted teeth. "And you shouldn't go either, if Misha's wandering around."

Arel glared at me. "I cannot sit here waiting to see what Misha might, perhaps, do. I am here to seal this treaty. I must attend the dinner."

"*I* am here to look after your safety." If something went wrong, it would be my fault.

"You are here because I needed a guide, and because you refused to take no for an answer. Because you have your own agenda here in Harin." Her voice was very aristocratic, and she stood very straight. "This, Sir Cade, is not your decision."

She held my gaze until I threw my hands in the air and turned away.

"So," she said, voice light again, as though the last few seconds hadn't happened. "There is little we could do about it just now in any case. The treaty is more important."

"You could authorise me to resolve it," I said, irritably.

"You may not kill xem," Arel said, without looking up from the pile of dresses. "Not unless xe forces you to, in which case make sure you have witnesses."

"I'm not going to kill xem unless xe tries to kill me. Or you. I'm not politically affiliated, remember? I can only do what's necessary to protect my client."

"Misha has not tried to kill me," Arel held a green dress up in front of her and grimaced at it. "To kidnap me, yes. To discredit me and my family, absolutely. But even on the road xe was not aiming to kill. It does not matter just now, because whatever you might do must wait until after dinner." She rubbed the fabric of another dress between finger and thumb.

"Why?" I knew I sounded plaintive. "I'm not noble. Or involved in this. I'm unaffiliated, remember?"

"You are in my entourage."

"*Entourage*? Get lost." Who was the guide, exactly?

"Thus, you are expected," Arel said, ignoring me. "This is *important*, Cade. I am responsible for making this happen, and suitable behaviour is part of that. We must be seen to be reliable. Trustworthy. Misha can wait."

If Graf and I were right, and Misha was waiting for Arel to leave the palace, she was probably right. But I felt like I was missing something.

"I don't like formal meals," I grumbled.

"I have full faith in your capabilities, Sir Cade," Arel said, giving me a blinding smile now she'd won. She put her chosen dress, a deep blue velvet number with lace around the bodice and an unreasonable quantity of skirt, over the back of a chair, and began to wriggle out of what she was wearing. "Now, if you could do me up at the back, and then, perhaps a spare, clean, surcoat? There are clean trousers for you on the chest."

The formal dinner was about what you'd expect. Big hall, lots of well dressed people, excellent food. I became less dubious about Arel's claim that I was required to be here when the seneschal greeted me by name and sent me to an

empty seat at a table near the door. Arel he escorted personally to the top of the hall, to join the Prince and various other
fancy types.

My table-mates were pleasant enough, and respectful
in the way people usually are of us. If I'd been so inclined
I could definitely have gotten laid; the woman next to me,
who'd introduced herself as Sara, one of the Prince's archivists, kept putting her hand on my arm and leaning towards
me. I flirted back a little, just to be polite, but mostly I was
too busy worrying about what Misha was doing and how I
was going to stop it.

Halfway through the pheasant course—I don't like pheasant—that tug in my stomach twitched, and Graf appeared
right in the middle of the table. I jerked backwards and spilt
gravy down my front.

"Sir Cade?" Sara sounded worried.

"Misha's on xyr way!" Graf said. "Someone came in and
talked to xem, and then xe was just up and away into the
palace!"

"How long?" I demanded.

"Sir Cade?" Sara asked, more uncertainly. Everyone
around me had put their forks down and was looking at me
in concern.

"It's not bloody far, is it?" Graf said.

I could hardly just shriek across the room at Arel,
although when I glanced over, she was watching me with
concern. I stood up, shoving the bench back and nearly
tipping Sara over, and began to make my way across the
room, towards Arel and the Prince, trying to look as casual as
possible for someone who'd been having a conversation with
empty air.

Inevitably, one of the Prince's guards stepped in front of
me. Fair enough; I would have stepped in front of me, too.
"Excuse me, Sir," she said, deferentially enough, but her hand

was tight on her sword-hilt. "I'm afraid you need to sit down. Or leave the hall, if you feel unwell."

"I need to speak to my client," I said, and gestured at the top table.

Arel was making sit-down-and-shut-up gestures. The Prince was looking. *Everyone* was looking. So much for casual.

"If you'll just step out of the hall," the guard said soothingly, "I'm sure your client can come and talk to you when they have a moment."

I wasn't about to fight my way past this kid; it wouldn't just be her, either, there were half-a-dozen guards standing around. I looked back over at Arel and tried to make *xe's on xyr way* gestures. From Arel's baffled stare, I wasn't getting anywhere.

The doors flew open, and Misha stalked in.

Xe was also trailing a fair few guards, but unlike me, Misha didn't want to avoid a scene. Misha's main purpose, it became rapidly clear, was to make a scene.

"Arel!" xe declared in ringing tones. "I come to retrieve the Emperor's stolen seal!"

That got a gasp from the assembled throng. No one was eating now. They were all staring with their mouths open. I swore, a lot, *mostly* under my breath.

"Stolen?" Arel repeated, voice higher than usual. She stood up. The Prince was looking between them, frowning.

"You stole the Emperor's seal and brought it here. To betray him."

The Prince's eyebrows went up.

"I did no such thing!"

"She didn't," I said, loudly. Hardly anyone paid any attention—certainly not Misha or Arel, attention fixed on one another—but the Prince glanced over at me.

"The Emperor gave me the seal!" Arel said.

"Personally?" Misha folded xyr arms.

"No, but..."

"You stole it." Misha held something out on xyr hand. "And here is the proof. A true seal, bound to me."

The Prince's expression didn't actually shift, but I got the strong impression it wanted to.

"This is nonsense!" Arel cried. There were red spots on her cheeks. "The Bethene seek to manipulate the Emperor, to bring me and mine down."

"No need for that," Misha said. Xe bared xyr teeth. "Given your theft, your family is no longer welcome in court, *Arel*."

Arel—not Lady Arel any more, then—looked like she'd been punched in the stomach. She set her shoulders and regrouped. "Lies. Why would I come here to negotiate with a stolen seal, when it would betray me the moment I used it?"

"How would I know what your plan was?" Misha asked, contemptuously. "Perhaps you wished to insult Prince and Emperor both."

"Prove it," Arel challenged him, her back straight. "You are a bone-magician. You claim my seal is false, and yours is true. Prove it."

I bit my lip. It made sense, except... Surely Misha would have predicted this? Surely xe wouldn't be waving around a false seal that a little bone magic could reveal?

Could both seals be true? Could the Emperor be playing some complicated game that I didn't understand, attempting perhaps to annoy the Prince, or... I didn't know. I wasn't politically minded. But the pit of my stomach lurched with a sudden horrible thought. What if Arel had been betrayed? We'd taken that kid at their word, because Arel had recognised them, and they'd had the seal, and they'd bound it to Arel.

97

Misha's eyes flickered. Xe looked almost confused. For a moment, hope rose that xe had been bluffing all along, and Arel had successfully called it... but no, Misha spread xyr hands. "By all means."

Arel came to stand in front of xem, back straight, mouth set in a firm line. Misha was frowning, just slightly, as xe spoke quietly to Arel. Arel's chin went up and she held her hand out, the seal balanced on her palm. Misha's lips compressed, and xe took the seal.

"Very well," xe said. "The blood-bond, first."

A small table was hastily brought, and Misha laid both seals on it, keeping them carefully apart. Despite myself, I was interested. I'd never seen bone-magic before.

"If I may?" Misha held xyr hand out, asking for Arel's. Something about xem had changed; a certain seriousness. Silently, Arel put her hand into Misha's. Misha brought a tiny sheath on a cord out from under our tunic, took an equally small knife out of it, and pricked Arel's finger. Xe held the seal for a drop of blood to fall on it, then pressed the flat of xyr knife gently to the top, an expression of concentration on xyr face.

The hall was so quiet that everyone heard the tiny chime. Misha repeated the process with xyr own seal and blood, and I heard the same chime.

"Both blood-bonds are sound," Misha said.

Xe placed xyr seal back on the table, clenched xyr fist, and drew the knife gently across the back of xyr knuckles. Blood welled around the lines of the tattoos, where bone showed through skin and blue ink. Sweat beaded at the edges of Misha's hairline as xe wiped the flat of the blade into the blood, and it vanished into the knife. Misha balanced the knife point-down on top of the seal, holding it in place with a gentle finger on the end of the haft.

Xe began to sing, very quietly. I couldn't hear the words, but I began to feel a vibration deep in my bones, as if something were sounding far underground. It grew steadily more intense, until I felt as if I were inside a giant bell. The song finished on a single high note, reverberating through my skull, until Misha lifted the knife, and it cut off.

"The resonance of my seal is sound."

Xe moved in front of Arel's seal, then hesitated, and looked questioningly at her. She gestured towards the seal, expression resolute. Misha swallowed, and then, pin-scratch frown between xyr brows, began the ritual again.

Except this time, there was no vibration. Nothing to make my joints shiver and my skull ring. This time, there was only Misha's thin, quiet song, tiny in the silence of the hall, until xe finished, and lifted the knife.

"There is no resonance in this seal."

Xe didn't sound triumphant, and xe wasn't looking at Arel. Xe raised xyr left hand to xyr forehead, and I saw the traces of blood across xyr knuckles.

"But..." Arel began, her voice shaking. My stomach was clenched around the sour knot of what dinner I'd managed to eat. I wanted to go to her, but I couldn't.

The Prince stood up, and everyone turned to him. "Enough!" he said. "I will not have Ralian politics played out in my court. I have heard enough, and I am not interested. When the Emperor wishes to negotiate, he can send a valid seal, with no dramatic denouncements to follow it. I will waste no more time."

Arel turned to him and he shook his head. "No. Enough. Leave. Both of you."

Misha strode out. I couldn't read xyr expression, but xe'd done what xe came for, hadn't xe? No skin off xyr nose to leave now. Arel, walking after xem, held her head high, her face set and unmoving. I turned and followed her. When I passed Sara, she wouldn't meet my eyes.

14.

Tears were running silently down Arel's face by the time we got back to our rooms. I helped her out of her fancy borrowed dress and back into travelling clothes, and through all of it, she didn't say a word. Graf hovered worriedly by the door. He'd tried to warn me. It was me who hadn't moved fast enough. I should have insisted on staying away from the stupid meal, should have dealt with Misha, should have could have...

"How dare xe!" Arel burst out. "How dare xe tell such *lies*. Bad enough that they desire war, but to destroy my family this way... my *family*, do they believe I'm a thief too?" She scrubbed her hands over her face. "But I was given it! Why didn't it work?"

She was given it by a messenger, from the Emperor's household, and neither of us had questioned that. And now, even if some of what Misha was saying was a lie—Arel hadn't stolen anything, for starters—it certainly looked like xe had proven the seal false. Given which, it was entirely possible that *Misha* thought xe was telling the truth. The question was, why was the seal false?

Wouldn't help to go through it all now. We needed to get out, and we needed to get out safely, and I had no idea how to do either. My own bag packed, I started on Arel's.

"I cannot just leave," Arel said, into her hands. "I cannot just abandon this opportunity. I can *fix* things."

"Are you sure xe didn't fake it?" I asked. "The thing with the seal?"

"Cade," Graf said reprovingly. "That's a serious accusation."

"Xe is a bone-magician," Arel said flatly. "Xe would not betray that. No. If there was faking, it happened at home." Her voice was grim. "I should have —"

"It was the Emperor's seal!" I protested. "You could hardly have guessed —"

The door burst open. I swung round, going for my sword.

It was the Prince. He shut the door behind him, said impatiently to me, "Put that away," and strode over to Arel.

"You say you didn't steal it," he said.

"*No.* Of course I did not." She'd straightened, looking the Prince proudly in the face despite the tear-tracks on her cheeks.

"And yet there was no link."

"Would I have asked Misha to perform the ritual, had I known that?"

He was frowning at her. "Yes, well, that's the problem. You're not behaving like someone who expected this, and I know where the Bethene stand, politically. But the seal..." He made a frustrated noise, and turned to me. "Sir Cade. You said she didn't steal it."

"She didn't," I agreed.

"On your oath?"

I was mildly offended; yes, I can evade a question with the best of them, but I'm not going to break my oath with a deliberate untruth, and I needn't be swearing by it to be bound by it; but agreed, "On my oath, she did not steal it."

"So you were there when she acquired it."

"Yes. Someone from the Emperor's household delivered it. And blood-bound it to her." I paused. "Of course, I can't tell you *they* didn't steal it."

"It wasn't the Emperor himself?"

"They came secretly," Arel said. "Only Sir Cade and myself knew, no one else in my house."

"But your porter, or your guards, must have let them in?"

Arel shook her head.

"Came through the window," I supplied. "I'll be having a chat with the family's security when I get back." Though if they weren't in court any more, perhaps it didn't matter so much. Would they get to keep the house? How much disgrace were they in?

The Prince rubbed at the bridge of his nose. "So. Someone you believe to be from the Emperor's household brought the seal to you, secretly. And gave you the mission?"

"Yes." Arel sounded uncertain. "But they *were* from the Emperor's household. I recognised them."

"Could you too say that, Sir Cade?" He swung back to me.

"No idea. Never been in the Emperor's household in my life."

"I assure you I am telling the truth," Arel said, very stiffly.

"Yes. I believe you believe you are. It is hard, however, not to conclude that you have been misled. And yet, the Bethene... perhaps..." He paced the room, then turned back to her. "Lady Arel."

"Arel, now," she said.

"Lady Arel," he repeated. "It is not that I disbelieve you, you understand. But you no longer have a seal, and I cannot be seen to take sides between you and the Bethene. I have my own court politics to think about. You must leave."

Arel's shoulders sagged.

"But," the Prince continued fiercely. "I want this peace. You want this peace. Do you believe there is any chance that the Emperor will agree to it?"

"Until this evening I believed I could agree on his behalf," she said, bitterly.

"That is gone, now. But is there any chance that something else is going on here? That, bone magic or not, Misha is somehow mistaken about the Emperor's position?"

"I cannot say," Arel said frankly. "But I want this as much as you do. You know that. If I can get in to see the Emperor, if I can tell him that you are agreed, I can try to persuade him." Her chin set. "I *will* persuade him."

"Well. My proposal, then, is this. If the Emperor agrees to it, personally, I will hold to this treaty. But this promise must be between you, and me, and the Emperor, you understand? It cannot be formal, or public. And you must leave, immediately, and without my visible connivance."

"So I must trust you." But her eyes were alight again with hope.

"As I am trusting you."

I could see the lines of strain around the Prince's eyes. He must be as desperate to avoid war as Arel was.

"I cannot promise to do this," Arel said. "I wish I could. From what Lyr Misha said, I no longer have court access." I saw her jaw clench. "Whoever has done this..."

"You are resourceful," the Prince said. "And, not to put too fine a point on it, you are also my only option."

"I will do everything in my power," Arel said. "Although. It is not finished." She frowned. "And your reciters."

"I don't need my reciters," the Prince said. "We can conclude the last pieces now. Then you must go."

Eyes locked with the Prince, Arel began to recite the thing. Not that I could understand it. I mean, I knew most of the words, but I had no idea what they meant all together. A few stanzas in, the Prince interrupted, and the two of them began to argue fiercely.

I shoved the last bits in Arel's bag and sat down on the bed. Graf sat down beside me. I wanted, so badly, to be able to lean into his broad shoulder.

"Sorry I couldn't get there any faster. Misha moved bloody quickly when xe moved."

I shook my head. "Not your fault." I kept my voice low, even though the other two alive people in the room weren't paying me the slightest attention. "I should have skipped the meal and dealt with it. I only realised what I'd missed once Misha was already there. Xe had to move right then, or not at all. By the time Arel left, the treaty would already have been agreed. That was the point of the seal."

"The stolen seal."

"She didn't steal it."

Graf's face was solemn. "But it didn't resonate. Why didn't Misha sit back and let *that* happen?"

"Yeah, well. I'm not saying something funny isn't going on." I rubbed my hands over my face. "Maybe the point was to attack Arel's family, not embarrass the Prince?"

Graf sucked at his teeth. "Prince is pretty embarrassed right now."

"Would have been more so if they'd been doing the sealing and it'd failed." I scowled. "But if Misha's lot want war, wouldn't that make war even more likely? That embarrassment? Why not just leave Arel to it?"

"Beyond me," Graf said, frankly.

"I dunno. But apparently now we're going to go back home and Arel's going to... I don't know. Convince the Emperor that she's right? No idea how."

Graf shrugged. "Is that your problem?"

Graf always was better at staying focussed than me. And fair enough, I was pretty certain that 'sneak someone into the

Emperor's Court' wasn't within the scope of my oath. "In that sense, no, but do you want war?"

"Course not, but..."

"And I *am* responsible for getting her out of here, and home safely. Presumably Misha's still around?"

"Xe left the palace. I followed xem as far as I could, but all I can tell you is xe looked to be heading out of town in a hurry."

"So I have to assume xe's waiting somewhere. Shit."

Outside, it was full dark, between the moons. Easier in some ways, harder in others.

"Sir Cade?" Arel and the Prince had turned to look at me. "Are you all right?"

"Just talking to myself," I said, summoning up a smile. "Trying to work out how to get out of here."

"As soon as possible," the Prince said.

"Yeah, I got that part." I really wasn't in the mood for court manners.

Out of the palace, and then maybe I could convince the city gate guards to let us out? If the Prince could authorise our departure that would be ideal, but it was clear he wanted nothing official to do with it, which was understandable if unhelpful.

There were always secret ways out of cities, but it took time to find the people you needed to ask about that, and we didn't *have* time. How could I do this?

Light flared bright outside, and the Prince strode over to the window to look into the courtyard. "What the...?" His voice wavered somewhere between horror and wonder.

Another flare, this time definitely flame-coloured. And a lot of shouting. And something that sounded like a sort of pulsing wind, almost like... wingbeats?

Oh shit. I'd forgotten Theo.

15.

"There is a *dragon* out there." I was impressed by how level the Prince kept his voice.

"Theo," Arel, Graf, and I all said at the same time, in various tones. Graf hovered at the Prince's shoulder, peering out of the window.

"You *know* the dragon?"

"Long story," I said. This was, clearly, our opportunity. "Which I'm sure Lady Arel can tell you another time when the two of you are celebrating the treaty and all that, but how about we go, right now?"

"In the chaos," the Prince said approvingly.

"In the chaos, on the dragon. Are you two done with all the clauses and what-not?"

"Yes," Arel said. She bowed deeply to the Prince. "My great thanks, your highness. I will do all I can to be worthy of your trust."

"Let's get a move on," Graf said from the window. "Theo's not making himself terribly popular with the guards. No one's actually been fried *yet*, but..."

I passed Arel her saddlebags. Shit, I was going to have to leave Monty behind.

"My horse belongs to the Order," I said to the Prince. "If you could sort that out, I'm sure Siremos will smile on you and so forth. Arel's horse belongs to her, while we're at it."

"Certainly, Sir Cade."

I threw my own saddlebags across my shoulder. "Can we get down into the courtyard?"

"The stairs come out —" the Prince began, sounding startled, but I wasn't looking at him, I was looking at Graf, leaning out of the window. His edges seemed blurry; that must be the flame and smoke outside. I did hope Theo wasn't getting himself into too much trouble.

"Two storeys," Graf said. "Your rope's long enough. I can't hold the end, though."

I dug the rope out of my bag.

"Oh no. Not again," Arel moaned.

"Come on. We're in a hurry." I made it fast around her. "Out of the window, my lady."

"Not a lady any more," she muttered, and sat on the window ledge. She avoided Graf, I noticed, even though she couldn't consciously see him.

She was pretty calm as I lowered her; though I was going as fast as I could and she did squeak a bit. As soon as she was down, I tied the rope around the bedpost. The Prince still stood in the middle of the room, looking... amused? Impressed?

"I strongly recommend you get out of here before you get accused of assisting us to leave, Your Highness," I said, and went down the rope hand over hand.

I nearly landed on top of Arel, who was trying to untie the knots around her middle. In the chaos of the courtyard, no one had noticed us yet, but it was only a matter of time.

I drew my knife to cut the rope; but the rest of it slithered out of the window and down to pool at my feet.

Helpful of the Prince, I supposed, although Arel was going to have difficulty moving with it. I gathered it up in large unwieldy handfuls and slung it over her shoulder.

We hadn't far to go. It wasn't a big courtyard, and Theo was right in the middle, breathing fire at the guards and soldiers clustered round the edges trying to poke at him without noticeable success. The fire and the smoke provided cover, and no one had seen us; they were all, understandably, very focussed on Theo.

Someone went for his tail, which would have been smart, except Theo was both observant and bendy. He swiped a claw and they went flying. In the process, he spotted us.

"Where were you?"

"Long story," I called. "Any chance of a lift out?"

Now the guards had seen us, and some of them were starting towards us. "Run!" I shrieked, and Arel and I belted for Theo's side. Graf was already perched on his neck and whispering in his ear.

"Oh very *well*," Theo said irritably to Graf. He whipped his neck round again and huffed at the guards who were coming for us. They, sensibly, scattered. Arel and I cannoned into Theo's flank, and Graf offered us a hand up, which was of course entirely useless. Arel had dropped part of the rope and it was trailing across the courtyard behind her. I boosted her up and grabbed the rope with my spare hand, hauling it towards us only to discover, as it was yanked away, that someone had grabbed the end.

As it pulled tight, I remembered it was still attached to Arel.

"Cade!" she screamed, hanging onto Theo's spikes with both hands, then with one hand.

I still held my knife. I sliced through the rope, as hard as I could, once, then again. It was nice to know I had bought excellent quality rope, but really now was *not the time.* A third time parted the final strand. Arel thumped against Theo's flank, and Graf tried again to help her up properly, his hands slipping through her like smoke.

More soldiers were pouring into the courtyard.

"Now would be good!" I shouted at Theo.

"Get on, then!"

Which was all very well, but I couldn't. I'd been counting on a hand up from Arel, but she wasn't even solidly on board herself.

"Go without me!" I called.

"What the *fuck*," Graf and Arel said simultaneously.

"Honestly," Theo grumbled. "Humans."

He spread his wings, and I thought I was about to be left on my own, facing a courtyard-full of angry armed people who might not be in the mood to respect my surcoat; then he grabbed me between his front claws, and took off directly upwards.

I only screamed a very little bit.

16.

That swoop upwards, out of the palace and over the city walls, was hair-raisingly awful. I still have nightmares about it sometimes. I knew Arel must be barely holding on, and most of me was suspended in mid-air, dangling outside Theo's claws. Someone—several someones—shot at us as we flew upwards, which was unpleasant. One of them even hit Theo, but only the shielded part of his underbelly. He flew faster after that, which was even less pleasant.

"Are you all right?" Graf demanded, clinging onto Theo's leg.

"Really not at all. Is Arel?"

"More or less," he said, which didn't fill me with confidence.

"We need to land," I called, as loud as I could, but with the rush of the wind and the fact that Theo was in a terrible mood, he either didn't hear me, or didn't want to.

Graf disappeared. A moment later Theo snorted irritably, and shortly after that we were spiralling downwards into a dark field. I thought it was empty, until I heard all the panicked bleating as Theo's rear feet hit the ground.

He dropped me just before he put his front feet down. I landed harder than I would have liked, but managed not to roll over onto my scabbard, which I know from previous experience hurts a lot.

"Well, that was not at all what I expected from Harin," he huffed. "I was *honoured* the last time I went there."

Arel slid down his side and onto the floor. "Oh fuck," she said, very quietly, and folded down over her knees.

"Are you all right?" I asked.

"In one piece," she said, without lifting her face. "Don't ask more than that."

"You forgot me, didn't you?" Theo demanded.

I pointed upwards. "Is it second moonrise yet? No. Anyway, there was a lot going on."

Theo scowled. "I was bored. Moonset was ages ago. I assumed you'd forgotten me."

I kind of had. A little bit. Although I still wasn't actually late. And as it happened, Theo's arrival had been pretty timely.

"Just apologise?" Graf advised. I glared at him, but he was right.

"I'm sorry I was later than I intended, or you expected," I said. "Do you want to know what was going on when you showed up, though?"

"No," Theo said sulkily, then, "Yes."

"We were being kicked out of the palace because that arsehole you scared off before came marching in and accused Arel of theft."

"Nothing wrong with theft. Very draconic."

"Yes, well, humans aren't keen. So she was trying to finish the treaty, and I was trying to work out how we could get out without being ambushed by Arsehole and, presumably, whatever mates xe brought along. Things were a bit busy, is what I'm saying, which is why I didn't find you on time."

"Hmph," Theo said. "Oh, well, never mind. I suppose that was all quite exciting. And," he sounded like this had just occurred to him, "you did get out without being ambushed! Thanks to me!"

"We did," Arel agreed. I could just see her outline in the starlight. I couldn't face making a guide-light just now. "For which I am deeply grateful, and for which my family owes you. Once our name is restored, I will do what I can to pay the debt."

Theo snorted, pleased.

"Where now, then?" I said. "And *how*?"

"I need to get back to the Emperor," Arel said.

"Yes, but you can't just walk in there, can you?"

"I could fly you in," Theo offered.

"That may not help," Arel said, dryly. She paused. "Might your ghost-friend be able to do anything?"

"I'm a ghost, not a cat-burglar," Graf said, folding his arms. He was leaning against Theo's side.

"No," I translated approximately. "He'd probably need to be haunting the palace, anyway."

"And he's haunting you," Arel agreed, as if it were obvious.

I sighed. "That's what the ghost-whisperers said, yes."

"Oh, *that's* what you smell of," Theo said, sounding enlightened. "What did you go to them for?"

"To see if I can help Graf," I muttered.

"Help him to move on?" Arel asked.

"Not exactly." I didn't want to talk about it. Although, I realised with a sudden lurch, we'd left Harin now, and that meant we'd left the ghost-whisperers, and they'd said Graf had *days*. I chewed at my lip. Maybe, if he didn't have the option of being safely detached, maybe if time was running out, maybe he would be willing to consider, after all...

"Ohhh! You went to find him a body," Theo said. "Couldn't they get one?"

"They don't do that," Graf said.

"Really? They did when I was a cub."

"Apparently it's not ethical any more. And I wouldn't take someone else's body even if it was ethical."

114

"Don't see why not," Theo sniffed.

I was very, very tired. And I didn't want to get back into this with Graf right now, still less in front of an audience. "Look, far be it from me to stop this delightful discussion, but do we really intend to sit in a sheep-field until dawn? Because I have no idea where we are, so don't look to me to find a way out until I can see."

"I know where we are," Theo said. "But not in human terms. Do you know, I've just realised those are *sheep*." He lumbered off towards the other end of the field. I probably ought to stop him, but I couldn't for the life of me think how, and I had enough on my plate just now. Let him have his sheep. Saved me a problem.

"We need somewhere to stay while you work out how to get to the Emperor, Arel." I rubbed at my aching forehead. "The chapterhouse, maybe?"

"Uh-uh," Graf said. "The Archon won't want to get involved."

"You're welcome in my cave," Theo said, from across the field, sounding muffled. "These sheep aren't as good as the last ones."

"Hang on. You mean the catacombs?"

"Where you met me before. My cave. I think I'll go there, in any case. That was all very exciting, but now I need a nice rest." He belched. "Rest and digest."

"That could actually work," Graf said.

"Not far from the city," I said. "No one much goes there. And Theo'll keep the monsters off. It's not a great place to camp out, but for a few days..."

"Ugh," Arel said.

"Do you have a better idea?"

Silence. I raised my voice. "Theo? When you're done eating, could we possibly take you up on your very generous offer?"

"Just one more sheep," came from across the field.

"I shall leave some money by the gate," Arel said. "And hope the sheep leave it alone. Do sheep eat gold?"

"That's goats you're thinking of," I said. "Sheep stick to grass."

We sat, surrounded by panicked bleating, and waited for Theo to finish his meal. Hopefully he'd still be able to fly once he was full.

17.

Theo grumbled about flying on a full stomach but did it. This time both Arel and I were firmly seated on his back, Arel in front and me behind; but the whole thing was, to be honest, fucking terrifying anyway. We were a long way up. I could see that even absent any moonlight. Could sense the vast expanse of empty air underneath us. I shut my eyes and buried my head in Arel's back, and Arel reached back and patted me.

The upside was, it was a sight quicker to get to the catacombs on dragonback than it would have been on the ground. I was still never, ever doing it again. The worst part was right at the end, in the grey pre-dawn, when I saw the city away below us to one side, and then Theo folded his wings and dove straight down towards the ground.

I'm pretty sure I screamed again.

Then we were swallowed up by trees and rocks and vining undergrowth; crumbling mossy stones flashed past my shoulder; and Theo pulled up, backwinged, and thumped down to earth. We were down in the belly of the catacombs, right back where Arel and Graf and Theo and I had been—I would have counted on my fingers, but they were locked immovably into the folds of Arel's cloak—four days ago? Five?

"Fuck," I croaked. I didn't think I could move.

"You're welcome," Theo said. "Off."

Arel twisted round and gently pushed me upright. "Cade? Are you all right?"

"Fine. Fine."

She waited for a moment. "If I get down first, I can help you?"

"No. I can do it."

I uncramped my fingers, managed to swing one leg over, and slid gracelessly down Theo's side. I just about stayed upright when I hit the ground. Arel slid down beside me, looking much less terrified than I suspected I did, but about as tired.

"I need a nap," Theo said, curled up, and shut his eyes. As far as I could tell he was asleep immediately, or at least good at faking.

"It's not a bad idea," I suggested to Arel.

"I must work out how to reach the Emperor," she said, fretfully. She was, uncharacteristically, chewing at her lip; she didn't normally betray her tension that way.

"Which sleep will probably help with?"

A little way off, Graf was wandering around, kicking at fallen rocks that his toes were going straight through. The blurring at his edges that I'd noticed back in the courtyard of the Prince's palace was still there. Worse, maybe. But probably it was my tired eyes, not Graf at all.

"Back again," he said. I couldn't read his tone.

"I suppose you are correct," Arel said, and I jerked myself back to that conversation. "But it is just as true for you."

"Someone should be on guard," I said. Staying up long past when it would be sensible is, conveniently, part of knightly training, though it's never been my favourite thing.

"I will," Graf said. "Not like I can sleep."

"I..."

"Go on, Cade. You're no good to anyone when you're tired."

"Is your ghost volunteering?" Arel asked, yawning hugely. "Good. Get some rest, Cade." Her tone was decisive, even through the yawn. "I will need you tomorrow."

Getting her into the Emperor's palace was well outside my job parameters, but that was an argument for tomorrow. If I couldn't just avoid it. I curled up in my blankets and was asleep even as I began worrying again about Graf's blurred edges.

Arel and I had the argument right on schedule a few hours later, when I was making breakfast. Or possibly lunch.

"But I am your client!"

"And I can guide you to anywhere you like," I said, "but I can't break you into somewhere."

"You broke me out of somewhere."

"Sort of, sort of. I needed to break myself out, too. At that, if it wasn't for the Prince helping us, I'd worry about the consequences for the Order." Also everyone in the courtyard had seen a dragon carrying me away in its claws, with me screaming, so hopefully that was the—very embarrassing—image that would stick.

"Cade..."

"Look. I think you're doing the right thing. And you are my client, and I will look after you down here for as long as you like, and guide you out again when the time comes. But I cannot break you into the Emperor's palace, even if I had the first idea of how to do it, which I don't."

Arel didn't speak to me for several hours. She alternated between pacing around the square muttering to herself, and sitting by the fire muttering to herself. Graf wasn't talking, either. I wrapped myself in my blanket, kept the fire going, and thought.

Surely there was a way I could help Graf to a body. There had to be. I wasn't just going to give up, whatever Graf said.

Arel tried to refuse lunch-or-maybe-tea, but I over-ruled her. She sat sulkily by the fire, chewing bread.

"There *must* be an answer," she burst out.

I'd been thinking much the same thing about Graf. I'd been, or he'd been, handed a second chance. There had to be something I could do with that. If I could just think of it. "Maybe there isn't," I said.

"There *has* to be."

I badly wanted to believe her. For both of us. I wrapped my hands round my elbows and sighed. "I dunno. Not all problems are solvable? Maybe sometimes the only answer is to give up." That was Graf's usual line whenever I was stubbornly chewing on something.

"I will *not* give up," Arel said. "I have a treaty. It is my responsibility to finish it. I can—I must—fix this. There must be a solution." Her determination rang absolute in her voice.

I didn't bother attempting again to point out the flaw in her logic. *I want*, even *I must*, doesn't mean *it can be done*, last I checked. But it wasn't like I was any better with that than Arel, was I?

Some time later, Theo had woken up, made pointed comments about how dull we were after Arel once again rejected his idea of flying straight into the palace, and gone back to sleep again in a sulk. The thin shafts of sun that came through the overgrown trees high above us had the golden-peach tinge of early evening. A whole day gone. I looked over at Graf, poking his fingers into rocks on the other side of the cavern. Was he more tattered?

"Why should I not just go?" Arel said, for about the tenth time.

"If you go to the front door, they'll turn you away, and probably arrest you for treason," I said, also for about the tenth time. "And if you try to break in, they'll catch you, and the same applies, or worse. It's too dangerous."

"I have not committed treason." Her arms were folded. "I was sent by the Emperor."

"Except apparently you weren't."

"What if Misha lied? Just to destroy the treaty?"

"Well, that's one option. The other option is that you were deceived." I sighed. "And there was the whole bone-magic thing. *Something* screwy was going on, somewhere."

"I have a treaty," Arel said, obstinately. "If I can speak to the Emperor..."

"But no one speaks to the Emperor any more, you said." I was getting frustrated. "For pity's sake, Arel, you can't just go off and smash a palace window or whatever. Even if that would work, which it won't."

"This is not your decision." Her chin was up again, and her tone was freezing.

I scowled at her. "It's a terrible idea. You'll be caught, and you'll be killed. If you're lucky."

"And if I make no attempt, we will be at war with Perren by the end of the year, and many more people will die," Arel said. "I can *fix* this, Cade. I must try. That is my duty."

"She's right," Graf said, from the other end of the cavern. "And you know she is." He stiffened suddenly. "Surely not." He vanished, as I reached automatically for my sword, then reappeared looking massively pissed off. "That fucker Misha is here."

"What? Here? How did xe manage that so quickly?"

"Good horse, couple of changes, take the straight road along the river and ride non-stop?" Graf said. "It's doable. Xe'll be wiped, though." Good news if it came to a fight.

"Just xem? Anyone with xem?"

"Just xem."

That didn't make sense. Misha couldn't possibly fancy xemself against me. Unless xe was down here for something wholly unconnected; but that was way too much of a coincidence. I couldn't see how xe could possibly know we were here, but that was still more likely than that xe had

121

raced back from Harin overnight and just happened to head directly for the catacombs.

"What are you talking about?" Arel demanded.

"Graf says Misha's in the catacombs. Headed this way."

"Why? How? What *for*?"

"All good questions to which I have no answers," I said. "Unless you do? You know xem."

She shook her head. "I told you, we are no longer friends."

"Visitors?" Theo rumbled, without opening his eyes.

"A visitor," Graf said. "Nearly here. You ready, Cade?"

"Course." I was on my feet, sword out. "Arel, get back."

Misha appeared in the mouth of the alleyway across from us. "Lady Arel?" xe said.

"Just Arel, now," Arel said from behind me. "According to you, anyway."

"My lady." Xe bowed formally, then spread xyr empty hands. "Peace. Please? I want to talk."

18.

"**A**bsolutely not," I said, and levelled my sword at xem. Misha swallowed but didn't move.

"Give xem a chance," Graf said, who'd gone over to Misha to peer intently into xyr face. Misha shook xyr head as if shaking away a fly, then looked back anxiously at me.

"Talk? About what?" Arel demanded.

"I want to hear your side of things. I... I think I may have been misled."

Arel's eyebrows shot upwards.

"At least let me pat xem down," I said with resignation.

Misha didn't protest. Xe had a belt knife, but nothing serious. And that little knife around xyr neck. I didn't go anywhere near that. You couldn't attack people with bone magic that I'd ever heard, and if it turned out you could, we'd be screwed anyway.

"How did you even get in here?" I asked.

At which point Theo woke up properly, opened one eye to look at Misha, and said without apparent surprise. "Oh. It's you."

"Hello, Theo," Misha said, with the first proper smile I'd seen from xem. My jaw dropped.

"You *know* Theo?"

"I used to come down here as a kid." Xe glanced at Arel. "After you knew me." There was a painful tension in xyr voice. "It was somewhere to get away from my brother."

"Your brother is an arse," Arel said flatly.

"Yes," Misha agreed, equally flatly. "Anyway, I explored all over. And one day I came across Theo."

"I tried to roast xem," Theo said. "Hungry, you see. But xe dodges well. Gave up eventually. Xe tells a good story." He glared at Misha. "You haven't been back for *years*, though."

"Sorry," Misha said. "I ... it's been difficult."

"Hang on," I said. "You were roaming around down here as a *kid*? With all the monsters? And no guide-song?"

"At first I didn't care about the monsters," Misha said. Xyr tone was bleak. "It was better than... anyway. Then I got good at avoiding them, and I made up a guide-song of my own to help me get around. It wasn't all that hard. And all I had to do, by then, was practice magic." Xe flicked another glance at Arel. "I had plenty of time."

So much for our training-zone. I bit back my irritation. "Fine. So you recognised Theo in the courtyard?"

"Yes. I thought—well, I didn't know, but I thought, maybe Theo would bring you back here. You'd want somewhere safe, somewhere you couldn't be found."

"And yet, here you are." I eyed xem sourly. "With a lot more behind you waiting for your word?"

"No!" Misha said. "Not at all. I told you. I want to hear your side of things."

"My side?" Arel said. Her voice was cool. "My side is straightforward. My family, unlike yours, wants peace. The Emperor sent me a message, and the seal. Sir Cade can vouch for me."

"Yep," I said.

Misha was biting at xyr lip. "Go on, Lady Arel."

"The Emperor desired me to go to Harin and negotiate the agreement my family have been pressing upon him. In secret, lest I might be prevented. Sir Cade guided me there, by the back-roads."

"And Theo came with you?"

"I was bored," Theo said.

"It was all going very well until you arrived." Arel folded her arms.

"You didn't speak directly to the Emperor?" Misha asked.

"No. To a member of his household. I recognised them."

"Right," Misha said. Xe nodded, looking almost relieved. "Well, the problem there is that my brother is running the Emperor's household now. Has been for a while."

"What?" Arel looked horrified.

"You know the Emperor's not well. Nico's been taking advantage of that." Xyr shoulders hunched. "You know what he's like. He's good at... getting hold of levers. I'm not sure the Emperor knows, even, but the seneschal does what Nico tells her."

"I knew Nico was in the Emperor's confidence, but not... Yes. I see. He always has been good at that." She shut her eyes for a moment. "And now I understand why he has been happy to put himself out of the succession. He seeks a different sort of power."

"He can affect who does succeed," Misha agreed. "And more."

"And the household does not change with the Emperor." Sick realisation coloured her voice. "So. He had that message sent. To discredit my family, and insult the Prince."

Two for one. I saw what Misha meant about levers.

"After you left, the Emperor—well," Misha grimaced, "someone of his household—announced a seal had been stolen. The court bone-magicians linked it to your family, and said it was travelling east. You'd been seen leaving, and everyone knows what your family's been pushing for. It was obvious you were going to Perren, whatever you'd claimed. Nico sent me after you, and Theo chased me off."

"Sorry," Theo said. "I only smelt it was you at the last minute. All that steel and fear and anger flying around. I did hold off on cooking you or any of your friends, once I realised. But it was so much fun seeing everyone run away."

"Dragons," Misha sighed.

"I was going to talk to you!" Theo protested. "But you all kept running, so."

"And you didn't think to mention it to us?" I asked through gritted teeth.

"Misha," Theo said with dignity, "is my *friend*. One should not betray one's friends." He paused. "Even to one's other friends. I think. Anyway, I chased xem off, didn't I? Don't complain."

"So," Arel said loudly, "Nico sent the seal."

Misha nodded, without looking at Arel. "I didn't realise... I thought you truly had stolen it. But I didn't catch you, and Nico was raging. He said I had to go after you, fast as I could, and make sure whatever you were doing in Harin, it didn't succeed. I truly thought you'd stolen the seal." Xyr voice was desolate. "I thought I needed to stop you."

"From making peace."

"But it was *stolen*. You couldn't use it. I thought that would just make things worse, with Perren. Embarrassing the Prince in public." Which, of course, would have been a win for xyr brother too. Good strategy, however bad the goals were.

"You 'thought'," Arel noted, her eyes narrow. "Past tense."

Misha swallowed, and looked at her with visible effort. "I don't agree with Nico," xe said. "I've never thought war was a good idea. Nico says how much we'll make off it, but I know what the cost is. I've listened to the guards who used to be mercenaries, and you must remember my tutor who was a refugee. But Nico is the head of the family, and I thought it my duty to obey him."

" 'Thought'," Arel said again.

"I *thought* he was telling me the truth. I knew about the Emperor's household, sort of, but I didn't know... I didn't think he would have set you up like that. But he lied about you. If he's lied, I don't have to do what he says any more."

"You could have stopped already," I said. It sounded like a flimsy excuse to me.

"You make an oath, don't you?" Misha said. "To your Siremos."

"Yes," I said, stiffly.

"Do you break it? When you dislike what your clients are doing?"

"No," I said, even more stiffly.

"I chose to stay with Nico, years ago." Xe looked at Arel. "You know that."

Arel's jaw clenched, but she didn't speak.

"At first I thought he was right, perhaps. Then I knew he wasn't always, but he used to listen to me, a bit. I could talk him down, sometimes. And strategically, he's good at all the court stuff, and I'm not. He understands it, and he heads the family. He looks to the family's interests. These last couple of years, I thought I was talking him round to peace. But it's not working any more, if it ever was. Perhaps I was just deluding myself all along. I tried again, before I came here."

"You tried? Just now?"

Misha shrugged. "I knew he planned to leave the city. I rode as hard as I could, and I was lucky. I caught him just as he arrived at our wayhouse by the river. I said, maybe we should take advantage of this moment. Go back and apologise to the Prince, use the treaty. They *want* to be friends. It doesn't make sense for us to fight them. Peace will make everyone richer."

"It would make my family richer," Arel said quietly. "And the Emperor, and the realm as a whole. Not your family."

"But we wouldn't be bankrupt. We wouldn't lose anything. We just wouldn't rake in money for uniforms and marching-corn. But," xe sounded tired, and sick at heart, "that's what Nico wants. He wouldn't listen. He told me he'd gone to all this effort, what was I doing backing out now. He said, of course he'd sent you the seal. He said I was naive. He—he slapped me, in the end. And I left. So. I am here to ask what you were doing, and to help. If I can."

Arel and I looked at each other. "I don't know if I can trust you," she said to Misha.

Misha flinched. "I know. I—am sorry. Nico said, on the honour of our family, that you and yours were our enemies. I trusted him." That last came out with a betrayed intensity that made my own stomach clench in sympathy.

"Not sure if matters what xe's been like in the past, or how trustworthy xe is," Graf remarked, arms folded. "Do you have any better options?"

"Graf says, what are our other options?"

"Good point." Arel grimaced.

"Who's Graf?" Misha asked.

"My ghost sword-brother," I said.

Misha blinked. "All right."

Arel's foot was tapping. "So your brother set all this up. Does the Emperor know?"

"Not as far as I know."

"Is the Emperor still functional at all?"

"I don't know. I haven't seen him in months. Nico still sees him, but not often."

Arel sighed. "I still have no better idea."

"Than what?" Misha, Graf, and I all asked at once.

"The Emperor is the only one who can straighten everything out. Get rid of Nico, agree to the treaty."

"You did negotiate it!" Misha sounded genuinely pleased.

"I did. But the Prince and I could not seal it, could we?" A frown flickered on her face. "Though had you not interrupted, we still would not have been able to, with a faulty seal, and perhaps you are right. That might have been worse. But either way we have a treaty, and it needs the Emperor's seal. But as Cade keeps pointing out, getting to the Emperor is next to impossible. I am no longer welcome in court, even if the Emperor were ever seen in public, and how could we break in? We would be seen immediately."

"Still don't know why I can't just fly in," muttered Theo, who would definitely be seen immediately.

Arel's tension was visible, her shoulders tight. "I cannot see how. But I *must*. I must make this happen."

"I can get you in," Misha said, confidently.

All of us stared at xem.

"What?" Arel demanded.

Misha pulled something out of xyr pocket. I stiffened, then realised what it was: a piece of bone, yellow-white under the guide-lights. "I've still got the Emperor's seal. The real one."

19.

We all looked at the seal in Misha's hand.

"If I take myself out of it," xe explained, eyes wide with what I sincerely hoped was honesty, "I can add you in. It'll get you to the Emperor's waiting-room."

Arel was frowning, but Misha had already pulled out xyr little knife. Xe put it to the seal, and a drop of blood glistened on the knife's tip before vanishing.

"Give me your hand."

Arel held her hand out; and just like the Emperor's messenger, Misha flipped the seal over to reveal the pin and produce a drop of blood.

Except this time, the blood didn't sink in. It just sat on the seal's surface.

"Shit," Misha said. Arel had gone pale, eyes wide.

"What?" Graf and I demanded. I looked from Arel to Misha, heart in my mouth.

"She's been cut off," Misha said.

"Cut off?" I asked.

"My family are no longer connected. We no longer resonate," Arel said, tones clipped. "My blood will not work."

"Why not?"

"I imagine our foundational bone has been unlinked," Arel said.

"But didn't that happen before?" I was honestly confused. "When you were first down here? And you still linked to the old seal?"

Arel shook her head. "The bone was missing, then, but the link was there. Our bone-magician had only to connect the new bone."

I gestured over at the mausoleums. "And you can't do that now? Because there's, like, a whole heap of bones right there."

Arel began to shake her head, but Misha looked up, suddenly alert. "Say that again?"

"Uh. There's a whole heap of bones, right there? Can't Arel just link one of those?"

"The resonance is broken," Arel said.

"Yes," Misha said. "But I'm a bone-magician. I can recreate it."

The hope creeping into Arel's face was almost painful to watch. "You can?"

"If you have a foundation bone I can use, then yes. Similar to the ritual you did after, uh," xe looked embarrassed, "the last one went... missing."

I thought it was very restrained of Arel not to point out who had pinched it.

"So you could recreate the resonance, and I could use the seal?" Arel's voice rose in hope, then dropped back into uncertainty. "But should you? We have," she swallowed. "We have been banished." My heart ached for her. I'd only known Arel a few days, but it wasn't like you could miss her dedication, to both family and country. All this was her worst nightmare.

"Define 'should'," Misha said. "My brother will be furious. If the Emperor knowingly cut you off, I suppose he will be too. But my belief is that this is my brother's work and not the Emperor's. As a bone-magician, knowing you to be of the Family Xeria, I can recreate the resonance against your blood, without breaking any oath." Xe held Arel's gaze. "I want to help. Please. Let me."

Arel swallowed visibly, then her chin went up and she breathed in. "What do you need me to do?"

Once Arel had fetched another bone from the mausoleum, Misha began to carve a dip into it with that tiny knife. Now I could see it more closely, it looked to be made of bone, which ought to be ridiculously weak; but it glowed faintly, and it went through the new foundation bone like it was softwood.

Theo watched the preparations with interest. "You've got all your fingers," he observed. "When I was a cub, bone-magicians used their own bones. I knew one who was three fingers down by the time she was sixty."

"Urgh," I said, as Graf said, "*Cool.*" Death really hadn't changed him.

Misha didn't look up from xyr slow carving. "These days we access the power through ink near the bone, and blood." The scars from the ritual at Harin still showed across the blue ink on the hand that held the foundation bone steady.

"Whose bone is that knife, then, if it's not yours?" I asked.

"My grandmother's. She was our bone-magician when I became apprentice. She left it to me."

I really shouldn't have asked.

It was all ready in plenty of time. We waited.

"We're underground," Graf said, after a while. Impatient as ever. "Does it matter where the moons are?"

"I guess the magic knows," I said doubtfully.

"How will we tell the correct time?" Arel asked, unknowingly echoing Graf.

"I'll know," Misha snapped. "The resonance is only correct when both moons are in the same direction, okay? Ideally they'd both be risen, but you have to work with what you've got. We can't exactly sit around and wait 'til summer. Now shut up, I'm listening."

We all stood around in silence, until Misha opened xyr eyes and said, "Now."

Arel offered her open palm to Misha. Xe drew the knife across it, a long slash that immediately oozed red. Misha squatted down next to the bone and held it carefully, one hand on each end.

"Handprints," xe said quietly to Arel. She nodded, and Misha began to sing.

The song was gentle, pulsing heartbeat-warm in my ears. Arel placed her hand on the bone in time with it, and I didn't sense chiming or vibrating this time, but *belonging*. Something that fitted. Arel's bloody handprints initially stood out on the bone, then began to sink into it. By the time she'd made her way right along it, the first few had disappeared.

The last one vanished almost as soon as she'd made it. Misha, watching carefully, drew xyr song to a close as Arel stepped back. The bone pulsed a soft heartbeat-glow.

Slowly, intent, Misha placed the bone down, took xyr hands away from its ends, and knelt in front of it. Xe cut across the back of xyr wrist, where the ink turned around the knot of xyr wristbone, and let the blood drip into the bowl carved in the bone. It didn't sink in, just sat there, glistening under my guide-light.

Misha gestured to Arel, and she knelt on the other side of the bone. Misha put the tips of xyr fingers into the pool of blood, and Arel copied xem.

This time Misha's song was like the song in the hall at Harin; but more. Much more. At first I didn't think so; at first it was just Misha's voice, small but sure. Then I heard new harmonies, felt that same vibration under my feet. It intensified as more notes merged, until my vision began to blur and I could hardly think straight.

Then Theo, too, opened his mouth and sang. My knees buckled. Misha's eyes snapped over to Theo, and I panicked in case that was wrong; but no, Misha was smiling.

133

The reverberations, dragon and magician and world all together, ached in perfect beauty as my breath stuttered.

Then it was over. My heartbeat thumped in time with the last dying echoes, and Misha sat back, drained but smiling. The bone was clean of blood.

"There," Misha said softly, and held the seal out to Arel.

Xe pushed her finger into the seal. This time, it worked.

Once Misha had put the bone away, I made xem drink some water, and xe began to discuss with Arel the details of getting through the palace.

"You're going too, Lyr Misha?" I asked. "Because you're not authorised by the seal now."

"I am permitted to enter both on behalf of my family, and by virtue of my job." Misha gave me a half-smile. "I do not intend to betray your client, Sir Cade. I will be there to validate the seal if need be."

I still didn't entirely trust xem, but... well. Not my decision, was it? And it wasn't like Arel was swimming in options. Myself, I was torn between wanting to go along to see what happened, and wanting to return to the chapterhouse... There had to be a solution for Graf, and whatever it was, I needed to find it as fast as possible.

But what if Arel got in trouble that a sword could have got her out of? How would I feel then? Not to mention if we did wind up at war with Perren.

I wandered over to where Graf was examining the old graves.

"What you are, we once were; what we are, you soon will be?" I asked, quoting the inscription from the chapterhouse graveyard.

Graf straightened up. I could see straight through him now. "Morbid much? Anyway, it's not true for me, right? None of them were ghosts." He paused, and looked down at himself. "I'll be faded out pretty soon, I reckon." He sounded horribly matter-of-fact.

I didn't want to have this conversation. I didn't want Graf to be fading. I wanted to solve this, and I didn't know how. "Are you sure?" I demanded. "It might just be all that disappearing and reappearing. Maybe that just makes you kind of. I don't know. Fuzzy."

Graf shook his head. "I c'n feel it, Cade. Like when you're on short rations in the field, and everything's knackering. I'm nearly done."

"But..."

"Cade. *Listen*. I'm fading. You telling me I'm not won't help."

We both stared at the graves. "You could stop," I said.

"I'm going to," Graf said patiently. "That's the point."

"Not like that. I mean, stop being a ghost. Get a body."

"Fuck off."

"Misha," I said, desperation cracking my voice. "Xe's been a massive pain in the arse. You pinch xyr body, then..." Then everything could be like it was. Couldn't it?

"Cade. I am going to do us both a massive favour and pretend you didn't just say that, or maybe like it was a big joke. Ha. Ha."

"But you could be *back*. Why does Misha deserve to be here more than you do? Or someone else, I don't know, we could go into the city..." I knew what I was saying was wrong, even as I said it, and it wasn't even as if I knew how to do it even if it had been right, but I couldn't bear it. There had to be a solution. There had to.

"Right, first up, Misha's a bone-magician. Secondly, I'm not taking anyone else's body, however much of a pain in the arse they've been. And I know you don't really mean that, anyway. Cade. Love. Listen. I'm *dead*. It sucks, but it's true.

And you need to stop trying to push decisions on me. It's not your fault, and it's not your call."

There was water in the corners of my eyes. "I don't want you to be dead."

"Yeah. I don't want me to be dead either. Shit happens." He shrugged.

"We could get you back to Harin, at least?" I was clutching at straws, now. "For them to detach you." That would be better than him just...vanishing into nothing and nowhere.

"Pretty sure I don't have the time, love." He gestured down at himself, tattier by the moment. "But hey. *One of the great mysteries*, that ghost-whisperer said. That's pretty cool, right?"

"What are you two arguing about?" Theo rumbled behind us. Graf and I both jumped about a foot.

"Theo!" I said, suddenly inspired. "Theo, could you give us a lift to Harin?" I turned to Graf. "Theo could get us there in time, right?" I'd said *never again,* but for this...

"Well, I was intending to have another nap, but certainly, I suppose, if you really need one."

"Hang on," Graf said. "We're not going anywhere 'til after Arel and Misha have done their thing."

"Do you have time?" I asked, pointedly.

Graf shrugged. "Dunno. Do you have an oath you swore already?"

I scowled at him.

Theo was looking with interest between us, swinging his big head from side to side. He looked as if he were about to say something.

"Cade!" That was Arel, from across the cavern. "We think we have it."

"Come on," Graf said. "Just as well I'm still here, right? A ghost might come in handy, breaking in to see the Emperor."

As far as I could tell, the whole point of the seal, which was still a bad idea, in my view, but a marginally less bad one than anything else Arel had come up with, was that we wouldn't, exactly, be breaking in, which was, as I had told Arel before, emphatically outside my skillset. Still. Graf slung an arm around my shoulder. It went straight through, which was chilly, but the thought was there.

20.

"It will be dawn soon," Arel said. "We must go."

Go, apparently, via Theo. There wasn't time to walk, Misha's horse wasn't in a fit state to go anywhere, and Arel's and mine were still in Perren.

Theo was delighted. "I can take you *right* into the palace!"

"No," Arel and I said together, and Theo pouted, which was a weird expression on a dragon.

"You'll be seen. And shot down," I explained.

"I can..."

"We are not starting a fight with the Emperor's guards," Arel said firmly. "You can drop us, quietly, somewhere *dark* and *outside* the city."

"Ugh. If you insist," Theo said with ill grace.

"I'm still not sure *any* of this is a good idea," I said, as if I hadn't lost that battle already.

"You have made that point, more than once," Arel said, raising her chin. "Well. I am back at Jiral. More or less. You have completed your job, I am no longer your client. I release you. Stay here, and be done."

I felt my face do something strange. I had to get Graf to Harin. Theo could drop Arel and Misha, and then take me and Graf on to Harin, and maybe, just maybe, we'd get there in time. But just leaving Arel with Misha, with no idea of what was going to happen or whether she was going to get in to see the Emperor, never mind what else... What if they ran into early morning footpads going into the city? She wasn't at the end of her journey, and she wasn't safe. My oath still held.

And in any case, client or no, Arel was my friend. If something went wrong that I could have prevented, if she was hurt or the treaty lost, I would never forgive myself. And I was good at not forgiving myself.

"I'm not going to remind you about the oath," Graf said. "But I am going to say that you are bloody well not staying here, because if *you* don't go, *I* can't, and I want to see what happens. There's time for Harin afterwards. It's my decision, Cade. Remember?"

Arel had turned to talk to Misha again. Her back was stiff.

"I—ugh. Fuck's sake." I stomped over to Arel. "You're not releasing me, don't be stupid. I'm coming with you, and I won't say anything more about how this is a terrible idea. Just *please* let me do anything that needs a sword?"

"Thank you, Cade." She smiled at me. "I would much prefer that, if you are willing."

"Better not be anything that needs a sword," Misha said. "The palace guards will be there even if no one else is."

I gave xem my best maybe-I'll-just-use-it-on-you glare, and xe blanched and changed the subject. Xe wasn't wrong, though. If Arel needed me, she was screwed already. Still, I just couldn't leave her to it.

Theo dropped us, not quite literally, in a field a mile from the city. It was after second moonset, not yet pre-dawn. The stars gave just enough light for us to pick our way across the cabbages towards the torch-lit city walls.

Once there, we had to wait until just before dawn to be let in, but after that things went remarkably smoothly. We walked up to the palace through empty streets; the main gate was the first time anyone spoke to us. Misha's bone-magician black hood and knife sheath, like my surcoat, acted as a pass through most doors; and Arel had the Emperor's seal. Twice, Misha had to do the thing with the knife to demonstrate the seal was truly bound to her, but it was treated like protocol, not like any of the guards specifically doubted Arel. I was worried someone might recognise her, but either they didn't,

139

or Misha and the seal overrode any questions they might have.

I'd asked if we weren't at risk of running into Nico, if he consulted regularly with the Emperor, but Misha reminded me he'd been out of the city already, headed to the family estates, when they'd argued.

"He won't be back for a couple of days," xe said confidently.

I really should have questioned that more thoroughly.

The guard on the door of the Emperor's waiting-chamber looked with surprised recognition at Arel, at the seal, then up at Misha.

"My brother sent us," Misha said, with aristocratic aplomb, and she let us in without even asking Arel to lose another drop of blood.

The room had the thickest rug I've ever set foot on, and lots of very expensive panelling and paintings all over the walls. But there wasn't time to appreciate any of it, because in one of the fancy chairs, one booted foot over his knee, sat Nico of the Family Bethene.

We were *so close*.

"Misha. How nice to see you," Nico said, with a broad and unpleasant smile.

"But I thought..." Misha said, surprised into honesty.

"You thought I was away? Whereas, after the little tantrum you threw last night, I wondered what foolish idea you might get into your head, to what risk you might decide to expose the Emperor. And here we are. Who is it, I wonder, that you're bringing into the Emperor's presence?"

I stepped in front of Arel. "Sir Cade, Knight of Siremos, my lord." I bowed, as broad-shouldered and pompous as I could manage.

"Not *you*," Nico snarled, but Arel had ducked around my other side and was over at the door that led to the Emperor's reception room, showing the seal to the guards. It wasn't working; neither guard moved to let her through. Graf hovered next to her, staring at the door as if he were trying to see through it.

"You're a liar, brother," Misha said. Xe was trying to sound loud and forceful, but xyr shoulders were braced as if xe expected to be hit. "You're a liar, and I'm going to prove it. Take me to the Emperor."

"Don't be ridiculous, Misha," Nico said. In contrast to Misha, he was all confident relaxation, still leaning back in his chair. "Go home and we'll say no more about it. Guards! That one stole the seal she's carrying. Arrest her at once."

One of the guards had a hand on Arel's arm. This was not going well. They all knew Nico, and they knew what Arel had been accused of. Nico seemed so assured, and I could see why—and yet, if he knew Misha and Arel were coming, or even just that Misha might try something, surely he could have had them turned away at one of the many gates we'd passed through?

But then, the further out we'd been stopped, the more public Arel and Misha's accusations would be. Nico was gambling, wasn't he, behind that confidence—gambling that he could wrap this all up in private and give out whatever story he chose.

"It is not stolen," Arel said, loudly, showing none of Misha's nerves. "I am Lady Arel of the Family Xeria, and I was given it. It is blood-bound to me."

"You've been banished, *Arel*," Nico hissed. "If it's blood-bound to you that doesn't make it resonant."

Arel ignored him, and spoke even louder. "The Emperor has been grievously misled in his household. I must make my case to him."

Nico leapt to his feet, taking a stride towards her, but I was quicker.

"I cannot permit you to hurt my client," I said, showing all my teeth.

I caught a glimpse of Graf moving towards—no, *through*?—the door. I had no idea what he thought he was doing, and no time to think about it.

"I am not going to hurt your client," Nico snarled.

"Then you will be happy to stay away from her."

"Sir," one of the guards warned from behind me. "If you draw steel here, we'll have to act." She sounded wretched. She knew that if Arel was my client, I was bound by oath just as much as they were, and I doubted she wanted to get into a fight in the middle of the waiting-room.

"I understand," I said. "If you could step back, Lord Nico."

Nico didn't step back. His head cocked to one side, as if he were listening, and for the first time he looked worried. What had he heard? He shifted his weight, as if he was about to rush me to get to Arel, which was odd, because surely if he just waited for the guards to get on and arrest her, he'd be wholly in control.

"I demand my right of audience as the bearer of the Emperor's Seal," Arel cried.

Nico's shoulders shifted, and I braced myself to stand against him until the guards knocked me down, probably in about three seconds time.

Then a door snicked open behind me, and an old, dry, querulous voice, said, "Let the young woman in immediately."

142

21.

"My lord." That was Arel.

I'd only ever seen the Emperor from a great distance, and that was years ago. I desperately wanted to turn towards the door, but didn't dare take my eyes off Nico.

Who, very unwisely, took a step forward, towards the Emperor. There was a sigh of what sounded like relief from the guards and the *schick* of a sword being drawn, then one of them stepped past me towards Nico, her sword low but threatening.

"Lord Nico. Step back, if you please."

I saw Nico think for a moment about disobeying. His eyes flicked to me, and I gave him a broad smile. He looked at the guard. He stepped backwards.

I took a half-step sideways, so I could keep an eye on Nico at the same time as watching what was going on in the rest of the room.

The Emperor stood in his doorway; a small, stooped, wizened old man, his ornate robes hanging off him. Behind him stood Graf, looking even more ragged than he had a moment ago, and utterly exhausted.

Arel was on one knee before the Emperor. "I am accused of stealing your seal," she said. "I did not. I demand my right to be heard."

"Come in, then," the Emperor said.

"My lord!" Nico cried out. "You cannot trust her."

"Nico," the Emperor said sharply. "I have heard enough from you. Indeed, I begin to wonder whether I have heard *rather too much*." His gaze wandered over the rest of the room. "Sir Knight."

"My lord." I dipped my knee, but not so much that I couldn't get up again in a hurry. I still didn't trust Nico.

"And you, you're here with your brother?"

"No, my lord. I brought Lady Arel."

"She is no longer *Lady* Arel," Nico said. "And I believe my sibling has used xyr bone-magic to evade that."

"Well, now, that's interesting," the Emperor said. "You," he pointed at Misha, "come in with her, and tell me what you've come to tell me. And if I am not impressed, I'll execute the pair of you." His voice didn't change at all. My back shivered. Arel's face was proud, her chin high, the way it was when she was determined. I was pretty sure she wasn't as unconcerned as she was making out, but she was doing a good job.

"I urge you, my lord, to let me come in and advise you."

"If you say one more word, Lord Nico, I'll execute you too," the Emperor said pleasantly. "Stay here. And the knight, too."

He turned to hobble back into his rooms. Arel and Misha followed him. The guard still had Nico at sword point.

"I suggest you sit down, Lord Nico," she said without inflection.

He backed up to sit on one of the ornate chairs. His face was set and unreadable. He'd gambled on keeping all of this away from public court, at the risk of having the argument right in front of the Emperor's rooms, and just maybe, that hadn't paid off.

The guard put her sword away. "You too, Sir Knight," she said, with more warmth.

Well. If Nico was sitting, I might as well do the same. It was nothing at all to do with how my legs were shaking.

Graf sat down next to me. I could see straight through him.

144

"Are you all right?" I asked as quietly as I could. Nico still glanced over at me.

"Tired," Graf said. He looked it.

"What happened?" I tried covering the question with a cough.

"He's nearly dead," Graf said, with a sigh. "Close to the, you know, thing. Veil. I dunno. It was hard going, but I managed to get him to hear me. Warn him he was maybe being lied to. Talk about his legacy. That sort of thing. Once I got him over to where he could hear all the shouting, he finally got interested. Fuck, but I'm tired."

Nico's gamble probably would have worked, then, without Graf. But, quite clearly, it had cost Graf dearly. I couldn't see his feet any more. His legs just sort of ended at the ankle.

"Do we need to find Theo?"

"Pretty sure those two," he nodded at the guards, "won't let you go."

"*You* could find Theo."

"Too far."

"Graf..." I'd forgotten to moderate my voice. Both guards and Nico were staring at me. I gave them a fake smile, which didn't seem to reassure anyone.

"'M fine. Just... let's get through this, yeah? It's fine."

It wasn't fine, not at all, but he was right that I wouldn't be allowed to leave against the Emperor's command, ghost-sword-brother or not. I set my teeth and waited, stomach churning anxiously, glancing over at Graf every minute or so. He slumped towards me. My shoulder felt the chill of him, and the rest of me just wanted him there, really, whole and solid, the way he never was going to be again. But he was here, now, as he was. That was something. I would take what I could of my sword-brother, while I could.

145

It was about half an hour before the Emperor called me in. Graf stayed outside. The Emperor asked me to tell him on my oath what I'd seen in Arel's room, nodded, and dismissed me again. After that he called Nico in, and I sat back down by Graf, now frayed almost to the knee. Nico was in there a lot longer. Eventually Misha and Arel came out, but he didn't.

"You can all leave," the guard said, without any signal I'd seen.

"What did he say?" I asked.

"We're not going to be executed," Misha said. "Nico, I'm not so sure about." Xe looked bleak. Nico might be a shit-head, but he was Misha's brother, I supposed. "He's not head of the family any more, anyway. It sounded like the Emperor is going to take a good long look at a lot of things."

"He's not," Graf said quietly. "He's going to be dead in a week."

"He refused to agree to that treaty exactly, but we agreed something that is close enough. I can return and convince the Prince. I think." Arel looked exhausted, huge smears of purple under her eyes. "He agrees that we should avoid war, in any case."

"That's... something?" I said.

She nodded. "I could wish it were done already, but I can do it. I am certain I can." She did her best to smile at me. "Willing to guide me back to Harin? We can go the usual way, this time. Possibly with an entourage."

"Not sure I want to guide a whole entourage," I grumbled half-heartedly. "But fine. For you." Arel grinned at me despite her exhaustion, and my fondness for her flickered warmly in my chest. "Once we've both had some sleep." I paused. "You shouldn't waste time, though." I should tell her what Graf said, as soon as I could, but not in the middle of the Emperor's waiting room. She needed to get the thing agreed formally before all the noble jockeying around the vote for the new Emperor began. Everything would stop for months, and who knew who would wind up in power. But a fully sealed treaty would be hard to repudiate. If we took the usual way to Harin, without the need for secrecy, we could be there in a couple of days. The Prince was keen, and Arel would have the real seal. We could do it, if we hurried. We could make whatever Graf had said to the Emperor about his legacy true.

"I should... I don't know. Tell the family, I suppose," Misha said. "About Nico."

"I must *find* my family," Arel said, a little bitterly. "The Emperor has reinstated us, but they have already fled to the country. I must send a messenger."

"I've got something to do, too, before I take on any more guiding," I said. "May I...?"

"Of course. Then come back here, to arrange the journey?" Arel asked.

"It'll be a few hours," I said.

Arel eyed me keenly. "Is this about your sword-brother?"

I nodded. Water was standing in my eyes again. I pretended it wasn't.

"Of course," Arel said, gently. "Whatever time you need."

I couldn't speak. I bowed to her and to Misha, and strode off down the corridor. Graf was just by my shoulder, but my sense of him was fading by the moment. We were going to be too late.

22.

Theo was still out in the field where we'd left him, curled under a clump of trees looking more like a mossy stone than a dragon. He uncurled as Graf and I arrived.

"Did you manage all the whatever-it-was?"

"More or less," I said. "Arel and Misha both got some of what they wanted, and some of what they didn't, and they're both still alive."

"Sounds like as much as could be expected," Theo said, and humped his back up in a stretch. "Humans are far more complicated than dragons. It's much easier if you just bite each other."

"I dunno," I said, thinking of the Emperor. "Some humans are a bit like dragons, I think, that way."

Theo sniffed. "Your teeth aren't good enough."

He came to where Graf was leaning against my shoulder again, and sniffed delicately at him. "You haven't much longer, you know," he said.

"I figured that." Graf pushed himself upright, and looked at his hands, turning them over. "Cade, if you say anything..."

I shut my mouth before I offered again.

"Can you take us to Harin?" I demanded instead, of Theo. Maybe, just maybe, there was still time. I'd known, really, since that conversation with Emer, that return to the Lake was the best we could hope for. And it was all well and good that his life-stuff might return, but it wouldn't be *Graf*. He'd truly be gone, this time. I'd known, I'd just badly, so badly, wanted there to be another option. But maybe we could still...

"By all means," Theo said. "But I. Uh." He looked uncomfortable. "I don't wish to be rude, but I am not sure that both of you will *arrive*, is the problem. Even flying it's a fair distance."

"I don't have that long," Graf said.

"I fear not."

Not that, even, then. "Then there's no point." I slumped back against a tree, misery and exhaustion draining me.

Theo tilted his head at me. "No?"

"The idea was the ghost-whisperers would detach me," Graf explained. He shrugged ruefully. "I guess I'll just disappear instead. Which, hey. Sounds kind of interesting, I guess. Great mysteries, right?"

But it wouldn't be Graf that experienced them, would it? I felt empty. Sick.

Theo sniffed around Graf again. "I could eat you, if you like?" he offered.

Graf and I both blinked in confusion.

"I mean this in the nicest possible way, Theo, but—what?" Graf squinted at him.

"If what you're worried about is your attachment to Sir Cade here, then I could eat you instead, and that would solve the problem."

"The *problem*," I said slowly, "is that Graf won't return to the Lake unless he's detached."

"Oh, well, he won't return to the Lake straight away if I eat him, either, but whilst dragons live for a long time, we don't live forever."

A sort of desperate hope began to fizz up through my ribs. I felt light-headed, like I was floating an inch off the ground.

"I've hosted ghosts before," Theo continued cheerfully. "For a while they carry on being ghosts, just anchored in me, and then I suppose they just become me. A bit like those sheep, but more *metaphysically*."

Hope warred with discomfort. But Graf, when I looked at him, was looking interested.

"I'd be a ghost inside you? With flying and that?"

"The ghost-whisperers said, only one spirit per body," I said, trying to understand.

Theo spread his wings out pointedly. "Oh, well, *humans*. You are limited in such regards, I suppose. Dragons are more robust. Though I should be clear. It is only for a little while the anchoring lasts."

"Does sound a lot like being food," Graf said, but he didn't sound like he was put off.

"Would that mean you go back to the Lake, eventually?" I asked.

"I will," Theo offered. "So I've always supposed any of the ghosts I've absorbed will, then, too." He snorted thoughtfully. "If they haven't already, that is."

"You might just disappear," I said to Graf.

"I'm not going to make it back to Harin anyway," Graf said. "At least this'll be interesting."

I was torn evenly between hope and sorrow. I opened my mouth to say something else, then closed it again. It wasn't my choice, was it? It was Graf's.

"I do quite fancy flying," Graf mused. "Theo, are you *sure*?"

"My scales are your scales," Theo said, with a generous wave of his wing. "My wings are your wings."

"Eh. Go on then. It'll be a laugh, won't it?" He looked at me. "Stop looking like that, Cade. I've gone already, really. This is just a very shabby echo, I guess, by now."

"I'm sorry about everything," I said. Him being dead. Not being able to save him. Not even knowing whether this would bring him back to the Lake or not. Even if it was the only option left to us—to him—now.

"Don't be daft," Graf said. "Shit happens. None of this is down to you, Cade love, and it never was. Okay?" He was almost entirely transparent now.

"You might want to move it along," Theo warned.

"Love you, sweetheart," Graf said quietly. He put his arms around me. I closed my eyes and for a moment, it was almost like he was really there, solid in front of me, my forehead resting on his shoulder; then that was gone, and only a faint chill remained.

I opened my eyes, and Graf stepped back. "Go for it, Theo."

Theo leant forwards, and engulfed Graf in his jaws. I felt a deep, sharp, pain in my middle, anchored in the tug of Graf's connection to me; and then it was gone, leaving only an aching hollowness; and Graf had disappeared.

Theo was pulling faces, like he was eating something surprising, or chewing toffee. Finally he swallowed, and yawned again. He spread his wings. "There we are. He'll need a while to settle, but I promise you, he's perfectly well. Do come and visit. But, if you please, *after* the nice long nap I'm about to take." He huffed a cloud of smoke at me, and while I was still coughing, took off straight upwards, a black dot shooting up into the sky.

"FUCKING BRILLIANT," came floating down from above me, and I laughed despite the wetness on my cheek, because that was definitely Graf.

I sat down with my back against a tree, and stayed there for a while. The sun rose further up the sky; the shadows slowly shifted. I'd need to go back to the chapterhouse at some point, and explain everything to the Archon, including

Graf, and Theo. We'd have to come to some kind of agreement with Theo, now we knew he was there. And there was Arel's and my return to Harin to arrange, which at least meant I could pick up Monty.

And after that... after that, there would be another client, and another journey, and then more after that. The world out there for me to explore. Maybe the next one would be one of the long guide-songs, right out across the sea and beyond. Graf and I had always wanted one of those. I could come back and tell him about it, and he could tell me about flying, and whatever else Theo might get up to now he wasn't a secret. Graf would get to explore, too; Theo could probably go places humans couldn't. I'd better make sure I kept up with him.

Thinking of the future felt good—a little sore still, but good—for the first time in a while. Belaran had been right, hadn't he, to kick me back out there. I was a better guide than an archivist, I'd always known that really; and if he hadn't, well. A lot of things would have gone differently. I had things to do, didn't I? A friend-and-client to deal with; guiding to do; a war to keep avoiding. And Graf to catch up with afterwards, to share tales of our adventures like we always had. At least for a while.

I stood, and began to walk slowly back towards the city, towards Arel and the job and the future, feeling heavy and light all at once. It could be worse. It very nearly had been. I looked up at the blue of the sky, thinking of Graf up there with Theo, and smiled even as my eyes prickled. Yeah. This was fine.

* * *

Bring Me Home

E.M. Faulds

For Doug.

**And for everyone searching
for someone to be.**

E.M. FAULDS

BRING ME HOME

1. The Hole in the Girl

Selen

"You're thirty-six, still young," the mod technician told me as I perched on the edge of the procedure couch. "Are you sure you want a body tunnel, miffren?"

Patronising. Of course I did. What this technician didn't know is that sometimes you had to surrender to inevitability. And my path towards *becoming* was inevitable.

I looked around at the studio, pretending to think. Yes, it was a big decision, but one I'd already made. However, I couldn't say yes too quickly. He'd make assumptions, the kind people make about younger women. I'm not even that young, had my first telomere binder shot a decade ago. While the tech waited for my response, he removed a modular cushion from the couch so there was a gap where my back would lie. He lined the edge with medical sheets. I tried to ignore the crawling sensation on my skin.

This modification studio was much like other ones I'd been in with pals: an uneasy mix of sterile therapeutic furniture and spiritual art, the smell of grease and cauterised flesh covered over with aloe vera, orchid, and sea minerals. There were polished stones, flocks of origami cranes on silksteel filaments, and the cantilevered mechanical arm of the tunnelling bot poised over the treatment couch. I'd had a couple of things done. Nothing major: a dream-stream chip behind my ear, a biotrinket stud in the back of my wrist, easy stuff. Nothing this big.

I was here alone. No pals this time, no-one to giggle and hold my hand while I got it done. To be fair, there was only one person I wanted here, and he'd still be sleeping off last night's performance. I wanted to surprise Jayce. To show him who I was. At the shibboleth last night, the raucous beats and the chant cycle all hinged on one word: becoming. It had been as if my soul had been written for his soundtrack, and I danced, head back, laughing at the night sky while the lights of space traffic streamed overhead, moving in uncanny time with his music. Had he timed everything so perfectly, or was that the effect of his mod on us? To make us think the world was synchronous with his music? It didn't matter, it was all so breathlessly beautiful. So art. I wanted, I needed something like that for me.

I'd selected a full through-and-through body tunnel in one hundred percent elagite with anodised blue rims, seven centimetres in diameter. It sat waiting on the sterile tray, still in its wrapper. I could change the rim colour, but the base material had to be the expensive spacetech alloy, or I might take a catastrophic allergic shock. I nearly had with my cheek piercing.

A weird bonus discovery from researching how to grow spaceships like giant, kilometre-long gourds, they found that elagite could mimic your cells, be a stealthy little implant that didn't activate the immune rejection as with some other substances. More importantly, there were some funky exploits it unlocked. The webbing inside the rim would be invisible, but I would know it was in there, pearlescent twines of DNA-like fronds, interacting with my nervous system, rewiring it.

"What do you do with the stuff?" I asked the tech, putting off my final answer. "The stuff you scoop out of me, I mean?" I had this vision in my head that there would be a massive corer that would take a plug of my flesh and pull it out, glistening fat and scarlet blood. Repulsive, but I wanted to see it.

He pushed his instruments around on the table, an apologetic little smile on his face. "We don't remove that much, just kind of push things to the side. There's some stretching, expanding, but it's not a case of taking stuff out."

"Oh, yeah. Of course."

There are channels, we're told, in the body. Where you could tunnel in and not hit too many vital organs or blood vessels. Why people used to survive getting shot sometimes, when it looked like they should be killed outright. Mine would be right through my abdomen, slightly to the side, an easy opening, no rerouting of spine or artery, no slow and painful expansion of ribs.

I wanted this. I wanted the change. The first known body tunneller was Ogawa, and people said that was why his art was so evocative. It had killed him, in the end, they also said, but things have advanced since his time. I wanted to be like Jayce, so driven, knowing what made him special. So, I had chosen the biggest, most expensive tunnel I could get.

"It flexes with you, to an extent," the tech went on as he finished his preparations, talking as he adjusted machinery and unpacked sterile attachments for the tunnelling bot. "It has to. The body changes a lot during a day and of course there is bloating after a meal and such. Of course, pregnancy would make things awkward. Or sudden weight gain. The tunnel flexes, but not enough that those things won't cause complications. You're still young, you might decide to change your mind, and we can remove the channel but the webbing... different story. It integrates closely with you, makes it basically impossible to remove."

I snorted. Pregnancy? No chance. And I wouldn't be getting this done if I had any thoughts about taking it out later.

"There are some employers who take against body tunnelling," he went on. He had several smaller tunnels in his arms and legs, visible even in the backs of his hands – which must have been a complicated rerouting of thin bones, tendons, and nerves. I supposed he was a walking advertisement for his own skills. "I'm obligated, legally and morally," he said, "to tell you that. And about the other complications, the random effects." I waved this off. I'd already done my own research on the known effects body tunnelling could have — sensory shifts, nerve annexation, identity changes. The randomness could be awkward or amazing, but that was part of it too. I wanted something to make me special. Something other people couldn't take from me because it was mine.

I hadn't told my parents. I knew what would happen. "You're risking disability for some fad!" Dad Rob would say. Daddy Arjun would look at me sadly, like he had failed me somehow. Mum would storm around. She'd start aggressively rearranging things – curtains and cushions and knick-knacks – as a substitute for doing the same to me. All these things would still happen, but they were consigned to the future, locked away until I ran towards them. But I wouldn't until I was ready. I wanted to be unassailable. To say, *see, it all worked out.*

"Miffren?" he said, gently prompting with his hand hovering over the controls.

"Yes, I want it," I said, too loud. Then, for the contract impression, said it again, with my name — Selen A. Muir — and today's date — the twelfth of March 85 Post Deluge — and the place — the Tunnelporium in the heart of Ben Lomond City. Then I lay down, my back across the gap.

I'd dismissed the idea of taking a funicular this morning, and instead walked up BL's teetering switchback streets from the ferry port, wanting to exercise, or exorcise, my nervousness. Of course, it just meant I was embarrassingly sweat-drenched and had begged to use the studio toilet to wipe down my armpits before starting. I'd looked at myself, for what felt like a goodbye, in the dented piece of aluminium they had in place of a mirror in the dingy cubical. Thirty-six.

In the past, that would be my life half-done. Or maybe I'd already be dead. I hadn't even hit my stride yet. Not like Jayce. Not like my sister, Phoebe. I could have asked my parents to pay for it, but they were still up to their eyeballs in obligation to the space port's mother corp for their leveraged lives. They had no choice. I did. I'd saved up my pitiful bursary. For this. For this, and maybe a shot at a new life without leaving the Craig. I loved where I lived. I didn't want to go to space or 'find myself' on the other side of the world, like Phoebe.

But I did want change, and here it was.

"If you can lift up your top a bit, and scooch your waistband down, there. That's great."

The antiseptic swab chilled my belly, bringing up goosebumps. Then the prickling itch as an analgesic patch worked in thousands of tiny needles into me. Everything was happening, much too fast. I was ready, but it was all happening *now*. Should I live-splash this? Would it get me fans and motes?

Too late. The arm of the tunnelling bot hinged over and plunged in. I felt nothing physically except a push-pull sensation where the skin stretched and moved, but I wanted to claw my way off the sofa and climb up the walls.

On the ceiling, a poster, held by sticky tack, one corner drooping. It was faded by light and time and said, 'This is but one moment in the flow of eternity' and I held this in my eyes as the horrific sounds and smells of cut and cauterisation threatened to overwhelm me.

I remembered, quite deliberately, the aluminium mirror in the cubicle. How I'd felt the shame of my nothing body, of not being enough. Of anything. To anyone. All this was worth not feeling that again. I kept pinning that to the front of my mind as the horrible thing plunged, buried, burrowed into me.

159

Finally, it was over. A rivet that ran through me, deftly placed to nudge my intestines and an ovary out of the way. Tiny metallic pings sounded as it warmed to my body temperature. The blue rim crowned from my flesh.

"You can sit up now, but take it easy," the tech said. My brow crinkled. It should be impossible to rise, I should be pinned to the couch like another piece of upholstery. I shuffled upwards, first on my elbows, then enough that I could swing my legs over the side. Moving felt odd, stiff. "Go take a look," he said, nodding and smiling towards the full-length mirror in the corner.

I took a few steps. A wave of nausea washed through me and I stopped, but it passed quickly. I pulled my top high and studied my reflection.

A view from front to back, a gap of air. I had been punctuated. My own full-stop-period, to put in front of any of this world's arseholes. And there were so many of them.

The tech's voice came from over my shoulder, where he was cleaning his instruments. "The effects will come after a couple of days. You might not notice anything until you mesh up with it fully. But the webbing, it'll already be branching out."

The fronds of elagite inside would reach out, divide, wriggle around, rooting themselves into my nervous system like a chaotic work of living art.

"And then," I murmured to myself, "I'll become."

"Hmm? What do you mean? Become what?"

I ignored him and pulled my top down.

Phoebe

"Lil Sis," Phoebe groaned. She shook her head and dangled the phone over her knees, unable to look at the image Selen had sent for more than a few seconds before needing to break off and stare back at the barren landscape out the passenger window. It was no use, she could still see her sister's eyes, baby-blue, filled with a mix of exultation and anxiety. And that ugly cylinder cut out of her belly.

Her younger sister had a remarkable ability to one-up her last fuck-up. Before this, she'd had a spectacular row with the lecturer of her previous course and quit the night before her final exams. Phoebe had thought that was the low point; that after that, Selen would get her life back on track. But here she'd sent a picture of her *full through-and-through body tunnel* and a note not to tell Mum and Dads yet. All this while Phoebe was on the other side of the planet and too far away to give her a good shake.

The aircon was drying out her eyeballs. In theory, it should be much cooler inside the cab of Harro's car, but after the hundreds of kays the convoy had travelled on red dust roads, all that blew out of the vent was a slightly less-hot air that ripped the moisture out of a person. It was too stifling to not have it, though, and if they stopped there was no shelter from the sun. The last rest break had been at a piddling artesian well with some biodiesel bowsers, a shade cloth, and some hard-eyed individuals who charged a hundred bucks a litre for water. The convoy had drunk from the spigot at the side of the water tanker instead, and everyone had eyed each other suspiciously.

They weren't scheduled to stop again for another four hours.

Harro—*real name Arthur Harrison, Caucasian New Australian, male, sixty-three*—was singing as he drove, tunes only he could hear, sieved through lips mostly closed to keep the moisture in. All the songs came out high-pitched and hoarse but it was probably a sign he was happy. That was a good thing. Phoebe still wasn't sure how she felt about this guy, or the people he represented. Most of the time, he seemed

161

as serene and unmovable as the endless outback plain they drove over. His anger was like gun-drones diving out of a clear blue sky. Phoebe normally kept her distance, not wanting to trigger him by saying the wrong thing, which was easy to do.

She wasn't on the same wavelength as all the rest of Harro's Horde, either. (It was a stupid name, half a joke, she found out once she'd embedded with them.) They all wanted this, wanted to go south with Harro and join the secretive group in the middle of the desert that called themselves 'Us'; she hadn't even heard of them until a week ago.

The handheld radio crackled. "Roadblock," the lead car sent. Harro shifted down a gear so he could pull out on the other vehicles—a school bus, a camper, several cars and utes—and get to the head of the convoy. They cleared the dust plume and the obstruction revealed itself. Passing under the shadow of the tanker, Phoebe looked up to see the driver, Reggie, frown beneath his sunglasses. Shan was up there, she knew, in the passenger seat. She'd trade for it right now.

Every time, every roadblock, some different little pissant would try to shake the convoy down. It was literally highway robbery, but they had the guns, and no-one cared out here. And a route avoiding their territory would add a week onto the journey.

"Fuck," she muttered to herself. She'd wanted to be in Harro's car in case he dropped any interesting titbits of information on the organisation's plans, but now she was going to be stuck here while men waved scary guns around and Harro tried to argue his way past them.

"Veil, veil!" He clicked his fingers at her, and she pawed through her bag for the charity shop scarf she'd been using as a head covering, that she'd forgotten to put on. Out here, where women were forced into modesty. At the point of a gun if necessary.

"Now, keep it chilly, they just want to talk," he warned as she looped the fabric round her head and shoulders. He pulled up slowly to the militia, who had their own scarves pulled up to sunglasses. They wore them for intimidation and dust protection rather than modesty, and finished the look off with berets. Always berets, the stupidest hat to wear in sun this strong, even if you weren't as sandy-white as Harro. He pressed the window button down and waited for the men leaning against the vehicles. They'd parked their flashy dual cabs across the road. It was more of a symbolic barrier than anything. There was nothing to either side of the track, but the matte black of the automatic weapons cradled casually in their arms discouraged this idea of skirting around.

"Yeah, Boss? How ya goin'?" Harro called as one of the gunmen swaggered to his window and pulled his scarf down to reveal a lizard-like grin. The hot wind blew in. Every prickly bit of scrub and shiny sun-baked pebble on the side of the road, the dome of the sky, the glint and flash off the sunglasses of the man gained instant clarity as the barrel of his automatic pointed into the cab. The thing was much smaller than she would have imagined, but she still had to resist the urge to fling open the passenger door and roll underneath. *And, what?* Burrow her way out?

Harro must have sensed her muscles tensing. "Sit tight," he breathed between gritted teeth.

"G'day," the man with the gun said, his friendliness a thin veneer. "Where you mob going?" His short-sleeved shirt let him flex his juiced-up muscles at them. Not subtle. New Aus Fasica were the worst. They'd taken the old white settler mentality and amped it up to ridiculous new heights. Phoebe saved her sneer for a better time. If there was one.

"Passing through. We're going south," Harro said cheerfully. "Heading for the Pans."

"Got a permit?"

Harro pretended surprise. "Didn't know you needed one. How much are they?"

The man looked down the line of vehicles, visibly calculating what he could get away with.

"Hundred bucks a head." He paused. "A grand for the tanker."

"Aww, mate," Harro said. "That's a lot." The barrel of the gun suddenly became active again. "Reckon we could come to some arrangement," Harro said quickly.

The Fasica grunt looked deeper into the car, and for a horrible moment Phoebe thought that she was going to be part of that arrangement, but then he changed his angle to look in the back seat. "What's that?"

Harro winked at her, then leaned out the window, speaking so low she could hardly hear him. Her fear shifted down a level or two. The militia man was taking the bribe. They'd be let past.

When she'd first joined, the many containers of K-fire had seemed like an insane thing to haul across a desert, but the Fasica loved it. Their leaders had banned alcohol consumption, no drugs of any kind, but this was a loophole. It was mildly stimulating, refreshing on a hot day. When they were loading it up for this leg of the journey, Harro had finally explained the second part of his convoy's nickname. Like the Mongols, sweeping across the plains with a mare's milk beverage tucked in their saddlebags, they were a horde, carrying their ayrag. This stuff was made of soybeans and some molecule cribbed off betel nut, but it was similar enough, and liquid gold out here.

Harro got out to make the transaction—some cash and some containers to be let through. He climbed back in the cab and clocked her shaking hands. "I told you, you don't kill the golden goose if you want more eggs," he said breezily as the men hauled their prizes back to their trucks. "They can't buy this stuff out here. They'll want us to bring some next time."

She kept her mouth shut, wondering if the tension in her chest could stop squeezing her like a python anytime soon.

There might be a time when this didn't work. When they'd take everything at gunpoint, including her. But Harro knew the roads, knew the tricks. He'd done this convoy hundreds of times, he'd claimed, bringing people South, like the fabled birds of old Europe winging their way to better lands.

As the dual cabs trundled back to open up the blockade, and the rising heat distorted the view of the opening road and the miles and miles of dust, how could they be going towards any kind of paradise?

Selen

It was late afternoon, two days after the fitting of my body tunnel, that I got the first tiny signpost for the effects to come. I was snooze-watching shows on my bed while waiting out my recovery time. My favourite today was a soap about Spacers. All the actors were hauntingly beautiful, tall and willowy, drifting balletically around their space station. They were a dynasty of space mining colonists and most of the emphasis was on the boardroom-to-bedroom antics of a driven, ambitious oligarchy. The format was a wraparound shell, but I had balanced my phone on my chest and couldn't be bothered using the walkabout facility, just watched it passively. When I nodded off, it dipped into dream-stream with long, compressed-time side stories that supplemented the main arc.

But then I fell into natural sleep and had a restless, vivid dream about Phoebe. I couldn't see her, not properly. It was as if I was looking at her through a keyhole or something, but I was also there with her, and she was in danger. I woke, upset. It was ominous, but not that unusual, frankly. I enjoyed a plethora of rotten anxiety dreams, even without the massive upheaval of a body mod fitting.

When I sat up, my stomach griped, the pain around the operation site edging its way back in, so I took a pill and nestled back down. My arm slipped down my side and pain jolted up my hand to my shoulder. I snatched it back to my chest, swearing. Had something stung me? But then I clocked what it was. My hand had fallen into a beam of sunlight from the high storm window. It had given me a reaction, like eating lemon sorbet too fast, but all up my arm and into my head.

Okay, I got the principle. Synaesthesia, when your senses overlap so you start hearing colours or smelling sounds. It was mostly supposed to be a good thing, a lot of artists experienced sensory overlap and it made their work richer or helped their memory. In my case, it felt like the sunlight had punched me in the head. With a fresh, citrusy aftertaste.

I cradled my arm protectively, but then curiosity took over. So of course, I had to do it again. I stretched my fingers back towards the white-yellow rectangle of light, rendered into a miniature landscape by the rucked-up bedcovers. This time I was ready for it. Faint static whined, as I pushed the tips of my fingers into the edge and encountered not resistance exactly, but *thereness* like the meniscus on the surface of water. Now the sensation was warm, buttery. I laughed.

Unconsciously, I stroked the anodised blue collar of the elagite tunnel with my thumb, rubbed over it like the rim of a wineglass. The sound was confusing, an echo of a distant conversation, or an earthworm turning over the dirt somewhere. Then the sensations collapsed, and my hand was in normal, warm sunlight again, my mod sounding just as it would for any brushing touch.

"Take it easy," the tech had told me. "Take a few days off, just sitting with yourself until you get used to it. The webbing will do some strange stuff until it's fully bedded in. It'll mess with the wiring, so to speak."

I poked the beam of light a bit more, but nothing else interesting happened, so I went back to my shows and watched the bit from when I'd fallen asleep. The story wasn't dragging me along with it, and I found myself fidgeting. It'd be better to stay in and ride out the changes. But I could show my mod to Jayce. Tell him about that weird effect. Maybe he'd be interested, impressed.

Time to go. I had to get out of the commune, preferably without comment, discussion, or drama. Flick and Senna were good as far as housemates went, but they sucked at this kind of thing. At understanding what I was trying to do with my life.

I'd known them since school. When they'd got together, they'd advertised for a room-mate to share the commune and get the required occupancy for free residence. They'd been glad to take on someone familiar, but we've grown apart since I started hanging out with Jayce.

They were sensible. Gainfully employed. Called me perma-student when they thought I couldn't hear. If I were a perma-student, I'd have already enrolled in the next course. I hadn't. I was enjoying my life for a bit. What was wrong with that? I mean, I'd have to pick something soon, or my bursary leftovers would run out, but that was another future-me problem.

I got myself together and slipped through the living area like a ghost, down the steps, then out. I held the big metal storm door with one hand while I stuck the other out into the sunshine to see if there was any more of that effect. Nothing happened, so I set off. Down the street, no problems, no weird stuff, pills properly kicking in. Maybe I'd get away with it.

Jayce held court, as usual, at the FenderBender. Everyone sat around a table diorama of fast food and drink; half-eaten protein patties, Kelpy's sodas, all salt and fat and sweeteners. He was deep in conversation when I came up; at first, he didn't notice me. I held off from interrupting, though I wanted to punch his shoulder. Then he saw me, noticed my stomach, and his eyes popped.

"You did it, you crazy knuck!" Worth the wait.

He swung his arm across the table, nearly knocking over drinks and bowls, his mod, a purple and gold tunnel through his forearm, casually visible. I'd cut two clumsy holes in my t-shirt with nail scissors, just so people could see. He snagged my elbow and drew me in closer. "Jude, jump out for a sec, hey?" Jude was a hanger-on, a face but not a name on the scene. They'd got forearm extensions so they looked lanky, simian. It was a weird mod to get, didn't really work for them. They gave me a dirty look, but slid out of the booth, to go look for a spare stool to pull up, muttering. I didn't care. I was here. I'd arrived. I bumped up next to Jayce, right up to him.

"Sel, what are your effects?" Diddy asked from across the table. Diddy was Jayce's pal. They hung out. Always around.

"Not sure yet," I said. "Hoping for something big. Useful. Like Jayce's."

I'd met Jayce three years ago at a festy. He'd been hyping a show, working behind the scenes, waiting for his break, hustling. He'd made a ton of bucks off his live shows, stream-dreams, shibboleths, and dubh-drop nights. Apart from working hard, he'd also been smart enough to reinvest his money into his brand. The only ostentation on him was his mod and he'd been lucky enough to get a talent that aligned with how it worked. During his shows, he'd just lift his arm in the air, and everything would somehow come together. He said it made a 'standing wave' but I've no idea if that was just marketing. Whatever, it felt good. Weird, but good. When he pulsed his arm back and forth, everyone went off, bouncing, part of the music. *Inside* the music. You had to experience it to get it, really.

It could have been the opposite, an effect that killed it, made his tracks sound shit, messed up his sense of rhythm, but he was brave and did it anyway. Brave, like me. Nowadays you can't go anywhere in Alba without someone having a Jayce story.

A man across the FenderBender was frowning, deliberately not looking at us. Disgusted. To be expected from the older generation, I suppose. He must have been at least a hundred. Born in a time before mods were a thing. But this was our place. We came here all the time; it was his problem not ours. It was much more interesting over here, big smile spreading on my face, Jayce putting his warm arm round my shoulders, him smelling like hot, salty fries and body spray, pulling me in for a pic.

"This is my sib, Selen, got the mod!" he told his splash feed and I posed, pulling down my bottom eyelid, goofing off, looking down at my body tunnel and acting shocked. The motes piled up, 'shocked' or 'zazz', retro smiley faces. I didn't even know who was sending them. I wish he'd told me he'd be doing that. I mean, none of my parents would pick it up, but still.

"Maybe I should get a drink," I said casually pulling away to look up at the dispensary boards.

"Nah, we're just leaving, meeting some folks at the pier." Jayce was all sly confidence. "Coming?"

The abandoned pier at the end of the Craig. Party central. It was probably too soon. I should recover some more.

"I dunno," I said, "I guess."

"Get my bag?" Jayce called across the table as he shoved his hip against mine to shunt me over and I giggled, half-falling out of the booth. It was sore, but he wasn't to know that. Diddy swung out Jayce's bag, and we left the table strewn with bowls and bottles and wrappers with their picnic-chequered red and white, past the disapproving man who still didn't seem pleased, even though we were leaving.

We walked down, me uncomfortable with the wind whistling through my middle and humming across the rim. Jayce whooped at the sound, delighted, so I experimented with what angle worked best. He turned his own to get the sound. "We need more of us, make a pipe organ," I said, mostly to cover my surprise. I'd get used to it soon enough, sure.

The evening light sparkled off the choppy seas round the Craig. A backhoe dredger mined up soil for the mountaintops, out by the tidal power booms. It dipped its huge scoop in and lifted out silt and metal and we stopped to watch it for a while. There wasn't much else to do round here. Used to be a lot different, so my folks said, before the depop. I was a baby when it happened. Apparently, there used to be twenty billion people here on the planet and around here used to be hoaching with art, noise, culture. Then the Deluge and after that, the depopulation. Only the lottery winners, key personnel, and their families got to stay, and the rest were rafted up into space. The world got dull and empty. My parents banged on about it all the time, how it was a privilege to stay here, how we're the lucky ones. Didn't feel that way though.

"My da found a bicycle once," Diddy said, contemplative, watching the black sludge from the machine's bucket.

"What you on about, ya knuck?" Jayce wasn't pissed, just liked to keep Diddy on his toes.

"Dived down to Glasgow, bought back up this battered piece of metal. Turned out to have been a bike. Old but. That weird design they used to have. The kind that looked like it would cut you in two to sit on."

I was going to ask him what they did with it, if they sold it for scrap metal.

"Your da was a case, though," Jayce said before I could. That closed the conversation because Diddy went off ahead, sulking.

I touched my mod gingerly. Maybe I would regret not taking a day extra to recover. The skin on my belly felt red, angry.

"Don't poke it," Jayce said, like it was a dire warning from experience. I put my hand in my pocket instead.

He lifted his chin and watched a lone seagull patrol the sky. I hated them. Bigger than they looked on the wing when they came down to harass you for food. Evil-eyed shits.

"What did your folks say about it?"

"Haven't quite had the conversation," I told him, eyes still on the bird. "I guess I'll wait until I have something to report." What if my mod did nothing special? What if I got a great big version of fuck all channelled right through my guts?

We reached Diddy looking out over the sea again, back to us. Jude slouched up against one of the pier's piles, looping their arms all the way round it. "When's Charles getting here?" they asked.

Jayce sat down and stretched his legs out over the side. The little waves lapped nearly at the soles of his shoes. "Dunno, it's a shibboleth, innit?"

Charles was another of the hangers on. And there was Mira, Addie, Dilayne, Rhona. Others. People would turn up and use the password to join in. Probably something like, 'Let's get wasted!' It was always something like that. Jayce reached into his bag to get out his mixer and fiddle with it, tracks lighting up the air in front of his face. When the others got here, there'd be a party. Drugs, booze. Jayce's mod bringing the noise home.

I sat down next to him. Near enough I could feel the warmth of his body. Nearly touching. It felt like the right moment to share. We had that bond now, the body tunnels. We were closer.

"When me and Phoebe were little," I started, "we'd sit here, tell each other stories about Old Glasgow. About the things we'd find down there. She'd make me giggle or tell spooky stories about giant tentacle beasties hiding down there hidden in drowned tenement buildings. The light would shine off the water all the way up to join with BL City and the space traffic. I'd call it the staircase to the stars, and Phoebe, being practical," I chuckled, "would tell me a staircase couldn't be big enough to get to the stars."

Jayce didn't respond, just poked about with his tracks and mixer. I nudged him. "Wonder what we'd find if we dived down there?"

"Nothing," Jayce snorted. "Nothing left, dragged it out to build up BLC."

"Huh." Well, he was probably right, but I felt myself going red. I looked out across the water.

Most clear days you could see across the straits to Ben Lomond City, the biggest settlement round here. They'd built up the terraced slopes of the mountain. At night it was a ziggurat of blue and red and lights that poured up into the sky as launches floated up to meet the star traffic out of Killie, the first proper space port on Earth. The one that all my parents worked for.

"Maybe I'll go to space," I said. "Yeah, I got spacetech now, this is all elagite." I flicked a fingernail off the tunnel rim. "So lucky, such a privilege to stay down here on Earth they always keep telling us, but I can't see what everyone's so jammed about. Not like there's that much to do down here. And anyone can give up their place, let a spacer return. If they want." I had no intention of ever leaving but I wanted to prod Jayce. Make him say something.

"What? And leave me here with him?" he joked, finally as he looked up at Diddy, who grinned back uncomfortably. He was always around. Always hanging on. But it didn't matter when Jayce turned his smile back to me. I felt warm inside. So, I kissed him. Diddy grunted with disgust and walked away.

Little lights floated about us, bokeh fireflies of red, orange, and green. I broke off, breathless. "Can you see them?" I asked, but they faded away before he looked. "Was I doing that?"

"What? Dunno," Jayce said. "Don't care." And he pulled me, greedily, back in.

We kissed until the shibboleth started.

2. Family as Given

Phoebe

Phoebe had backpacked around the New Australian coast-line for six months on her work-to-travel visa, taking temp jobs here and there. When she got bored, she'd look up the vacancies in the next town near a nature park, then move on when her application was accepted. A receptionist job in a small real estate agency. Bar worker at the local pub. She'd even cleaned the public toilets at a national park camp-ground, and gained a healthy respect for, if not downright paranoia about, the local fauna.

It had been interesting, learning how little she needed to live. A bed for the night, meals, a limited set of clothes that she would swap out at local charity shops when her roles changed. A phone with a pre-paid grid plan, and a can-do attitude, had got her halfway around the continent.

The Aussies were strict about keeping tabs on casual workers, and Phoebe was sensible, she knew not to mess about. But then something strange had come over her, a kind of malaise. The heat had bleached out all her punctil-iousness, made her fuzzy. She'd looked at her old life as if through a window that had grown foggier and foggier until she could barely see it any more. She'd put her leave date out her mind, buried herself in getting by day-to-day, until it had been too late. Her supervisor at Food for Less had been alerted to the visa expiry and abruptly told her to pack up her things and get out.

She'd been piddling away her last pay cheque in the beer garden of a shabby outback pub, wondering if they'd jail her or just deport her with a black mark against her on the international register, when a man had approached. She'd assumed he was looking for one thing, but he'd been looking for another.

"You're perfect for it," this strange man had told her as she'd gazed, shocked at his proposal, up past the biolume light strings to the night sky. The New Australian skies were frighteningly clear, with all that space traffic and junk almost close enough to touch. "Morgaine likes her women young and ambitious." He'd grinned and she'd felt a squirm of disgust.

And that's how she'd ended up in Harro's Horde, caravanning down south to the Pans, to meet up with the imaginatively named 'Us'. All of this from an encounter in a bar by someone who offered her a way to keep going. Because she hadn't wanted to go back. And she hadn't wanted to go to jail. And, if she was honest, out of embarrassment for being so stupid.

When she'd posted about staying a bit longer, going on a retreat with a bunch of strangers in the middle of the desert, the reaction from family was more or less what she'd expected, but she'd hoped they would have been kinder. Her fathers were disappointed, her mother had demanded she get on a flight home straight away. Her sister... Selen was Selen. She'd been an annoying child and hadn't changed that much over the years. She was a grown adult but still hadn't done anything in her life except be a student and hang out with dubious characters, and since Phoebe had taken a year out of her life to go travel, Selen had acted as if she'd been abandoned instead of just realising she needed a life of her own. Then she'd posted that picture of a horrifying mod that went right through her. It was legal. Most things in Alba were, short of outright murder, but still.

Maybe Phoebe felt guilty about not being there. Maybe. But there were other concerns right now. Like being in the cabin of a tanker truck cabin high above the road and filled with a terrifying sense of momentum.

Shan had jumped at the chance to sit in Harro's car when she'd suggested the trade. It might be further from the action, but after the roadblock, Phoebe had few fucks to give about what she was supposed to want. The tanker cabin felt solid as a fortress, lofty. It was above most of the dust the cars kicked up, with a view out to emptiness that stretched on and on for days in any direction.

A starred shape of darker earth splayed out on the land. Reggie must have spotted where she was looking, because he lifted one hand from the steering wheel to point at it and laugh.

"Splatellites. Bits of space junk and old satellites that the techfucks didn't want to pay to clean up. You see them out here all the time."

'Techfucks' seemed to be a term popular with them. She couldn't blame them, really. She stared at the scar on the landscape as it slid by.

"You want to be lucky, or you might wake up with one of them punching a hole through your bivouac," he said, gleefully.

"Great," she said. "A total gift."

The splatellite passed out of view. The desert wasn't what she'd thought it would be. She'd pictured huge dunes, but here it was just sun-baked red earth littered with wind-polished stones they called gibber, some stunted bushes, and far off hazy plateaus. Every now and then they would see a dead animal mummified by the side of the road. The only living thing she'd seen were kangaroos, mostly near human settlement water sources.

"Penny for your thoughts," Reggie said. He was friendly, but he was Harro's offsider. There was nothing she could say to him that wouldn't get straight to the Horde's bossman.

"Just thinking about my sister," she said. Well, it was true. "She got one of those body tunnel mods." Reggie grunted

176

but left a space for her to fill. That's what he did. A little light family chat was good, though. Safe. "She's always been an annoying little liability. And my folks aren't hard enough on her."

"Like they were on you?" he said, and she caught a smile beneath his omnipresent sunglasses. "Got a little brother. Know exactly how you feel."

More silence.

"Why'd you decide to do all this?" she asked, trying to go for casual and to fill up that dead space. It sounded mawkishly amateur to her ears, but then, she had never done anything like this in her life.

"You mean driving a tanker truck?" Reggie looked over at her for a second. Not too long, or he'd risk a collision in all this dust. Kangaroos might be rare, but they'd still belt out of nowhere to bound in front of vehicles and catapult off the roo bars. Cars coming the other way wouldn't take a hint and pull off to the side, but try pass them on the table drain, looming out of the dust cloud with a spray of gravel that starred the windscreens. There weren't any autostop or AI safeties built into any of the Horde's vehicles, it was like getting into a time machine and going back fifty years or more. They were suspicious of anything that could be hacked. Someone could, theoretically, send a ping down from a satellite and make this tanker flip. It made strategic sense, she had to concede, to keep things old-school, even if it was like skydiving without a parachute.

"You know what I mean," she said, laughing. "Us. Her, Harro, all of it."

"Why'd you?" he countered, a challenge underlying his friendly shell. She'd have to make this good. *Don't have your story down too pat.*

"I dunno," she said. "Looking for something. You know?" She stared out the window for a moment. "Like, is this it?

We've been saying stuff for years about how things needed to change, how we should get better. Fuck utopia, just something better would do."

"And you come from Alba, right? Isn't it 'better' there?"

Phoebe fidgeted. "It's different." When people heard her accent, they tended to make assumptions. Alba. The Highlands That Were, the Islands That Are. The glittering jewels in the Britannic Archipelago, and ground zero of the second great space race. But most people never got to see that wealth. Most people were leveraged up to their eyeballs. "Every place's got its problems."

"Sounds like your sister's been looking for some of them."

"She's a good kid, really. Ha, 'kid'. She's in her thirties. Old enough to know better than to fuck around with that body mod shit. And god knows what it'll do to her." She held up her hands. "Sorry. Yeah, just been on my mind a bit."

"Well, you never know. Heard some pretty scary stories about people getting them. Maybe you're right to be worried."

Phoebe had heard them too. People who got chronically ill. People who changed personality completely, people who died. No rhyme or reason to any of it, and no way to predict what would happen. The losers that Selen hung out with had no doubt egged her on.

"I dunno why it's still legal," she muttered.

"It's alright to worry about your fam," Reggie said, softer now. "It's natural. But you got a new fam now." And he reached across and patted the centre console, a gesture that was meant to be reassuring, but it made Phoebe's stomach turn icy cold in the middle of a desert.

Selen

I woke up alone in bed with jagged shards of memory filtering in. Jayce being a dick, leaving me alone while he schmoozed at CeòlFest, us fighting, him storming off and me angry-marching home alone. I struggled out of bed and threw up into my mouth as I ran to the toilet.

It took a while and some heavy medication to get myself together, but I had stuff to do. I hoped like hell Jayce got over it by tonight. I'd apologise then. I took a long shower, dressed up primly as I could given my wardrobe, and shuffled down to the station. The train I got on was apparently host to a clown convention. I kept my head down and my ambient filtering on my dream-stream chip up. The gentle rock and hum of the train was normally comforting. This morning it was nauseating. I leaned my head on the seatback in front of me. It was sticky but I couldn't care.

What had we even been fighting about last night? I'd over-indulged, wasn't as used to the chemicals in snorts as he was. Or the strong drink. I'd been trying to keep up. And there was something else. As he came off the festival stage, I had to push my way around to the back through a bunch of rands to meet him. I'd tried to talk to him about my anxiety about today, but instead he'd left me standing at our spot in the bar tent while he 'networked' with talent scouts and festival managers and minor faces on the scene — which looked a lot like drinking, flirting, and laughing — and I couldn't work out if I was irked because he'd left me or because I wanted to be the one meeting important people, the one in demand. So, I'd drank and snorted toxic amounts just to make that question go away. In the end that hadn't even been the thing we fought about. Something stupid, like a turn of phrase taken personally. I couldn't really remember what was said, just the rage in his tone. But we'd both been out of it. It would be okay.

I dragged myself off the train at Killie just as a big ship was launching from the space port.

It was only a stager, getting folk up to the orbital park, but I had to slam my hands over my ears as the boom of its ascent rolled out over the town. It seemed so much louder than when I grew up here. Mum and Dads' house was ten minutes' walk from the station, but it was a marathon when your head was made of clay, fuzz, and needles, still ringing from the launch. The Atlantic was playing its own part, getting ready for a storm in the near future. The leaves on the avenue's lime trees swayed and tumbled ominously in the sticky breeze. I had to get back to mine before it hit because I did not want to be stuck there with my parents while it blew over. Not after this.

Their commune was a bustling one, half buried under a mound of grass. I went to press the buzzer button and a lanky older man, came out. Could never remember his name. I usually tried to avoid the other communards. "Selen," he said. He pointed at my belly and stated the obvious. "You've got a body tunnel. Does Remy know?"

"Morning," I said instead, pulling past him through the storm door. It might have still been morning. I stymied any further conversation by not letting my feet stop. "Got to go, sorry."

The interior was cool, and my headache was grateful.

I'd made sure each of the parentals were off shift at the same time before coming over. If I had to tell Mum, I was going to do it in front of all of them, for safety. The dads reined her in, helped her stay calm. I needed all the help I could get, what with the chance I might vomit on her carpet and really tear things. I swallowed a few times before opening the door into their living space.

Mum was reading something. Like, on paper. So typical. She'd always manage to find some ancient book at a market or in someone's attic. It was a disturbing passion for her, dead words on dead trees. Like some kind of necromancer hobbyist.

Daddy Arjun was making something in the kitchen, I could see his back through the pass. Mum looked up.

"Selen," she said, with a dreamy smile, just swimming up from wherever that book had taken her. Then, more distinctly and with her tone taking a nosedive as she looked at my middle, "Annelise Muir." Full names were not a good sign. She levered herself up out of the chair. "What is that?"

"Remy Mhari Muir," I greeted her back the same way, enjoying her eyes narrowing. "What does it look like?" For the longest time, she just stood and looked at me and shook her head slowly, mouth pinched up. She let out a laugh, but it wasn't a nice one. *Stay unflappable.*

"Arjun, come and see what your daughter has done."

He came out, wiping his hands on a dishcloth. "Hey, babbykiddo, what's..." He froze, fingers still splayed. Then he quickly resumed and balled up the cloth to plop it on the counter. "I'll get Rob."

I closed my eyes. "Do you have any juice? I am not feeling great."

Mum looked as if I'd just spat in her tea. "Were you intoxicated when you got this? Because if you were, I will sue the absolute waterfall who did it—"

"—No, I was sober." I shrugged. "And I wanted it." I pulled off my jacket and Mum hissed through her teeth now that the tunnel's *throughiness* was more apparent, but I ignored her, and turned to the coat hooks. I fussed a bit, hanging up my stuff, and by the time I'd finished, Daddy Rob had literally skidded into the room. He, too, froze and looked at my mod like spiders were crawling out of it.

"That's..." he began. He seemed to run out of words and glazed over with his hands over his mouth. Arjun trailed in too, completing the little tableau of staring, furrow-browed gawpers.

"Just go with it," I said, pleading. "Come on."

"I mean, it's just a lot—" said Daddy Arjun, while Dad Rob said, "—You need to understand it from our—" while Mum said, "—So, this is what you've been spending—"

I held up my hands. "Speaking stick!" I shouted at them. To be clear, we did not have a stick in any form, but they shut up, so I dived in. "Listen, this is something I have wanted for a very long time."

"Yeah? How long?" Mum said, sardonic in her tone. "Because I don't think you could have taken long enough to—"

"I'm still speaking," I thundered. Fuck, this was hurting my head and my muscles were all tensed up. I breathed deep and made calming motions with my hands. "I know the risks, and so far, it's all been fine."

"But you could get all sorts of problems from having elagite inside you, rewiring your nervous system," Arjun said. "We still don't know the consequences yet." He worked in the material sciences division of space services, so to be fair, he probably had a point. It just wasn't one I wanted to hear.

At the same time, Dad Rob was muttering something with worried eyes to Mum, which ended in 'personality shift' and it did nothing to improve my mood. I hadn't changed, I was just done with their bullshit.

"We didn't know the consequences of a lot of things," I snapped, "but we still did them. I used my own fucking money, so it has nothing to do with you." It was a lot meaner than I intended. This was going badly, and I wanted to just crawl under a blanky and not come out until my head stopped hurting. The medication I'd taken earlier felt like it was about to eject itself from my stomach. And my body tunnel's rash was choosing this moment to flare up.

"I get it," Rob said. "You want to feel important, special, but you already are." He reached out towards me.

Important. Special. "I'm leaving now," I said, giving him a withering glance. I turned back to the coat hooks.

"Fine, flounce off," Mum said. "But don't expect to come crying to us when it all goes wrong, miffren!" She yelled that at my back as I pulled on my jacket and walked down the corridor.

I'd been in Killie less than a quarter of an hour, in all. I'd have to wait ages at the station for the next train back, but when I got back to the Craig I'd go find Jayce. And then we'd make this fucking well work.

Phoebe

Walking beside Shan, Phoebe carted the bunches of twigs and branches on the homeward leg of the wide loop they'd taken up over the low escarpment. Down by the roadside camp, Apolline blew on the kindling and each breath lit up her face, then hid it in a blossom of smoke. The land out here produced very dry brush, the occasional eucalypt, and it all burned with the intensity of wood desert-dry. The scent was amazing. They needed more, and vegetation was sparse around here. Better to start before dark to avoid stepping on snakes and scorpions. The sun was a thumb-width above the horizon, and it was still baking hot, but it would vanish shockingly quick compared to the long summer twilights of Alba. Soon the fire would be welcome, as would the billy tea.

"The colours out here," Shan breathed. She was the earth-child type, with wide, soft eyes and a soppy disposition. She'd only joined the Horde a few days ago at Emerald on the trek up the interior highways before they turned south-west and the land turned from green to straw-yellow to red. Phoebe found her the least intense of the new recruits, so didn't mind her company, but it would be nice to be alone, even for five minutes. They staggered and slipped down an eroded washout, something that looked as if it could have last been wet a century ago.

"It's a bit less green than Alba," she said. "But I like it."

"Back home," Shan asked as she bent to pick up some more stray twigs, "you got a partner waiting for you?"

"No," Phoebe said. There had been a few relationships. Mikki had been the last and one of the reasons she decided to go travelling alone — a wish to get away, wash off old habits and hurts. It seemed like a lifetime ago now. Not something she wanted to get into. "You?"

"Nah, if I had, I wouldn't have come out here," she said. Her sudden peal of laughter was loud in the emptiness. Reggie, down by the roadside, turned his head up towards them as he carried a cooler bin from the vehicles to the fire.

"That's the point, I guess," Phoebe said. "Meet new people, find some adventure."

"Not for me," Shan retorted, grinning as she kicked at a small deadfall, to scare away any nasties before she broke off a branch. "I'm here to work. I want to bring an oasis to the desert. Morgaine is gonna turn New Australia green. Maybe the world."

She really believed that. Phoebe merely raised her eyebrows. Morgaine was the leader of the group at the endpoint of this convoy. As to the stated aims, she was reserving judgement until she saw it herself.

"You don't think... you don't think it's a bit of a cult or something, right?"

Shan laughed again, that uninhibited yelp. "No, no, nothing like that. It's just about doing good for the earth. No praying, or meditation." She put a hand to the middle of her back, stretching, "Mind you, if they've got us doing yoga, I wouldn't complain. Nearly there."

They carried their gathered sticks down towards the camp chairs that had been put out. Phoebe had claimed a seat she used every night, a silver and purple camouflage monstrosity that no-one else had wanted. After stacking the wood near the fire, she sank into it gratefully.

Apolline had pulled cooking duty, so she used the fire to bake some potatoes and a grill for some lentil sausages. Harro and Reggie handed out water from a jug siphoned off the tanker. It tasted faintly of dirt.

Darkness fell like a thrown switch.

"Anybody got any snorts?" Louis said lazily, and there was some awkward tittering. "Go well with stargazing tonight, eh?"

"You better get that shit out of your system before we get to the Pans," Harro drawled.

"Why?" Apolline asked, apprehensive. "Is it forbidden?"

"Nah," Harro said, and his lip curled up. "You're gonna be too fuckin' tired for it."

Night-times, this split between recruits and recruiters became more obvious. Reggie and Harro were watching the rest of them. Not that there was a huge number of people in the 'horde'. They were a few cars and a tanker. The campervan was Louis', the van where they kept all the backpacks belonged to a man apparently called Dag, though it was unclear if that was an insult or his actual name. A few assorted strays and weirdoes with not much more than the clothes on their backs. Like Shan. Not that Phoebe could judge. She'd thrown out her nice office clothes and loaded up her bag with hard-wearing work shirts and army trousers. To better fit in.

There'd be a point later on, after the regular small talk, when Harro would ask if anyone had any questions about Us, or the Pans. And Phoebe would keep her mouth shut. But until then, she could lean back in her purple and silver chair and look at the stars. She could watch for passing satellites and wonder if they were watching back.

3. Going Through Changes

Selen

Icouldn't believe I'd allowed Daddy Arjun to emotionally blackmail me into this, but he was all sad and worried in his messages, so I sat in the café, waiting on him to show up. He was like that, quiet in front of the other two, preferring to speak one-on-one. I sipped gingerly at my extra-hot, double strength Kelpy's boba and toyed with the idea of getting a scone. I couldn't blame him for choosing to do things this way. Rob usually took Mum's side, and she ran the family with an iron hand. I no longer lived with them thanks to her refusal to ever budge an inch.

Arjun seemed happy bobbing around, being kind and neutral. The parentals had refused to tell me and Feebs what our actual DNA mix was, saying it didn't matter, they were each as much a parent as the others, but I couldn't help but see my sister when I looked at him. Maybe that's why I was such a sucker for his puppydog eyes.

In my reflection in the window, all three of them chased their way across my face. I got blue eyes from Rob, my stubbornly nothing body from my Mum, cheekbones from Arjun. Phoebe was clearly not adopted, clearly the daughter of all three of my parents too, but the genetic combination made her look more like Arjun, more like she was *his*. How did I feel about that? What did it mean?

My confusion was broken by him entering the café and coming over to me, ducking his shoulder in that shy, awkward way that I loved so much. "Hey, Sel," he said and then there was the dance while he offered to buy me something even though my boba was still steaming and nearly full, then he had to go order his own, then there was sitting, rummaging through the sweetener packets and so on. Finally, he took a deep breath.

"I don't want to give you any hard time about... the thing."

"You can say it. Body tunnel. Or mod. They're not rude words."

He scrunched up half his face and looked askance for a second. "They're not, of course they're not. But yeah. I wanted to talk about it. See whether we can mend some fences. Get your Mum back down from the ceiling." He laughed. I just spun my boba cup with fingertips a while.

"What did she say?" I eventually asked, in a little voice.

That made him uncomfortable. He got a reprieve as the staffer brought over his drink, a coffee-style milk thing that no-one ever asked for any more. He faffed about, thanking them, and stirring in sweetener, tapping the drips off his spoon. Then he looked at me, all soft and earnest. I'm sure I rolled my eyes reflexively.

"I mean, she's still mad. But it comes from a place of protectiveness."

"I'm thirty-shitting-six," I snapped, folding my arms. "If I still need protection, you've done something wrong as parents."

He sighed. "Okay. Maybe protective is the wrong term. Concerned. Loving. Worried. Nothing wrong with thinking about your kid's future, no matter how old they are, right?"

"And what do you think?"

He sipped, stalling. I didn't care. I've had a lot of practice at stubbornly waiting people out. Tutors, interviewers, boyfriends. A lot of people over the years who've crumbled in the face of my sheer pigheadedness. It's a minor superpower.

"Listen. I heard about some really worrying talk from colleagues over in China." He paused for a minute and a I glanced at his face. He was wrestling with something. "I don't know how safe elagite is long-term."

"I chose pure elagite because I got reactions from other things, remember?" I said flatly. He had helped me bathe the cheek piercing infection, for god's sake. "I can't believe you, a scientist, are listening to nightmare stories about backyard botched tunnels. You know they just play that stuff up for the splashes."

"That's not what I meant. Yes, there are things that me and your mother and Rob are concerned about, I won't lie to you. About how elagite works on the nervous system. But I'm not even talking about that. You've got to look at it with a wider lens." He spread his hands. Quite the hand-talker, him. "There's a ripple effect to every great innovation, and that includes artistic ones. Everything is linked somewhere. And this stuff is important to Alba, so it's important to everyone up there in space." There it was. A lecture on cosmopolitics. My favourite.

"Shit!" My cup had chosen this moment to somehow fall off the table and shatter and splash hot liquid all up Arjun's trouser leg. He yelped in pain.

I swore and leapt to grab some napkins. "I must have knocked it. Did it burn you?" I dabbed at the mess, but it was everywhere.

"No, it's okay," he said, hissing a little through his teeth.

"I'm so sorry," I said. I felt tears come unexpectedly. I don't know if it was just for the tea.

Such a fuckup. Not the good daughter. Never like Feebs, steady, solid, achieving.

"No, it's fine, don't be silly," he said and other things people say when lying about the amount of pain they're in.

The server came over with a mop and I took the opportunity to grab my bag. "Sorry, Daddy A, I'd better go."

"No, wait," he stammered and tried to get up, but the server was blocking his way with the dour attitude of someone who'd had to clean up a lot of people's messes. I used the moment to escape.

As I hurried up the street, I swiped at my eyes with the back of my hand. Something must be wrong with them. I could have sworn the Kelpy's boba cup had fallen right through the table, in a little puff of coloured lights.

Phoebe

Even after spending so long in the convoy, Phoebe hadn't known, really, what to expect from Morgaine. She'd seen a detailed rendering of all the main players, head and shoulders, but that hadn't captured the weirdness, the presence of the woman in long, flowing linen shirt and wrap trousers who came to the circle of chairs under the tin canopy and sat down, as if she was just another one of the group. Her spindly frame was reconditioned to Earth, but still with that drawn-out, elegant look of a long-term spacer. Most of all, it was her eyes. They were dark, large, troubled. Gravity differences aside, she seemed to carry the weight of the world, and this made her sad. A trace of simmering anger. And now she greeted the new recruits to her little cult, or terrorist group, or whatever it was, and Phoebe was officially becoming one of them. One of Us.

The 'new spuds' sat on sun-perished and powdery plastic chairs. They'd each been asked to say their names and say a piece about why they were here. Phoebe copied Shan's homework on this one and said she loved green spaces and wanted to help turn back the clock to a time before the Deluge. Not that she thought it was possible, but she'd had to say something. She spent the rest of the introductions looking around as if distracted by the movement around the place.

190

There were long tables for communal eating set nearby, under the canopy of a hot tin roof supported on metal poles, open at the sides. They'd called it the Pavilion, and it was the central gathering and dining place. It smacked of the little outback pubs and sports club associations Phoebe had worked at, but at the same time, it was fundamentally different. Above their heads came the clonk of feet as the man in the crow's nest on the roof with the proton rifle moved about. Camp security, they were told. Self-defence.

And Morgaine, right in front of her.

"Maybe you're wondering, what kind of name is that? Wasn't what I was born with. I took it from a female figure from European culture," she was saying. "A great disruptor." Some kind of witch or druid thing, popular with the hippy crowd. Others in the circle were impressed, though. Shan, in particular, had a face filled with devoted rapture.

"But now I kind of regret it." The woman chuckled wryly, an unexpected sound. "I mean, look at Us." She gestured around at her gaggle of followers, some working, some listening with the bright, toothy grins of people who'd heard this before, in on the joke. Phoebe could hear the capitalisation of 'Us'. It was something special to this woman, holy maybe. Her accent had a tinge of Aussie, but she also had the staccato delivery of a spacer.

"We're not European any more. Not Aboriginal, not Asian, not African. We're of Earth. I spent a lot of time up in space just to learn that here is home. We should never have deserted it." She smirked. "Or desertified it. I have no idea what we were thinking as a people. Running so fast to get away from here, we left it in a mess."

This was dubious. First of all, the depop of earth had been a good thing for the environment, a huge pressure release. There was just no way they'd have been able to feed everybody with the world's ecology. Phoebe believed it, had never heard anything that convinced her it was sinister.

Why would a person born out in space care about a place they'd never lived? Everything she said made sense, on one level. But it was fundamentally weird as shit on another. For example, this part of New Aus had always been desert, hadn't it?

Annoyed, she let her eyes wander again at the Us members who bustled about, stacking water containers or cleaning cutlery. A big man with short curly hair and intense denim-blue eyes stood by the circle of chairs, hulking arms crossed. Milo Broughton, Morgaine's second-in-command. He affected detached, casual, but he was studying each of the new spuds intensely, including her.

When they'd got here this afternoon, the whole camp had come out to greet the newcomers. And to help get the water from the tankers, store supplies the convoy had brought, all under the gaze of a rooftop gunman in a sniper's nest with a little shade cloth right in the centre of everything. It took up a lot of space in a person's mind. Gave things a certain extra gravity.

"You might wonder what we're doing out here, and that's a fair question," Morgaine went on. "Out here on the Pans, worthless country, soil sowed with salt. The shittiest part of the entire continent. Well, one of the reasons is the land was cheap." She smiled, self-deprecating again.

Watch for moments where she disarms people, the handlers had told Phoebe. Watch for when she seems vulnerable. That's when you've got to be most wary. That's what these people do.

"But it's also a symbol. A long time ago, this place was a paradise. Then we came. We humans. And we *raped* it." Goosebumps rose on Phoebe's skin in spite of the heat at the sudden vehemence. "Governments won't unfuck this land, they won't spend precious money on rehabbing it, when they could spend it on missiles, asteroid mining stations. All those little toys."

She unfolded her long, lean body and stood up. "I'm not going to lie to you. It's a hard life. And when we succeed in getting somewhere, people are going to be jealous. Look to take what we've made here for themselves and fuck it up all over again." She looked each new spud in the eye and as she came to her, Phoebe's buttocks clenched involuntarily. "Because that's what humans do. But if you're here, I want you to give yourselves to this life. To Us.

"We're going to regreen this world, starting here. It's not going to be without its hardships. Each of Us has made sacrifices. You can walk away; I won't keep any of you against your will. But right now, you have to make a choice. A commitment. Okay?"

And she left the circle, nodding to Harro.

He stepped in, something hessian in hand. "Your mobiles, please and thank you very much." He went to Phoebe first, holding the seed sack open. She pulled her phone out of her pocket.

They'll isolate you. Cut you off from the outside world. Be prepared. That's what they'd told her. Still, she hesitated for a second. Her lifeline to her family in Alba, splash feeds, all her friends, almost all help.

She stretched out her hand and put her phone in. Harro grinned at her. There wasn't a glimmer of malice, but he was enjoying himself, that was for sure. After he'd been round with the sack, another Us member passed him a small hand-held device with a little old school LCD screen. "Now, you all told me you had no implants when you joined the convoy. We're going to make sure you weren't telling me a lie."

Apolline's eyes went wide. She started fidgeting. Phoebe tried to ignore it as the scanner hovered over her own skin.

193

She'd been warned about this. She'd never been keen on implants and other ways of fiddling with yourself, much to her sister's scorn. She didn't even have a biotrinket – she'd just go to the doctormat if she wasn't sure about her health. But Apolline was sweating by the time Harro came to her. He waved the device up and down, and it beeped manically.

"It's medical," she said and looked like she'd melt through her seat. "I have a weak heart."

"Be that as it may, you're a liar, and we don't like liars." He jerked his head and some of the watching Us members took her upper arms and jerked her to her feet.

"What are you going to do with her?" The words were out of Phoebe's lips with a humiliating squeak before she could stop them.

"I'll take her home with me tomorrow. I'm going out on convoy again in the morning. Don't you worry, no harm will come to her." He looked at the other Us members and laughed. Apolline was herded away, her eyes appealing for help, not quite believing it was happening. And, to her shame, Phoebe melted back into her seat. The odds of Harro's words being true swung drastically in her head, but she couldn't jeopardize things before she'd even started.

Selen

I positioned the video of Ogawa on one side of the splash collage piece. It was about me, my journey, so there were renderings of my face I'd run through a few sketch filters to make them look arty. I'd decided the piece should have the scent of hibiscus and incense, high-end aromatics. I put a little bit of Jayce's cologne in too because I liked the smell. Why not? He was a part of me. The Ogawa clip was context for the curation. He was a 2-d artist, and nobody really cared about that anymore, not since everyone got splash feeds, dream-stream chips. If you couldn't walk about in a piece, what was the point? But the retro nature of the digital footage I'd scraped out of archives was pretty cool.

He was in a small house, somewhere in the Japanese Archipelago, I guessed from the tatami and decor. It was filled with paint tubes and brushes, fabric folded in haphazard piles, books, datapads, food containers with contents in varying states of decay, and in the centre sat Ogawa on the mats, a small man with long dark hair that Dad Rob would say was in need of a good brush.

"How do you make your life as an artist when no-one values art except as a commodity?" Ogawa asked. Quite right. Ever since the space race had taken off, science was the number one priority for education. I knew that all too well. "But art isn't an object for sale, it's not a formula or algorithm; art is humans. Art doesn't exist without an artist. You know? The smile I give to you doesn't exist without my face. Lately we've been... I don't mean to be impolite, but we've been disrespecting those who bring us art, those who comfort us in this time of difficult living."

I've only realised how true those words are since I decided I would become a splash artist. Who cared what the fam would think? Mum would say, "All those qualifications! You could get a job at the space port right next to us!" No, thank you very much. I'd seen what amazing lives it had brought them — humdrum, soulless grind, working to someone else's timetable. Not really a way to get to the truth. Not really a way to be somebody. Once I'd built up a portfolio, I could put on a launch party, maybe put some feelers out to local artists to see if they'd come. Ideas about virtual gallery gatherings, shibboleths with art. Jayce could provide the music, give it all an extra edge.

"Why?" Phoebe would have asked if she were around. "What's wrong with a normal job? Why are you always seeking attention?" She never understood.

I prodded at the dataslate to create a tunnel in the centre field of view. I didn't want it to look to literally like my body mod, so I made it more like a space warp or a wormhole. I teased its edges out into radial arms. Where would I put the far end? I wanted people to enter it and go somewhere. But where did I want it to go? That was the question.

Another world? Another place? Perhaps they could enter it and come out in an auditorium of rapturous applause? Something about the nature of our need for adulation? No, too pretentious. I focused back on the Ogawa clip. Perhaps he could inspire me.

"You have to make the art a part of yourself. Not something that is able to be separated from your name, your being. And so that is why I decided to make such an extreme modification."

He stood and bent down to raise his pantleg, revealing his body tunnel. It was rough, and tiny in comparison with mine, but then it was *the* prototype. It went through his calf muscle. A smile flashed over his face as he straightened up. I wished they'd had walkaround technology because I'd have loved to tilt the view back up from the tunnel to see his face. He was humble but you could tell it brought him joy. He didn't know the early version of elagite was already eating the nerves around his heart. They've fixed that now, even if effects are still unpredictable. And you could get scans. I stopped myself thinking about it and watched him create.

They showed him flicking a paint-loaded brush at a canvas. It was old-school, and you could tell it wasn't a real work, but he was into it anyway. Streaks and splatters of paint, thrown with joy, abandon. "The body tunnel produces an effect within me," he said, eyes still on his work, hand still moving. "My art is different because of it."

Make art a part of yourself. The tunnel was part of me. If I connected the end of it to itself, they could go in and keep going around and around it in an infinite loop. Say something about the nature of introspection as a never-ending process, maybe? Show my body mod as part of my journey to self-actualisation, or some shit. Would people get it?

I kept waiting for my mod to kick in, to contribute in some way, to make a difference to what I was doing. I felt nothing, but I did remember another feeling I'd had recently.

Jayce had looked at me funny, his hands paused in the air in the middle of a mixing session, when I'd got back from Killie, from showing my parents. The glow of the controls lit up his face and gave it a green cast like I was seeing him at the bottom of a column of murky water. And he'd had that expression all through me telling him about my dust up with the parentals, about how I'd had enough of their bullshit, how I was going to make it work with him or die trying.

And he'd said, "Yeah, sure." And given me a half-smile, a half-chuckle, and half a hug. And then he'd carried on mixing.

I looked at the tunnel again. Something bothered me about the radiating tweaks I'd made. Then I realised what the black, sucking, puckered hole looked like, and I erased it angrily.

4. Salt

Phoebe

Sweat had nearly stuck her to the plastic chair, but they handed out water frequently. The induction had gone on for some time about camp safety, how they should be alert for people 'causing trouble', though that was nebulous at best. What trouble? Who would cause it? People from outside or inside the camp? People like Apolline? What had she been up to anyway? Was she telling the truth about her implant being for heart problems? Had Phoebe's handlers sent more than one person in with her? Or was she acting on behalf of someone else?

Harro could have easily scanned everyone as they joined the convoy, saved a lot of time and resources by weeding out the unacceptable, but they'd waited until everyone was here. And made a much bigger impact in the process. How many of Phoebe's predecessors had tried that idea — an implant in your skull transmitting everything up to a satellite, walking around as a living breathing bug? Her handler had been very careful not to mention what had happened to those who'd gone in before.

Another member of Us, a peppy individual called Ceecee, had taken them through the rest of the details after all that unpleasantness. Apolline had been herded out of sight and though she'd started arguing as she'd left, saying words like, 'can't do this', and, 'embassy', at one point her protests had cut off abruptly. Hopefully, it was because she'd been shut in somewhere with good sound insulation. It was a smaller hope than Phoebe liked.

The induction droned on, and if a woman hadn't just been dragged away, it would have seemed ordinary.

Logistical. There were protocols for water use, food, recy-cling, toilets, every aspect of life.

Ceecee split them up into teams, Phoebe was with the grow team, whatever that entailed. And finally, they were to be taken to get their bags from the convoy and be assigned to a bivouac.

Ceecee lead them off. Phoebe trailed along, with Louis and Shan, and other new recruits. Or acolytes. Whatever. She couldn't see any signs of Apolline, no evidence of a struggle or blood soaking into the dust. Whether that was good or bad was uncertain. She had to stop thinking about it, or she'd be unable to function, let alone carry out her mission.

Shan walked beside her, looking around at everything while they crossed the hot dust, gawping. It was getting later. And desert sunset was fast. Phoebe wanted to get to their digs before it got dark and resisted the urge to grab Shan by her scruff. She should be acting wide-eyed too, like she hadn't seen any images of this place at all. She should take everything in, see if she could figure out the sightlines for that gunman on the roof, for one.

They passed sheds of varying sizes, huge water tanks on stands with grass growing in their pools of shade, domed tents pimpling the ground, and shade cloth arrayed in a patchwork of drab taupes and sun-bleached grey-blues. On the fringe of camp, a solitary hard-battled eucalyptus stood. Behind it stretched rows of younger, bushy trees, presum-ably the whole point of Us' regreening efforts. A large white yurt stood apart from everything else. Morgaine must sleep there. The whole place smacked of an Outback music festi-val, one where the facilities had been rigged up but none of the bands or fans had arrived yet.

Phoebe subtly searched the faces of the people she passed for signs of zealotry or abuse but found neither. It should have been a relief, but it made her position in this little microcosm even less certain. And then there was the giant, three-walled metal cave they called the grow shed, her place of work while she was here. It was an intimidating sight from this close.

They arrived at the row of bivouacs, ugly khaki canvas tents.

"You're splitting up," Ceecee told them. "One in each bivvy." This divided them into their teams but was an obvious security tactic as well.

The way Phoebe's brain was working now. Appalling.

"Aww, well, we'll still see each other," Shan said, squeezing her arm. "Probably catch you at tucker time, since I'm doing catering yeah?" And she walked off. Phoebe hesitated in front of the tent.

"New spud!" A man called from inside the bivouac, an Aussie accent. She went into the gloom. Inside was a reek of sweat and dirty socks. The speaker sat on the bottom bunk but rose to front up to her with an arrogant nonchalance. She unshouldered her backpack and swung it around in front, where he grabbed it. "Got a spot for you," he said, and made a face that wasn't quite a smile. He plonked her backpack where he'd been sitting. This all felt like some kind of test, or setup.

"Ah, thanks...?"

"Jerome," he told her, hard-eyed and with a nasty grin. "Don't thank me yet."

Dear god, what was she getting into? The convoy with Harro's weirdness and sleeping in vehicles or little tents on the side of the road was one thing but she could move around with that arrangement, get to know a few people. Shan was sweet, Louis was chilled, Harro and Reggie had been edgy but looked out for them on the road. This guy had a definite vibe to him.

Sleeping with one eye open was always on the cards, but things just kept getting worse.

"Hello, hello, welcome." Another voice. Someone else had come in, sweeping the bivvy door flap open. "I'm Sweetie." Phoebe had never been so glad to meet a person covered in sweat and dirt. "We all work in the grow team in here. I'm a her, he's a him." She grinned at Jerome, whose brow creased up in annoyance. "Alexis who sleeps here too is fluid, doesn't mind. And you?"

"Phoebe. Her."

"Nice to meet you. Good to have you in here, we always need more women. With all these smelly boys." She laughed and Phoebe felt herself relax a little. Jerome exited the tent without saying more and Sweetie carefully watched him leave, then turned up the smile again.

"Now, let's get you settled. You know you have to bang your shoes out before you put them on in case of creepy crawlies, right?"

Selen

Jayce and I lay in the sheets; for a time we were one person with eight limbs and two bodies and two heads. Until he rolled over and said, "Sorry babe, not comfortable." After sex, he just wanted to sleep, no talking or cuddling. He'd get tetchy if I tried. I stared at his back for a while, basking in the afterglow of feeling of him inside me, the gasp of his breath on my neck, the resonances from his mod making me feel good, the way he could make a whole crowded room feel, but just for me. My own mod was uncomfortable during sex, but it wasn't worse, really, than any else I'd had.

I'd tried so many ways to find my own art, but that hadn't happened. I'd even asked Jayce to teach me music stuff, but he hadn't been keen. Too busy, he said. Whatever I tried, though, the mod hadn't kicked in at all. It still looked the business, but it might as well have been a fake. I had to admit, it had crossed my mind a couple of times to go beat the hell out of that mod technician. He'd clearly messed it up and I was left with an elagite turkey. And so, this bed, these moments, were probably the best I was going to get in life.

I could never be special, but I could be *with* someone special. It wasn't what I wanted, but what other choice did I have?

My hand drifted up onto his shoulder and he didn't flinch it off. His skin was warm, soft bronze. The angles of his shoulder blades were like architecture. Of a home. My home. I could keep the memory of it through the day when he was gone. His arm lay on his side above the sheets, a little port-hole picture of the bedroom wall showing through his mod. I wished I could see into him instead. I wished he could see into me.

I lay awake for ages like that, with this small connection between us. How could I make progress? Nothing I did seemed to get us to the place I wanted to be: sharing our art, sharing our dreams. It wasn't always easy to get his attention. He was an artist, hard to please, so when he finally realised I was one too, really *see* me, it'd be special. I wanted him to be proud of me. One day, maybe, in awe of me. It was my fault, I didn't try hard enough.

A ray of morning sun fell from the high storm window onto the bed, crept up his body until it hit my hand. Pretty little bokeh lights streamed up. I smiled at them; they looked just right. Air whooshed abruptly and something spasmed under Jayce. He lurched sideways and fell from the bed. There was an ugly smacking sound. I lay frozen, my hand still poised where it had been.

202

He pulled himself up from the floor, blood pouring down his face and I sat bolt upright.

"Oh my god, I'm so sorry!" I said at the same time as he screamed, "What the fuck was that? What did you do to me?"

"It wasn't me!"

"Don't lie! Did you hit me?"

"I... I think it's my mod," I said, and clapped my hand over it. It vibrated and there was a high-pitched groan underneath my palm. "I didn't mean it to do that."

It hadn't showed any other signs of producing effects on this scale, just those colourful lights, the odd feelings and the weird noises, just on the edge of hearing. Oh god, trust me to have the weird shit that injured people.

He put a hand over his forehead, but blood was trickling between his fingers, dripping onto the floor. I scrambled out of bed to and grabbed my dressing gown, the unflattering, scuzzy grey one but there was no time to be pretty. I ran to the shared area, ignoring Flick and Senna's stares from the kitchen table as I grabbed the first aid box. "Can't talk," I pre-empted and fled back upstairs.

Jayce had wiped his face on the edge of my sheets, I saw, but that didn't matter. He'd hit his head on the corner of my bedside unit. An angry swelling already darkened over his eyebrow. He was pulling on his clothes.

"Sit, here, sit," I said while I opened packets of sterile wipes and sticking plasters. I apologised to him, over and over again while he brooded, and I patched him up.

"Shut the fuck up and hurry up."

I felt like the one who'd been thrown to the floor. "I didn't mean it. I think you should go see a doctormat," I said. "I'll pay for it, obviously."

"Don't bother," he said, and finished getting dressed, picked up his bag with his mixer from the corner of the room where it had been discarded last night. He rolled his shoulders, and looked at me, eyes now flat, and said, "It's not that bad."

And with those words, everything ended. He walked out of the room, leaving me in my horrible dressing gown. I collected up all the pieces of the first aid kit, scrunched up the wrappers, compiled everything neatly back together, and clicked the lid shut. Then I hurled it on the bed.

Colourful lights flared again, and the box hit the floor.

I knelt and lifted the dangled edge of the blood-smeared sheet, gazing into the dust bunny haunted space beneath the bed. The kit lay there as if it had always been able to fall through bedding, a mattress, and bamboo slats to land on the floor. I opened the dressing gown to look down at the mod, which was similarly innocent.

"What the fuck?"

Phoebe

Her head swam with the heat. It was lucky the work was so mindlessly mechanical – strip down pods from the salt wattle to collect the seeds, test soil pH, plant up in small degradable sacks made of coconut fibre, redistribute trays of seedlings around the various long benches. The seedlings, when they were ready, would go out to the hardening-off area for a period, then be planted into the long rows that radiated out from the encampment. They were battered by the wind and wizened, but hardy. Some of the oldest plants were only as tall as a person, but they were never meant to be much bigger, apparently. Like the lost icebergs, most of their mass would be underneath, roots that penetrated deep into the concrete-hard surface of the Pans.

The best moment in the grow shed was when the watering system came on to ooze drips of greywater like milky tears onto the tiny leaflings and made the air fractionally cooler, humid for a moment, but right now, Phoebe was about to collapse or vomit. She leaned on her arms on the grow bench, head down.

"All right, take five. Here." Mandy, the grow team supervisor, pushed a cold gel pack into her hand. "Go sit in that corner, you'll be right in a minute." She pointed to a dark spot, blessedly far from the sun.

"Why on earth would you make a roof metal out here anyway?" Phoebe grumbled as she pressed the cool pack to her face and wrists. "It's insane."

"Only thing that'll stand up to the conditions," Mandy called out as she bustled on with other tasks. "They tried laminated bamboo in the Outback a long time ago." She threw over a wolfish grin. "Kept spontaneously combusting. Ceramics would crack overnight... These are quick to put up, cheap, and don't tend to melt. Or go on fire. Look, I don't know why on earth you'd want to come here from Alba. Heard you get heaps of rain, and it's lovely and cool."

"Funny thing is," Phoebe said as she sat down on the concrete slab floor, "they'd say the same but opposite."

She'd been woken up in the bivouac on that first morning by Sweetie. The quiet, shy Alexis had shepherded Phoebe over here to work under Mandy, a young woman from the Queensland and Pacific Republic who'd been snaffled by Us straight out of university. She led the grow shed and planting-out teams, dividing her time between the nursery and the long, radiating lines of young trees that surrounded the camp. Her degree dissertation had been on tweaking the salt wattle to not only tolerate salt but uptake and sequester it from the soil. In the early part of its lifecycle, the plants had to be kept from direct sun and the harsh saltpan winds.

Hence, the current setup, and the team leader who looked like she should be taking part in an intra-mural sports competition. But someone younger in charge was alright; Phoebe had so little training, she needed every edge she could get.

The crew in here was small, to cover such a large floorspace. Sweetie, from South Africa, Alexis from somewhere in central Europe, and Jerome, who looked like he could fit in well with the Fasica she'd seen on the roadblocks.

Of course he'd be here too, she thought bitterly. The one proper weirdo who kept looking at her would naturally be on her team. Fortunately, most of his job involved him shuttling seedlings to the hardening-off area, bringing collected pods back in, so he wasn't in the shed for long. Still, he was around more than she was comfortable with.

They were allowed tea breaks, called smoko, a name from some obscure old Aus tradition. It seemed weird to drink hot drinks in the middle of the desert, but that's what they did. And it involved sitting down in folding canvas chairs for a minute, which wasn't to be sniffed at. It was an opportunity to talk to the grow team, so she asked questions. Slowly, naturally, like she'd been trained to do. *Never seem too curious but do ask normal questions that anyone would.*

"How did you all end up here with Us?" A reasonable first day question.

"How'd you?" Jerome fired back. She decided to take the question at face value.

"I was backpacking, looking for something to do with my life. Met Reggie in a bar, and he told me about Harro, about the Horde, about Us, and..." she spread her hands, "The rest is history."

Alexis and Sweetie had nodded. A familiar story to them, at least.

She'd looked at Jerome, but he'd just pouted, so Phoebe ignored him.

Alexis and Sweetie had been wandering, separately, lost little lambs, around New Australia before they were picked up, brought here. "But the police were looking for me," Alexis added. "I attended one too many protests for their taste."

Interesting. Us liked people who had issues with authority?

"What we're doing here," Mandy went on while Phoebe mulled this point, "it's not just for our own entertainment. If we can show the world how to fix centuries of environmental abuse, it'll bring others on board. And we'll build some sort of momentum." A party line to be trotted out and not looked at too closely.

Little questions like this over the next few days, normal conversation, some about sport, shows, the shittier parts of life outside Us, and she had a better picture of her immediate team. They didn't seem like cultists. Or terrorists even, despite Jerome's demeanour. She wasn't sure exactly what they reminded her of until it struck her: they were like the young people who went overseas for a year to help build a well or a school. They spoke about Morgaine with reverent awe, if at all.

And here Phoebe was, sitting on concrete trying to avoid heatstroke. With a bunch of gap year students and some possible terrorists, playing games.

Mandy came back over to her. "Feed time," she said cheerfully and put out her hand to help Phoebe up. "Better leave that here." She grinned at the cool pack. "Don't want them to think you're some softie foreigner, eh?" Phoebe put it reluctantly down on a planting bench and followed her out. Mandy waved off to the left. "Go get Sweetie, will ya? Then yous can head to the Pavilion for lunch."

Phoebe shambled off as quickly as she could towards the hardening-off area, a parasol of cloth covering rows of bigger seedlings. As she trotted along, glad of what little shade her unflattering hat provided, she felt every jolt of the iron-hard ground jar all the way up her calves. She'd always thought of herself as fit, but conditions out here pushed a body a long way past what was reasonable.

"Food," she called out, and Sweetie straightened up and nodded.

Phoebe waited for her to shuck her work gloves and saunter over. They walked in silence. Jerome trailed them and she tried to speed up without looking like it. If Sweetie noticed, she said nothing.

Under the shade of the Pavilion, they joined the back of a line for the catering tables. More people tagged on the back of the queue, and she was glad of a buffer between her and Jerome. She looked around at sweat-soaked shirts, brick-red skin on the white members of the planting-out team, to see if she could spot Louis. They had a much harder time of it on his team, often without any shade for hours at a time. No sign. There were more of them, and they took shorter shifts, so he might have already been and gone.

Phoebe was glad they'd clocked her as too much of a wuss for that kind of labour. They'd obviously thought similar of Shan when they put her behind the trays of beans, spooning out people's lunch.

They shuffled along until they reached the catering tables to pick up plates and cutlery. She tried her luck with Sweetie, since she was here. "How do we afford food and water anyway? Morgaine never asked me for any money."

Sweetie snorted. "Donations from rich people I expect," she said. "They never talk about money. It's not really the main thing here."

Would be if you were a proper cult, Phoebe thought to herself. In fact, from the small amounts she had gleaned, nobody here had sold their belongings to give everything to Morgaine. It was a strange setup. No-one had forced her into a bizarre initiation ritual. Yes, they'd taken away her phone, but she was told she could have it back if she wanted to leave. They might even let her use it to contact her family if she was good, jumped through their hoops a while. There wasn't any prayer, fasting, affirmations of dying for the cause.

So why all the secrecy? Why the bloody gunman on the roof if all was as innocent as it seemed?

She held out her plate for the mix of beans and lentils on offer and Shan gave her a quick grin but was onto the next, so Phoebe took her food and left, awkwardly. Sweetie had headed across to find a seat at the other end of the Pavilion, but Phoebe spotted Morgaine, on a table that had a free seat. She was holding forth, and there was laughter that seemed much louder than necessary. Phoebe drifted over and tried to sit down as if it was an everyday occurrence, but glances flicked at her like a peasant had just sat down with royalty. Morgaine didn't seem to notice, but there was a definite feeling of hostility from her flunkies.

Just like a family, really, Reggie?

"Jump up." A voice came from over her shoulder and there was Milo, the second in command. His rugby player frame loomed over her. The tone had been light, but there was a 'take no shit' expression on his face.

"Oh, I thought anyone could sit anywhere."

"They can," he said leaning in. "And you can sit over there," he rumbled in her ear, jerking his head meaningfully.

She collected her plate, humiliated, and found Sweetie. "I could have told you that was a lost cause," she said between shovelling food into her mouth. "Why you trying to suck up, anyway?" She grinned to show she wasn't serious, but it still stung as Phoebe sank into the seat opposite.

"I just..." Her face was burning. "I just wanted to know more about her." She pushed some beans around with her fork. "Come all the way out here, don't I get to do that?"

Sweetie was already scraping the last remnants of her meal together on the plate. "Work hard, be good. She'll notice you eventually." She must have inhaled her food because she was already getting up to go. "I'm going for a siesta. It's not a bad idea, you know. Chin up, you'll survive." She reached across and patted her arm in a conciliatory way before going.

Phoebe stared at the people at the Pavilion, faces from everywhere, all seeming to know their place. It was like school again, going back to being a nerdy little kid. She was supposed to be back in Alba by now, starting back at her job. Not breaking her back and getting bitten by insects and burned by the sun for some crazy people who seemed to enjoy living in a desert. She sighed and tried to work up an appetite. If she didn't eat, she'd probably regret it.

Jerome appeared at the table and sat down. She ignored him and started forking the gritty mixture into her mouth. "Tastes better with salt," he said. She grunted but kept her eyes down. "You got to eat salt out here or you'll get cramps."

She would have slapped anyone else who reached across to season her food for her. Instead, she just waited until he put down the cellar.

"Okay, you did that," she murmured. She stifled her urge to throw her plate in his face. She just couldn't afford to blow things up. Not until she had found out what she needed to and arranged an exit. Until then, she'd have to eat the salty food. She stared at him defiantly as she lifted her fork again.

5. The Dirt

Selen

I'd made a fleecy igloo about myself on the bed from a duvet and a shell of pillows and throw cushions, just enough of my head sticking out for air.

"You appear to be having a trauma response," my bio-trinket told me. "Consult the nearest doctormat." But I ignored the incessant alerts and eventually turned them off. It wasn't an injury. Not of that sort. I pulled a pillow over my knees and pressed my face into it.

My mod had finally done something. It had blasted a human body a distance of maybe half a metre. How it had done this, I don't know—air pressure? A static charge? I wasn't sure. But the salient point was that the body had been that of my boyfriend. (Or squeeze, we'd never made it official-official.) There hadn't been any burn marks on his skin or the bedding, so it couldn't have been something hot like plasma. My hand was normal-looking, everything about me was the same.

I hadn't wanted it. He should understand about body tunnels. They were unpredictable. That was the point. Jayce's tunnel brought people together. What did mine say about me? I didn't want to go there. I just wanted him to cool down. Come back. We could talk, if he wasn't ghosting my messages and splashes. I made an even bigger fool of myself trying to make a vague, detail-free confession on my public feed. I got 'confused' and 'concerned' motes from Mum and Dads, but I couldn't explain it without sounding like a case, so I deleted it.

I still had no idea what was going on, even after I'd read as much as I could about mods and dream-streamed a few hundred hours of theory. There was nothing I came across that mentioned any mod ever having an effect on the physical world. I mean of course not, or the bastards would have made weapons out of it by now. Even external mood alterations like Jayce's were seen as fringe theory and 'more like group hysteria'. What my mod had done was so far beyond any of it. What the hell was going on?

He had been there, sleeping, I'd put my hand on his shoulder, then the sunlight hit that spot, and he was on the floor, connecting with my nightstand on the way. I hadn't been thinking anything, certainly hadn't commanded my mod to hurl my boyfriend out of my bed. That wasn't even including the way the first aid box seemed to go through the mattress. I must have hallucinated that part somehow. I must have. Just like the boba cup at the café that had splashed on Arjun. There must be a reasonable explanation for all of it.

I scraped my thumbs over my aching brow. God, what if it was just broken? What if I was?

I'd tried to replicate the scene with a big pillow, see if I could push it off the bed. I'd even waited until there was a sunbeam, and... nothing. So there was only one thing to do, and that was build a blanket igloo and ride the waves of self-loathing that threatened to drown me.

"You useless piece of shit," I said, louder than I should have. I stuffed my face into the pillow once more.

There was a soft knock on the door, and I uncovered my eyes to reveal Flick and Senna. They stood on the threshold of my room, expressions filled with concern, but they weren't fooling me. I knew how they really felt, about how much human effluent I was to them. "Are you okay, Sel?"

I didn't answer, just looked at the dark, wet smudges on my pillowcase. I'd made a snot angel. I started laughing, though it might have sounded more like a whimper. It was the most artistic thing I'd ever done. Flick stole forward and sat gingerly on the edge of the bed, as if she might startle me away. Senna remained in the doorway, doubtful.

"Breakups are hard, right?" Flick said as she patted my leg through the bedcovers like I was a pony.

I flopped back. The bedding igloo meant I didn't go back quite as far as I'd intended, and I bounced gently. "I'm fine, just... Look, something is going on with me right now, and I just need some space to work through it," I said. Probably not as coherently as that, but Flick's face as she turned to look back at Senna said a lot.

"Maybe we can get you something to eat? To drink?" Senna supplied.

Flick grimaced. "You might not feel like it, but you should eat, get something in your stomach." She reached for my wrist. "You might feel better after?"

I flinched away and rolled over. "I told you, just need space." I slowly pulled the pillow up over my head again. They got the hint and left.

It was so typical. I got a mod to make something beautiful, some gorgeous art. Instead, it had ended up hurting my boyfriend and now I couldn't even make it happen again by trying.

I groaned again into the safety of Pillow, my only friend now.

#

Phoebe

"Feebs."

So clear. Selen, saying her name, trying to wake her. Phoebe opened her eyes. The bivouac was empty of a sister-shape. Or anyone standing in the dark. Everyone still asleep, though dawn light couldn't be far off. She didn't have a phone or implant to check the time, but the snoring of bunk-occupants was a good enough indicator. There. It had been a dream. Shit, it had sounded so real. There was a space where her sister's silhouette should be, Selen clutching one hand to her elbow, toes pointed inward. A note of urgency, anguish, tickling the edges of her face. But that memory of her sister was wrong. That there was that *thing* in her, and a dark feeling came down and rinsed the anxiety out.

She slithered quietly out of her bedding and pulled on her trousers before Jerome could wake up and leer at her bare legs. Exiting the bivouac, she headed for the latrine area. It was early enough to be chilly. The sun was still under the horizon for the moment. Watching the sun come up over the desert was a mixed blessing. It wouldn't be cool for long. Dawn colours were more subdued than at sunset, silver-blue for the most part, but it was quiet, and she was alone for once.

She could turn her face up to the sky and mouth words to the eyes in the sky, except there wasn't anything astounding to report. Weird people planting salt wattle. Hardly world-breaking stuff. And the camp was rousing now, little beeps of alarms coming from the supervisors' portacabin where Mandy got to sleep. What she wouldn't give for a bed with four walls around it and no-one else in her space.

Shan wandered up next to her, toiletries bag in hand. She looked out at the sun-lined horizon where Phoebe still stared. "It's really a spiritual place, isn't it?" she said with a sleepy drawl.

Phoebe grinned. "We're still sure it's not a cult, right?"

Shan gave her a playful bump, shoulder to shoulder as an answer. "See you at the barbecue tonight, yeah?"

"Shit, is it the weekend already?" That had snuck up on her. Not that such things were respected here. You got a day off in a rotating shift. But the barbecue could be a good opportunity to actually speak to some folk.

She walked on. The sun was rising now, blinding already. She passed the large, enclosed shed that squatted near the grow shed and thrummed with the sound of machinery.

She'd asked about it one smoko, nodding across the dust to its corrugated iron sides. Not one window on it, unlike most in this open-air camp, and a code lock panel beside the only visible door. Not asking about it would have been odd. Not curious enough.

"Supervisors and above," Mandy had told her, her expression brooking no further questions. Phoebe had grunted like she didn't really care one way or another, didn't look at it again.

Now she wanted to trail her fingers along its metal carcase, leave trails in the morning condensation. She wanted to feel the vibration, read its insides. Machinery of some kind? But she didn't dare, kept her eyes on the short line forming in front of the latrine area.

What were they keeping in there? What could this hardscrabble lot have that was possibly worth stealing? Drug production? Explosives? She'd have to wangle access somehow. At least now she had a purpose, a direction. She'd have to become a supervisor. Or maybe suck up to one of them until they entrusted her with the knowledge of what was in the mystery shed.

Perhaps it was where they kept Apolline's body, reused and recycled, like everything else around here, like the latrines and their moisture reclaim systems, the greywater filtration... could it be used on a person? On Phoebe when they found out she wasn't who she claimed to be?

Too morbid.

Harro's Horde was going off again soon, to find new recruits, haul some more water to make up the inevitable loss in a place where sweat evaporated almost instantly, no matter the recapture systems in place. Word was that he was looking for big machinery to turn over the earth, though they couldn't hope for crops so it must be something else. Maybe she would try to join him on one of his jaunts, see if she could make contact. She had no doubt they were watching from high above, spying from the edge of space, but she could ask if Selen was okay, if she hadn't killed herself by idiocy yet.

Selen

My eyelids drooped and I slapped myself on the cheeks. I'd nearly dropped off. And I had no idea what that meant any more. Flick had finally enticed me down to the commune's shared area with food. She'd practically laid out a breadcrumb trail for me. I'd dodged their attempts at coaxing me into talking, I'd just tried to eat and drink. But I kept putting a cup or bowl down on the table only for it to fall through the surface and shatter on the floor until Senna shouted at me to stop smashing things and I'd fled up to my bedroom. Had they not seen the things go through the table-top? Seen the glitter of lights that puffed up each time? Had they just refused to believe their eyes? It wasn't me!

Now I was terrified of falling asleep. Things happened. They only happened when I wasn't concentrating. First

Daddy Arjun, Jayce, now this. As soon as I stopped thinking. As soon as I stopped trying. Ergo, I had to keep concentrating. No more blanket igloo. I sat on the floor, let the cool parquet keep me from drowsing.

I had to fix it, had to fix this mess somehow. I couldn't get to Jayce directly. I needed to speak to Diddy. It was early afternoon. Jayce would have gone home, resting up for the next shibboleth. I wrapped my hand in a towel and stuck it out the window, and nothing seemed to get blasted, so I got dressed in long sleeves, trousers, and a sun hat and hoped it would be enough.

"Going out?" Senna said as I went by. Her splash feed lit up the wall in front of her. She wasn't at work today, which was shitty timing. "Couldn't take out the bins for a change, could you?"

She knew I was having a bad time. This was insensitive at best. "I'd appreciate you dropping the tone," I said. She didn't reply to that, and I didn't look at her as I left, but I did get the bin from the commune's close and hauled it over to the digester. The odours that came out of the thing as it ate the garbage hit like smelling salts. I should have thanked her.

Diddy would be at his day job. It was something I wasn't supposed to know about, but Jayce had giggled about it behind his back, about how he was embarrassed by it. I didn't see anything wrong with being a patty pusher. Not really. Not everyone could be an artist. Maybe I would end up working there, serving protein patties in buns alongside Diddy.

I knew the foodstop well enough from when we were kids, before we'd found the FenderBender. It was nestled down in the town centre's arcade, serving workers and students. Diddy stood behind the counter, wearing a neatly pressed, steel-grey cook's apron.

He groaned as I came up to him. "You're fucking kidding me on."

"No, listen, you've got to tell Jayce what happened." I pleaded with him with my eyes.

"Gonna buy something? I'm only supposed to talk to customers." He was surly but he hadn't told me to get out. I brought out my bursary chip and put it on the counter, concentrating, praying it would stay there.

"Just get me whatever's cheapest," I said. He grunted and fumbled around underneath, getting me a paper cup of something. It was my chance to explain. "Look. My mod's been acting crazy, and I don't know what it's doing. I tried looking it up, but I never saw anything like this. I think I'm sick."

He curled his lip as if to say *yeah, you're sick alright.* "Jayce said you kicked him square in the back, said you went nuts on him, beat the shit out of him."

"No, he..." I felt my voice wobble, caught myself. That wasn't true. "It wasn't that. I just touched him and then the sun..."

He raised an eyebrow. Another customer came in, waited right behind me, flustering me. Diddy picked up my bursary chip and swiped it, handed me the cup and looked at me like I was already gone.

"Look," I begged him, "meet me after your shift, I'll explain, I just..."

"Fine, just go," he said in a low voice. "Hello, miffren," he greeted the person behind me. "What can I get you?"

I came back to the foodstop a full fifteen minutes before Diddy's shift was meant to end, hoping he hadn't ducked out early to avoid me. I scuttled through the arcades, taking ridiculous detours to avoid crossing full sunshine. There was lots of indoor shopping on the Craig, places to hide when the Atlantic storms came in. I had a ridiculous hat and gloves on too, and I was boiling.

Diddy clocked me and groaned as he came out the side entrance (which I'd guessed he'd use). He was bang on time for the end of shift, so obviously he'd hoped I'd miss him.

"I'm going home," he said, "you want to walk with me, you got until I reach my commune."

It was the best I would get.

"Thanks, Diddy," I said and fell in beside him, a little way further into the shade of the shop awnings.

"First of all, don't call me that. My name's Dave."

"What?" He'd been introduced to me as Diddy, and nobody called him anything else.

"Jayce gets to call me that, but you're not Jayce."

A nickname? Whatever.

"Dave, I need you to tell Jayce that I didn't kick him, I only touched him and then the sun hit my hand and mod sent out some kind of... I don't know what, but it wasn't me, I didn't do it."

"Yeah, right, so your body tunnel gave you superpowers? Congrats, I'm sure you'll do well."

"Don't be stupid, come on, I'm trying to explain."

"If I'm so stupid, why do you need me? Can't you all just hang out and compare mods and leave me out of it?"

"You never got one," I said out loud, stupidly.

"Oh, you noticed, well done."

"I mean, why not?"

He rounded on me, nearly spitting in my face. "Because I'm not stupid! You got that elagite stuff. It's like metal DNA and nobody knows what it does to you."

"So, you were scared."

"Look at yourself," he said witheringly.

Such bitterness from him. Despite being pals with Jayce, all these years, he'd never got a mod of his own. I supposed working at a foodstop wasn't that lucrative, but even I'd managed to save up my bursary. Now the sourness on his face whenever he saw me, since Jayce and I started seeing each other, it all made sense. He resented it.

Diddy—I mean Dave—lived out by the Prentice, a grubby little area of the peninsula. The shady walks of town were going to run out soon, and I'd be stuck out in the sun and god knows what would happen. I had to talk fast.

"No, you're right. You're right. I keep smashing glasses, I don't know if I fall asleep if I'll wake up again. I'm just so tired."

He crossed out from under the last arcade, and I stopped. He turned, standing in the light, me in shadow.

"Guess you should have it taken out, then."

"I never asked for this, I thought I'd just end up good at art or something, like Jayce."

"You were always just another groupie to him, you know," Dave said and left me.

My mod whispered static to me as I stood with my mouth hanging open, watching my only opportunity to fix things with Jayce march away with his shoulders stiff.

"Yeah? Well, he doesn't think much of you either, patty pusher!" I shouted but it was too late, he was gone.

6. Perforations

Phoebe

" So, anyway, here I am, all of fifteen years old and trying to reverse a lighter into the docking station with the AI screeching in my ear..."

Morgaine was telling stories again, out by the campfire. Phoebe listened with half an ear, more interested in the faces of those members of Us, paying court to their queen.

She'd been denied the chance to go on the convoy with Harro, some flimflam about how the grow team needed everyone to stay for now until the next big plant-out. It sounded like an excuse. Hopefully her parents weren't panicking yet. The last thing she needed was some consulate bod coming out here to try to locate her.

She'd have to make the best of it. Get the right kind of information and get out sooner.

Most of the members of Us still on site had gathered on camp chairs, around a fire made of dead saplings, torn coconut fibre baggies, and broken crates. Shan and the catering team worked a barbecue grill of protein patties and sausages that threw off gouts of tantalising savoury smoke. There was even beer. Laced through everything was laughter, over-hearty. She'd heard that at the lunch table and out here so often that she took it for a kind of code. It said, 'notice me'. She laughed along in the same places as everyone else. Her face was starting to cramp from the plastered-on smile.

The stories weren't revelatory. Morgaine sounded like an ordinary Spacer kid, the kind you saw on any show. What was interesting was the reaction. Jerome, for example, had a ferocious focus on his face, as if there was a test he could fail if he missed a word. She'd made sure to sit on the opposite side of the circle and only glanced his way when it was natural, like when she got up to get another beer from the crate. It was cheap lager, the kind that had a yeasty aftertaste, and nobody seemed to mind how many she took. It would give her an excuse to get up, walk around site to go to the latrines but being too nosy wasn't really an option. There wasn't much to see in the dark, and the camp security patrolled the perimeters. The gunman on the roof must have night sights, because there was always someone up there, likely one of Milo's goons. So, she sat and watched.

Milo sat easily by Morgaine's side, as if with an old friend. Mandy and other supervisors were there, but they seemed further down the pecking order. After that were people like Sweetie, ordinary grunts but who seemed easy in their skin. Then new spuds like her, Shan, Louis. All listening. All hungry for Morgaine's words.

This story about a kid learning how to pilot a space vehicle with disastrous results was wrapping up to howls of laughter and even some literal thigh-slapping. But then, as the humour died down, Morgaine said, "Any of you new spuds got any questions?" And there was silence.

Phoebe glanced around. Apart from Shan and Louis there weren't too many newer faces. Some of her intake had already departed, she'd heard; work too hard, or not what they'd expected. Of the ones remaining, none of them seemed ready to get caught in the spotlight. She wasn't either. She sensed there were dangers in opening her mouth. But fuck, she was here to find things out, right?

"How'd you get back to Earth?"

There were snorts of exasperation from the crowd, but Morgaine shushed them. "It's a fair question," she said. "No drama." She went quite still. "Why'd you want to know?"

"Just..." Phoebe felt her ribs tighten up and her throat seize. She powered through. "I mean if you're down here, did you get someone to take your place up there?"

Earth's 'one in, one out' policy was ironclad. That didn't mean people didn't get around it all the time, though. If she was an illegal alien, it was something useful to know.

Morgaine gave a pained smile. "Look, what's your name, eh?"

"Phoebe," she said feeling all the eyes on her burning through her skin. "I just wondered."

The moment hung in the air, before restarting with a snap. Morgaine was all affability again.

"And you were right to. Because there was a swap. A man called Michael Warren, and you should all know his name." She looked around the circle. "Because he went up there so I could come down here. And that was very big of him. So, thank you for asking, Phoebe. It took guts." Morgaine lifted her beer. "Everyone, a toast. To Michael."

"To Michael," the awkward, murmured echo. And after everyone had swigged, Morgaine put down her beer and clasped her hands, leaning on her knees.

"Truth is, everyone could have stayed on Earth. None of this swapping nonsense. If we'd given up our luxuries. But we didn't want to do that. Did we?"

The fire crackled. No-one had anything to say to that, other than a few rueful grunts. Morgaine shifted back in her seat.

"Now, if you want to know what it's like to recondition to Earth gravity having spent your entire life in space, strap in because you're going to love it." Groans in anticipation of one of Morgaine's more excruciatingly detailed stories began and attention swung back to the leader, the guru. Away from Phoebe.

Morgaine ran out of stories eventually and left, suggesting that everyone else stay and socialise. Milo left too. Then supervisors. It seemed to be going in order of rank, some unspoken hierarchy. Soon only Phoebe, Shan, and Louis remained.

"How are you getting on?" she said, as the small flames of the bonfire danced as they died.

"It's getting better. The first few days planting out were hell on my back." Louis was tall and lean. He'd have had a heck of a job bending down that far.

"Catering's all right," Shan said, but she was laid back enough to fit in anywhere. She looked around ostentatiously before producing two small bars of chocolate that she handed over. "Don't tell anyone."

"Ah, Shan, you genius," Louis said, grabbing his bar and holding it to his chest like a treasure.

"Us new spuds got to stick together," Phoebe said around a mouthful. It had been a while. They giggled into the night.

Phoebe tried not to stand up too quickly when the fire had finally died, and they realised they still had to work in the morning. As she walked with them back to the bivouacs, head muzzy with beer, she pawed over her memory of earlier. Now Morgaine knew her name. If it was what she'd wanted, why did she feel like she was going to be sick?

She went to bed and closed her eyes, hoping to get to sleep quickly. Then woke to small sounds. Sweetie and Alexis? Were they at it again? It wouldn't be the first time they'd furtively shared a bunk. She opened her eyes. A dark figure in front of her. Jerome. She jolted fully awake.

He leaned over her and put his fingers to his lips. "Shh," he said softly. Then he left the tent. Had he been watching her? Masturbating, perving? Did she wake up right before he murdered her?

He didn't come back in that night. Phoebe knew, because she was not going back to sleep after that.

Selen

I got the earliest trip I could. The ferry left from the piers halfway between the Craig and the Prentice before the sun had started to climb the sky. Normally, I'd watch the sails raise and unfurl like massive wings turning to catch the wind, and the spray curl around the bow as it got underway. Normally, I'd look right down through the green water to see if I could spot anything of Paisley or Glasgow down there. Of course, I never could, but I loved thinking about it, cities lost beneath the waves, so mysterious.

But today, I hid right in the centre seating in the cabin, sunhat on, covered up again. Around me, snoring workers making their early morning commute from the cheaper peninsula suburbs to BL City. I wished they weren't so peaceful. I already felt sick from making myself stay awake.

The rocking of the boat wasn't soporific, it just made me want to retch. Thankfully, there wasn't much in my body to regurgitate. Concentrating on eating every bite was more of a chore than you'd think, and I was paranoid about putting things near my face. Last night, I'd put my teeth through a fork. I was lucky, it came out before anything broke off. The image of tines and teeth snapping and lodging in my throat wasn't doing much for my appetite.

If I concentrated, nothing should happen when the UV hit my skin, but I couldn't take that chance so I was swathed up in clothes and gloves. I felt like a vampire. My mod was quiet, doing whatever the hell it was doing down there in my guts without disturbing anyone else around me, but it was freaking me out anyway.

The mod tech would have answers. He had to. None of their public info said anything about effects even remotely like mine. In fact, the whole net was silent, except for some mad fringe theories about elagite poisoning that looked the usual conspiracy rants. Though, if I posted up my experiences, I guess I'd be a laughingstock, too.

If Phoebe were home, she would know how to cope with this. She would have listened, even as she judged me. But she was off being someone I'd never dreamed possible. A cult follower? I would have told you to get to fuck if you'd told me that was a possibility for my sister. I'd shared a photo with her when I first got the mod, then we'd got that family post that she was off doing some kind of weird retreat, and then... nothing.

The waves roiled and made my stomach heave like someone had punched me. I hunched over, hoping I wouldn't throw up, swallowing that horrible acid feeling down.

"What the—?"

Some guy had shouted, somewhere forward. People gasped and murmured, looking up through the forward observation windows. I sat up, craning my neck. Someone screamed, a kid, I think. I got up but the view was crowded out, so I edged out the door and towards the forward deck, trying to stay in shadow. The ferry dipped, like it was going down a big wave and then I saw what they were all looking at.

There was a hole in the sea and the sky, right in front of the ferry. No, not a hole. It was as if the sea and sky had been replaced, a bad image manipulation where a sphere of somewhere else had been patched over this part of the Clyde Straits. The trouble was, this other reality didn't have any sea there. A huge sucking vortex stood in its place. I recoiled, bashing into someone who'd huddled behind me, sending him sprawling. Not my mod this time, just my natural panic flattening grown men. "Sorry," I spluttered as I scuttled back towards the stern. I didn't stop to help him up but just ran.

Fuck, what if it was me? My mod was making a keening sound, like wind through wires, but loud. It wasn't the wind across the pipe, it was something else, something aggressive. Was I the only one hearing it? The ferry would fall down that great hole and I'd be killed. I'd be *killed*. We all would.

I stopped, gripped the guardrail. It was ridiculous, but since there wasn't much choice, I concentrated.

There was absolutely no way, the literature said, that a human biological modification system could affect the external world in any way more than a superficial, synaesthetic way. It could not be used for mind control, or telekinesis, but Jayce made people feel good with his, didn't he? Made the music pulse and sound better, made you feel better. That was real, wasn't it?

It wasn't like this.

"Fuck Jayce. Just think!" I shouted at myself, almost inaudible over the keening sound and the screaming of the panicked people ahead of me.

I closed my eyes. "Clyde Straits, BL City, all like it used to be." The sea fountained up in front of the ferry like a depth charge had gone off. The horizon tipped and lurched and I thought we were going down, but it was just a huge wave, surging beneath us. The ferry bucked like a beast, sails flapping and snapping, and dropped so hard back to sea level that my knees gave way and my teeth clacked painfully together. I could taste blood; water sprayed down on me. I hauled myself up by the guardrail again.

It was over. The void was gone, and my mod was silent. The boat bobbed about, settling from the spasm.

Later, after a lot of shouted questions and accusations from passengers turning their fear into anger, the ferry announced it would get underway and get us to our destination as quick as possible, and that they would be contacting the authorities to launch an investigation.

While younger people milled about and muttered theories, the old man in the row of seats across from me laughed and held his head as he rocked gently. "Pretty lights," he muttered to himself. "All those wee pretty lights."

My teeth ground together, and I felt my face tremble with anger.

I was going to get this thing taken out of me, whatever the mod tech said, if I had to threaten to throw his studio down a vortex too.

Phoebe

"God, he is creeping me the fuck out," she said to Shan as they sat on the steps of the catering cold store behind the pavilion.

"You should really tell someone about it," she said, sympathetic. Phoebe had found her on their breaks and together they hid from their supervisors, perched beneath the cold down-draft of the imperfect seal at the store's door. Bundy, the catering supervisor, was notoriously cantankerous and worked them unnecessarily hard. Mandy was fine, but so perky and efficient with her dataslate checklists. And this was the closest the camp got to cool air.

"And you reckon he didn't come back in at all?" Shan went on.

Jerome had been standing over her. Then he'd left the bivouac and not come back. That wasn't normal behaviour, was it? He hadn't been seconded to security, as far as she could tell, so what was he doing roaming camp in the middle of the night?

"I don't know, and I don't want to rock the boat," Phoebe said. "They don't like whingers here."

Or liars. She remembered Apolline and put her cheeks to her knees.

"Bundy's not great either," Shan said. "I think he's on the diamond dust."

"Uppers? Where'd he even get that out here?"

"No idea. But he's always nipping off, coming back wiping his nose on his sleeve like we wouldn't notice."

Petty drug use wasn't all that worrisome, but she'd need to do something about Jerome. Maybe he was reporting her movements to Milo. Not that he'd have much to tell, but it was the last thing she needed.

Then she realised. She could use his weirdness. An ace in the hole. A grenade in the pocket. She'd have to be careful about deploying it though.

"I'd better go." She got up and dusted the back of her trouser legs. "Got to go strip about a thousand wattle seeds out of their pods. That'll be fun. Then they're taking us out to the land farm tomorrow. I've no idea why."

"Custard for afters tonight," Shan called after her cheerfully.

Thank god for someone to talk to who was so thoroughly oblivious to the wheels going round in Phoebe's head.

7. To Dust

Phoebe

"Pesticides, petrochemicals, plastics, man's real legacy on Earth at this moment." Morgaine gazed out across the churned red earth in front of her. She wasn't talking to the people around her, the little group of Us members who had come with her on the field trip to see the land farm. She talked at the whole world. And Phoebe stood at the guru's elbow.

Automatic rotary ploughs turned the soil over in this small basin, the lowest point for miles around on a pancake-flat landscape, and the small group surveyed their slow progress across soil almost hard as concrete. Except for Milo, Morgaine's omnipresent shadow. His eyes were on the horizon, on the lookout for imagined dangers. The only danger out here was sunstroke.

Mandy was there, too, and did a short spiel on the concept of 'land farming', a peculiar term that that meant reclaiming polluted land by tilling the soil and aerating bacteria to break down the contaminants.

"This land was the downstream part of a river system. Farmers would use the water to irrigate their crops, then the run-off would leach salts out of the ground and back into the water. All that, not to mention their pesticides, would accumulate down here, making this some of the most toxic land to grow on, outside of nuclear waste dumps," she said.

That was hard to conceive. Something as innocent as watering your crops could create such a problem?

"But we can change things. Make this ground tenable again. Start feeding the world." Morgaine stood like a hero, posing on the brink of the small basin's rim. She spoke so confidently, as if it were destiny, as if this land should be farmed. Anyone could see that you couldn't make this place an Eden.

"Boss, dust coming," Milo said, looking out to the horizon where there was a brown smudge. "Better get back, soon as." Morgaine nodded and waved him off.

Mandy took up a handheld terminal, making some adjustments to the machines while the others headed back to the vehicles. Then she, too, strode off. Phoebe lingered, as if fascinated by the work below. But it was Morgaine that she wanted to be close to.

"You're with me, I suppose," Morgaine said, turning those large Spacer eyes down to her.

"What?" Phoebe said and turned around, pretending surprise that the other vehicles were leaving.

"It's okay," Morgaine said. "You've got me all to yourself."

"I hadn't... I didn't..."

"I told you it's okay." Morgaine was grave, resigned. "I'm used to people wanting a piece of me. Come on, then."

Phoebe trailed her up to Morgaine's car, the one no-one else touched in what was supposed to be a communal pool of vehicles. They got in and drove away from the auto-ploughs and the dust storm. The front wouldn't move that fast, but it was coming at an angle to the track back to the camp, so they'd be lucky to miss it. The camp should get battened down. If it wasn't, and there was grit in her bed, she'd be pissed.

"Hope it won't strip too much of the ground we just turned," Morgaine muttered, looking in the rear-view.

"Couldn't we cover it or something?"

"What with? You have seventeen hectares of agricultural sheeting you're not telling me about?"

Phoebe bit her lip and kept quiet. Morgaine sighed and slowed to stop at the side of the track. The dust cloud towered up over and enveloped them, and soon it was dark as night, with tiny pebbles pinging off the chassis. "No point in clogging up the aircon," she said and turned the fan off. "It's going to get pretty stifling in here."

"How long do you think?" The hiss of fine grit scouring the paint off the car sang behind their words.

"Who knows? You've got until it stops, though."

Phoebe didn't like how final that sounded. Was Morgaine about to throw her out of the car to walk home? Or did she have a gun secreted somewhere? Was her body going to be dumped somewhere in the middle of the Australian outback?

They'd given her an escape plan if things went rotten. "All you have to do," the man had said, when he was recruiting her, "is to be outdoors, turn your face up to the sky, and mouth the words. Our monitoring equipment will pick you up, read your lips. If you find signifiers of illegal or terrorist activity, or if you're in trouble, just say 'crash, crash', and we'll come in and get you."

That plan really fell apart in the middle of a dust storm. She wondered if they were even watching. She had no way of telling. Would they burn their entire operation just to save one Alban backpacker?

"You've got more questions, I can tell, so ask them."

So, that was it. Morgaine had remembered her from the other night by the campfire. "A lot of the new spuds do. Fire away. Don't use too many words, or you'll fug up the cabin with your breath."

Phoebe tapped a finger on her knee while she thought. She didn't know how long the dust would last, so she'd better make it good.

She could ask about the shed. No, she couldn't. It would be too obvious. Maybe she could work around to it somehow. Perhaps she could report Jerome for his creepy behaviour. He hadn't done anything, just stood there, but Phoebe was having a lot of trouble sleeping now, and any noise of a person turning over in their bunk set her on edge. But grassing him up to the boss seemed too short term. She could still need to use it.

She realised she hadn't spoken for several minutes now. Anything. Just say anything.

"Why did you want to do this, to start Us?"

Morgaine gave her a look. "You not been listening? I talk about it all the time."

"Well..." Phoebe dropped her head, smiled. "I mean you tell us about how it's a good thing to do, but not why you wanted to be the one to do it. If you see what I mean."

Morgaine curled her lip, halfway between a smile and a sneer. "Nobody else wanted to. Spacers, Earthers, all want to ignore it. We've been ignoring things for centuries. And here it is, the Deluge wiping out half of the old Australia, crop fields washed out to sea, salination spoiling the ones that weren't. And what did they do about it? Walled themselves up in compounds inland and hoarded food, that's what. Didn't lift a finger to fix anything. And I spent too long watching my home dry up and burn to a cinder."

"But it's not your home. You were born in space, weren't you?" It was an innocent question, a logical follow on, but Morgaine's expression turned ugly. She beat the steering wheel in time to her next words.

"Why'd you think I called it Us? Earth is my home, all our homes. Every human, every single living thing comes from here." Spittle flew out of her mouth and Phoebe flinched, wondered if she should start making plans on how to survive running through a dust storm.

But Morgaine breathed in deeply through her nose and calmed a little before continuing in a more measured way.

"The only reason I wasn't born here was because my parents lost the right to stay on the planet. Running away from it instead of trying to fix it was the dumbest fuck mistake we ever made. I'm not sure you could ever understand."

Phoebe bit her bottom lip. She couldn't fathom what it must have been like to live in an asteroid mining colony all her life, with earth as a fable, some Shangri-la.

She was blowing this opportunity, though. All this ideology wasn't giving her anything to use, to exploit. And the mysterious locked shed squatted at the back of her mind, too, but now was not the time to make Morgaine's face any darker. There could still be a gun, an outback execution. She reached her fingertips out to rest on the dashboard, as if she dared to touch Morgaine's hand but held back. She put as much emotion into her voice as she could without sounding corny.

"For what it's worth, I think everyone would like to see New Aus green again. You're doing a great thing." She could mollify Morgaine, get her onside. *Narcissists love praise and attention.* That's what they'd told her.

It seemed to work. Morgaine stopped looking angry, but then it was as if she stopped even seeing Phoebe. She turned her head slowly and looked out the window as if she sat in the cabin alone and was surveying a vista, instead of looking at the pattering dust inside a dark cloud.

It grew intolerably hot and stuffy in the car. "Can we turn on the aircon for a minute?" Phoebe said, when the sweat started to drip down the side of her face.

"Not as pleasant a climate as Alba?" Morgaine said, almost cheerfully.

Phoebe froze. But then, everyone knew where she was from. Her accent. She laughed off the question. "It's a bit different, that's for sure."

"Britannia's winners of the space race," Morgaine went on, cutting over her. "Must have been lovely to grow up with a space port right near you. Nice jobs, fewer people put onto the lottery from Alba."

Phoebe felt like she was swimming out over a deep drop off, no idea what monsters would come up beneath her. She made a non-committal noise.

"Do you think we were ready? For space, I mean," Morgaine asked in a tone that could not have been more leading if it held a rope. Morgaine was a Spacer, an exile returned to the world, and Phoebe was the daughter of people kept on earth for their skills and service to the space industry. She was part of one of the most privileged echelons of society, though it didn't always feel like that.

"Probably not," she said, carefully neutral. "But I'm not a scientist."

"No, you're not." The other woman looked at her and this time Phoebe felt a needle-stab of ice in her core. "Grants administrator at an Education Fund, wasn't it?"

No, that was better than an educated guess based on accent. She was just another new spud, why the fuck would this woman know anything about her? Maybe this was a trick Morgaine pulled on every recruit, make them feel like she knew everything about them, like she was omnipotent. She had to say something.

"Yeah, it wasn't the most rewarding job. I felt like... like a cog in the system, just turning on the spot." She was a prey animal pinned by something big and toothy. Perhaps if she didn't struggle, if she just waited...

Morgaine broke the spell by snapping on the aircon. "Gets clogged, you'll be the one cleaning it."

Phoebe made herself not pant with relief. She put her hands out to the vent, cooling fingers stretched and swollen.

"Sure, boss, no problem." Boss. That's what Harro and the others called her.

Morgaine relaxed and returned to looking out the window. "I'm dying, you know."

"What?" This conversation was like mental whiplash. Dying? This would change everything. The Bureau could relax. She'd stop posing a threat, wouldn't she?

"We all are. Up there," she pointed to the sky. "But most people don't know it yet."

"How?" She winced at the bluntness to her own question, but Aussies were blunt. Morgaine was unfazed.

"The human body wasn't built for it. Not even with our genetic tweaks, clever machines, radiation shielding." Morgaine looked at her with a foreboding expression. "Cancer. Everywhere. A new type. Systemic. And everyone who stays up there too long will get it, eventually."

"You can't get treatment, therapy?" Cancer. It was like saying someone was dying of leprosy, or typhoid. The telomere binders that people took to delay ageing had all but wiped it out.

"They keep treating it, it keeps popping up elsewhere. That's what systemic means. And in the meantime, the person grows weak, tired of living. You watch them slowly be erased." The anger was deep, primal. Phoebe wondered who the woman had watched die.

"And nobody knows about this?"

"Well," Morgaine said, and a smile like a knife blade settled on her. "The authorities do. And that's why I'm doing what I'm doing, miffren. We've got to resettle everyone on Earth, as soon as we possibly can. We've got to get them all back. And the only way to do that is by making it green."

Phoebe slumped back in her seat. The only sound was the ticker-ticker of dust against the window, and the aircon, straining.

Selen

I hadn't remembered the tech's name, so I told the Tunnel-porium's reception he was slim, dark-haired, with mods in the backs of his hands.

"Ken matches your description," the droning AI reception bot told me. "Please take a seat and I will inform him you wish to make an emergency consultation."

I stepped out of the privacy booth and sat down in the row of seats. The only other occupant was a man with three piston mods in his right calf. "Are you alright, miffren?" he asked. I kept my eyes on the floor, concentrating on memorising the pattern in the parquet, anything to keep my mind from drifting, and didn't look up until footsteps came towards me.

"Selen, what's up? Everything alright?"

I got up and scuttled away from the other customer, who made noisy throat-clearing sounds, but fuck him. There wasn't room in the privacy booth for two, so I spoke low. "I need to talk to you right away. Urgent. Now."

Ken looked disconcerted. "Okay, we can go into the office for a moment."

I grabbed his arm, shockingly invasive, but there wasn't time for nicety. "No, to the treatment room."

"There's someone inside, just undergoing a mod." He looked apologetic but also seemed to be picking up my vibe. "Let's go in here quickly and at least tell me what the problem is."

He let me in, and I covered my face with my hands. "I don't know what's happening!"

He tried to soothe me. "Listen, sometimes people have a more extreme adjustment gradient. What is it, synaesthesia? Memory issues?"

"I nearly put a fucking ferry through a wormhole!"

I mean, I have no idea if that's what it was, but it had sure felt like something that insane. I burst into tears.

He shushed me, like a child he was comforting. I needed to demonstrate it to him.

"Look," I said and put my fist through a window. Only, I was thinking about it, and I nearly broke my hand as it bounced off the glass. I bent double, howling.

It's like that old conundrum. If someone tells you, don't think about a zebra, it's damn hard not to. And even if you do, you can't think to yourself, *see, I did it, I'm not thinking about a zebra,* because now you are. If you want to show someone something that only happens when you're not thinking about it, how can you do it?

"Woah, hey!" Ken patted my shoulders. "Look, I can see you're distressed, please, just sit down. I have the contact for a pharma service, we can get you something to help you..." He didn't say *calm down*, which I was grateful for, underneath my physical and not-so-physical pain.

He made the contact, looking at me all the time under worried brows. When the packet of pills came through the printer, he squatted down in front of me and read the safety notices out to me. I nodded and shook my head until he gave me the meds with a glass of water. I focused hard on everything, squeezing my eyes up sometimes, just to make sure.

"I have to see the other customer for a minute, but please, stay here, I'm going to wipe my schedule clean for the next hour or so, just wait, please, okay?"

I nodded again and carefully put the glass down on the little coffee table by the chairs. He gave me one more wary look before exiting, closing the door behind him.

I had never had to maintain this level of concentration outside of an examination, and even then, that was only on one focused activity for an hour or two. My stomach flipped over and over but eventually it slowed. The meds were fast. Then I had a surge of adrenaline. What if they made me fuzzy? What might happen then? And my heart lurched in a new, sudden panic. Was the edge of the room getting blurry? Was I about to fuck everything? I very deliberately curled my fingernails into my palms and squeezed my fists until they hurt. Pain, that would keep me going, keep me here, alert.

The door opened and Ken came in again. How long had it been? It felt like hours.

"You managed to nod off?" he asked, kindly.

"No, I think that would be a very bad idea," I told him, my voice shaking.

"How long have you been awake?" he said and sat down to take some notes on a slate.

Asking me to do maths right now? I guessed wildly. "I don't know, I didn't sleep last night. Or much the day before that." He made a sucking sound with his teeth.

"That's not good for anyone, sleep deprivation." Implying I was delusional, hallucinating, I supposed.

"I know what happened. Didn't you see it on the splashes?" The news must have spread from the ferry at least.

"They said there was an incident, yes, but no-one's said anything about a wormhole." He came over and hunkered down right there in front of me and locked eyes, like he was trying to read my thoughts. "Are you sure it wasn't just a whirlpool or something? They get them from time to time out on the straits, you know."

"I know what happened," I said again. "Maybe they're not talking about it, but it did happen."

"Okay, I believe you." It sounded like something he'd been trained to say. "Let's start from the start. Tell me when you noticed the first strange thing. We'll work it all out."

I didn't want to tell him about Jayce, but I had to say something to someone. Or I'd really go insane. And then who knows what would happen?

"It... the first time I felt something odd was two days after the implantation." I started crying, and this wasn't even the worst part. "I woke up, and my hand fell into a patch of sunlight. And there was pain, like a shock. I thought it was just temporary. And it stopped. Everything seemed fine. But then, a couple of weeks later, the same thing, but it... I hurt someone else."

"Hurt someone?" I thought there might be a rising note of panic in his voice. Like he was worried about liability. "How?"

"I threw him across the room! I didn't mean to." I dropped my hand. "I just touched him and the sunlight..."

He stood up, quickly. "Alright, we will get you a scan. Umm..." His eyes darted between mine. "It isn't covered in your original payment, so..."

Anger. Anger focused me. I handed him my bursary chip and did not put my hand literally through his face. But it was tempting.

Phoebe

Phoebe humped the tray of little seedlings inside their coconut fibre baggies to boost it up onto the bench. Then she went back for the next one. Mandy eyed her, ticking something on a dataslate. "You're keen today," she said, drily.

Phoebe just grunted and boosted the next up. Her hands and back were sore from the job, it was hot, but still. She went for the next.

"Told you, didn't she?" Phoebe decided not to react. Mandy went on, regardless. "You know, I've seen it a lot. New spuds come out here with the idea that greening up a bit of New Aus might be fun. Then they hear what's going on up there. They either run for the hills," she gestured out the grow shed's open side toward some imaginary hills, beyond the dead-flat salt pans, "or they get a fire up their arse. Guess you're the second type."

"Guess I am," Phoebe agreed, realising she was starting to pick up on this Outback laconic thing.

"Well, good," Mandy said and put her dataslate away to hook up the irrigation tubes to the seedling trays. "I know when I first heard about it..." She looked away, at something distant.

It must have happened when Morgaine came to recruit her from her university. She'd probably planned to get a job at some research corp, a bright future. And then, she'd heard what Morgaine had claimed. She wondered how it would feel, having your career path upended with information like that. Then again, Morgaine had said the authorities knew already. And they had done nothing. So, the only people apparently bothered were out here in the desert?

"Why doesn't she just tell everyone about it? Like, make it public."

Mandy groaned in exaggerated frustration. "Are you that naïve? You don't know what they do to whistle-blowers?"

"I suppose."

Of course, she wasn't sure she believed it was true. Morgaine had said she was dying but she didn't look sick. Well, compared to the average Spacer who always looked a bit strung out. She couldn't take it as gospel truth. The handlers

241

had warned her about taking things at face value. Cult and extremist followers were always fed conspiracies and out-rageous theories. But whatever the situation, she wanted answers, or she wanted out. It was too much. She didn't have the training to know what to do with any of it and hadn't had any opportunity to discuss it with the higher-ups.

She went over the memory of the night she'd been shang-haied for what seemed like the millionth time.

"You'd be deeply embedded. You'd get out as soon as you found out their end game," the man had said. She'd never learned his name. He'd never told her.

"Why don't you send someone with training? Some of your super spies?" she'd asked, drawing circles on the table through the condensation from her beer bottle, that night in the bar, that night when everything seemed too surreal to be true.

"We might have tried already," the man had admitted, and he'd looked off to the side, not wanting to meet her eyes. "We might have tried every long-range surveillance we've got, too. You've got a clear, real record of who you are, who you've always been. You're impeccable. No-one's been watching you." That had been when she'd first realised what they were asking her to do was risky. And, if she was honest, it was the first time in a long time she'd felt any excitement. She worked in admin, for god's sake. But her work record was the right kind of boring to get her in.

They'd given her the basics, but not too much. Told her it was so she would react naturally. All she had to do was sit tight and keep her eyes and ears open. She hadn't seen any of the 'red line items' her handlers had told her to look for. No physical or mental torture, thank god. Voluntary hard work didn't count. No extreme ritual behaviour, no bomb-making ingredients. They didn't even use nitro-phosphate fertilisers on the plants. No sexual abuse, apart from Jerome being a freak, and one pervert did not a sex-cult make. Just a story about cancer and needing to bring back the Spacers on a planet too fragile to take it. Everything seemed reasonable; reasonable and extreme at the same time. There were no handholds to grab. She worked hard in the grow shed to try to exorcise the frustration and overwhelming sense that something was going to break at any moment.

"Anyway, Space corps and techfucks always have a way of suppressing things like this," Mandy went on, breaking back into her thoughts. "Makes it hard for the messages to get out. That's how the Deluge happened. Everybody knew about it but so many people wanted to muddy the truth for so long. Or just flat out pretend it wasn't happening. Bury their heads in their cushy lifestyle."

Mandy was only in her twenties. What the fuck did she know about the world? It was a spiteful thought, but Phoebe was feeling tired and petty. Mostly from lack of good sleep.

Maybe it was time to break things. It was a dumb idea, but it was time to lob the hand grenade and hope the shrapnel didn't get her. Otherwise, she'd just be out here repeating the same routine over and over and getting nothing. She had to do something. She had to get home.

"You know Jerome?" She didn't make eye contact, just kept working. Of course she did, he was a member of her team.

"Yeah?" Mandy said, warily.

Phoebe fought the rising anxiety down. She couldn't stop, had to see it through. "He's a bit of a creep, isn't he?" Too polite. "More than a bit. He's freaking me out."

Mandy stopped working and looked at her squarely. "What do you mean?"

"I think you, as a woman, know what I mean. Why do we have to share a bivouac with a guy like him?"

"Well, we don't have a lot of spare spaces, and we live and work as a team so what are you—"

"—You don't! You don't have to sleep in the same space as him. And I think a team leader should be able to work out a way the women in her team can feel comfortable."

"Sweetie and Alexis haven't said anything. And Jerome seems... Are you sure you're not misreading—"

Phoebe threw one of the precious saplings on the floor, where the baggie exploded sending dirt everywhere. Mandy looked at it with bulging eyes.

"I caught him looking at me the other night while I slept! Just standing over me, watching. If you can't fix this, then I'm out." Phoebe spun on her heel and marched out of the shed, heading for the far side of the campsite by the big gum tree. It was quiet and had a couple of canvas chairs in the shade. They were meant for planters on their break but were empty right now. A good place to look moody.

God, fuck. What had she set in motion? If she hadn't been so tired, maybe it would have been a different story. But it was done now, and nothing could take it back. She slumped into a chair and chewed things over. The risks were balanced against the fact the accusation was true. She hadn't caught him looking again, but she'd had to sleep sometimes.

Mandy came over to her not too long after. Phoebe didn't meet her eye, instead sipped water from her canteen and looked up through the grey-green of the gum leaves. The supervisor sounded contrite and worried. "I'm sorry if it seemed like I wasn't listening to you," she said earnestly. She squatted down and held onto the arm of Phoebe's seat. "I had a quiet word with Sweetie and Alexis and they... they didn't say anything that really disagreed with you..." Mandy was out of her depth but trying hard. "Look, I'm working on moving some people around, to see if we can't get Jerome into another bivouac but it might take a couple of days. Until

244

then, if you want, you and I can swap beds. You can take my bedroom in the supervisor's cabin. It's got its own door and everything. You can lock it and feel a bit more secure. And I'll take your bunk until we get things arranged. How does that sound?"

Phoebe tried not to smile, but act with wounded dignity. This was far better than she could have hoped. "I would like that, thank you."

8. Tether's End

Selen

I used up a lot of my commune goodwill by having a long shower, hoping the water would revive me or at least clean me. I staggered out and went through the motions of getting dry and dressed in my room. I put on the sun protection clothes again. I don't know why, perhaps I'd try Diddy again.

Every part of my body hurt. I couldn't even let myself sit on the bed too long. It was getting too hard to resist lying down and sleeping. I needed to get up and going. I sat down for a moment.

I'd got back to this side of the straits, got home. The scan I'd paid extra for had been 'inconclusive', medical-speak for 'we don't have a clue'. Ken had rounded up some specialist who clucked and said words over my head like 'Casimir', and 'photonic', as if I wouldn't understand. He was just trying to sound clever. I was already over that after years of academics. I'd re-referenced everything he'd said but I was too tired to process the meaning, to put it all together in my head.

They were going to get me to the big research hospital down south, but I didn't know how I could hang on until the appointment.

Seemed obvious to me that they'd put the thing in backwards. It worked exactly the reverse of what it should do. It should throw people across the room when I wanted it, when I focused. It shouldn't open up a giant, sucking void in front of a ferry because I got a tummy ache. How fucking typical for me. How art.

My phone started glowing ominously. Christ. It was Mum. What did she want? Didn't she see I couldn't talk to her about anything if all she ever did was make me feel like a piece of shit? Where was the benefit to me?

Daddy Arjun had left me some messages too, asking me to get in touch with them. 'Just to check you're doing okay.' I mean, he meant well, but I couldn't trust him either. He'd just run back to Mum. Any convo we had, she'd be vulturing in the background, getting all the emotional blackmail points in order.

I went to dismiss the notices, but I was so tired my body was swaying, fingers clumsy like I was on snorts. Mum's face splashed up on the walls, surrounding me. Fuck!

"Selen, there you are!" She sounded anguished, but also triumphant.

I fumbled with the phone, desperately stabbing at the off button. My mod started whining, keening. I was standing, no idea I'd got to my feet. Fuck!

"No," I shouted at the thing, it wasn't doing what I wanted.

I threw the phone at the wall and it went through, full, hard, in a shower of glittery lights. I heard a scream from the room next door.

Fuck...

I ran out. Flick was standing over Senna, who was clutching her head, crouched on her bed. There was blood visible. My phone was on the floor, with a thin stream of smoke curling up from it. Flick turned to me. Accusation in her eyes.

I bolted.

Phoebe

Supervisors had it cushy, Phoebe decided as she lay in the single bed in Mandy's room, door firmly locked. The little portacabin had a corridor with a row of doors that opened into the rooms. The space smelled of somebody else and it was tiny, just enough floor area and no more, but it was gloriously private and secure.

She'd avoided the other supervisors, who'd stared at her curiously as she encountered them coming and going. Fortunately, they were busy people. Bundy the catering supervisor, CeeCee the Operations supervisor, and the security supervisor, a guy called George. She passed them without comment or eye-contact where she could. She knew they had heard about why she was there, and they were staying out of her way. No doubt afraid of accusations that Us was a sex-cult or something. Good. They should have dealt with things earlier.

She drifted in and out of sleep, feeling the different patterns of people sleeping or moving around in the rooms that adjoined hers. Someone got up from the far bedroom, George it sounded like, and tramped down the steps in the early hours. Shift change or pee. His return less than five minutes later said if he had done any work, he'd not spent a long time about it.

She left it another hour before drifting up out of her light doze and putting on her boots. She walked to the door as normally as possible. As normally as George had. Opened the door. Surely the hinges hadn't squeaked that loudly for him? No matter. She was out and down the metal grating steps and off. She set off in the general direction of the latrines, yawning, hunching her shoulders against the chill. She'd forgotten to put her fleece on. A red dot like a firefly skittered at her feet and she resisted the urge to hurl herself to the side. The rifleman on the roof had spotted her, was tracking her. She kept walking.

Apparently, he was satisfied she was heading to the loos because the dot vanished. With a gargantuan effort, she untensed her shoulders, pulled her head back up. Tried not to think about her skull exploding like a coconut; she couldn't really feel the heat of that laser dot on her back, it was just her imagination.

She had never been so relieved to pull the rickety latrine cubicle door behind her. Fuck. Fuck this place. She squatted over the disgusting seat above the trench and squeezed out a few drops. They were always so unsatisfying, even after she'd consciously tried to up her water intake. She wiped and pulled up her pants before putting a handful of sawdust down the hole and getting ready to go back. She peered over the top of the cubicle door, through the crack of an inch or so clearance from the top of the frame. It wasn't much but she could see the camp laid out, flat and matte under the starlight. She looked towards Morgaine's tent. There was a light on.

She eased the cubicle door open and saw the gunman in silhouette in his nest. The rifle was angled down, it seemed. She could see shoulders, but he didn't appear to be looking her way. She drifted towards the white yurt, with its interior glow. Voices? She thought she could hear Milo's rumble. That would make sense, though it was pretty late. Maybe Morgaine was a night owl.

There was a snarl in reply to a question. Phoebe's stomach dropped. Jerome. It had to be. That combination of nasal and weaselly. The prick. What were they doing?

Was he talking about her? Had he been watching again?

Could she get any closer without the sniper noticing? Probably not. She was pushing it as it was. She decided to cut her losses and get back to the supervisor's portacabin.

She'd just turned around the lee of the grow shed, passing its huge, dark maw, when the sounds changed behind her. She ducked in, into the deeper shadow between the wall and one of the planting benches and squatted, pressing her ear towards the open air as best she could, but she couldn't hear anything intelligible. She nearly jerked a tray of seedlings onto the floor in shock as Jerome appeared into her field of view. But he was only walking past, and when he was safely out of sight, she got up and hurried back to the portacabin.

That was quite enough excitement for one night. The cold had started to get to her fingers. She was about to mount the steps when the door opened, spilling light. Jerome was there, with George, the security supervisor. Phoebe froze. The red dot played near them.

George picked up a radio and spoke into it. "It's okay, Vern, we're just going to pick up a catering attendant. Got some questions for her."

They padded down the stairs. "Where you been?" the supervisor asked, almost in passing.

"Toilet," Phoebe said faintly.

"Better remember your coat next time," he said, and Jerome leered. Phoebe crossed her arms across her chest. They passed, heading towards the bivouacs. Jerome lingered by the steps.

"Don't worry," he said to her quietly as George walked on. "I'm coming for you soon enough." He followed the supervisor out into the night.

She went back in her room and locked the door.

Selen

I sat down on the end of the abandoned pier at the tip of the Craig, after sundown when the blue-white of the sky had gone kind of green. I stared down between my feet at the water swelling and slacking, back, forth, Clyde, Forth, firth, straits, bubbling, black-green, white foam, darker kelp strands like monster hair.

I didn't know what I was doing here. I had to concentrate so hard on the moment, I had no idea where I wanted to go, where was safe. My fear had taken me here. The end of the pier, abandoned. Where we used to sit. Me and Jayce. Me and Feebs. My sister, yeah, meet her here. No, she was away.

My brain was quitting on me. I couldn't see an answer. If I slept, I didn't know what would happen. Maybe nothing. But if I opened a goddamn tear in the universe just because my stomach hurt, what could I do asleep?

I looked over my shoulder at the Craig. Home. Life. My commune wasn't safe from me. My family weren't safe from me. Jayce and even Diddy, I mean Dave... maybe I wasn't safe from them. I had thought we had something special. Jayce and me. I had thought we were fellow artists. I mean, would have been. It's all so jumbled now. But he was so angry. His face, so cold. "It's not that bad," he'd said. "It's over," was what that meant. Over.

I wanted Phoebe. Why was she so selfish, running off around the world, just because she and Mikki broke up? The stupid bitch. Why wasn't she with me?

Focus on the wood of the pier under hands, under legs. Silver, splintery. Look at the water. Green. Real. Really here.

A boom. Too tired to be startled. What was it? Back there, back towards the setting sun. A cloud rose in the sky like a sudden storm cell, but one that birthed a shining knife. The spaceport was launching another rocket that glowed in the last light.

I looked down at my feet again. The water had stilled. Some rubbish was bobbing against my feet. It glowed faintly. No, not rubbish, jellyfish. They pulsed, little white ghosts dressed like chandeliers. Possibly deadly, if enough of them stung you. But they looked so peaceful, like faraway clouds. That cloud of little lights rose up in my peripheral vision, but I could see them this time, reflected in the water, dancing above the jellyfish.

I leant forward to look in, to see them, the lights, the clouds, the forever nature of water. Then, an urge came over me. I think not to drown, but to swim. It was so strong, that before I could think it through, I'd pushed myself forward until my butt teetered on the edge, my feet plunged through the surface of the water, my sneakers soaked and heavy. I was weak, couldn't pull myself backwards if I wanted to, my arms shaking. No, going in there was crazy, what was I doing? I kicked, trying to get back up. My arms juddered, failing.

Just get it over with.

I let go, dropped. The water slid up over my body, a cold shock. The jellyfish were all around me, still glowing. Each with a different colour. Pulsing, faster, colours like a multicoloured city light blurred through a train window. A soft, noodley tendril caressed me, then a pain like someone stabbed me and my hands spasmed and clenched. I buckled. The water parted, I dropped further. My legs plunged into the mud. Bits of twisted metal scratched my legs, rusty scrap from a drowned city. I screamed, air around me to do it. The pier's legs, crusted in slime and molluscs, dripping next to me, blood running down my leg. I screamed again, in fear this time. The waters closed over my head.

9. Peeling

Phoebe

A good night's sleep and she would feel better, but that was a pipe dream. She was so tired her face was hot and fluttery, even with the cool night air. They might come for her. There was no way to tell. She lay awake, staring at the ceiling.

Shan had left the camp. Or been banished. Unlike Apolline, it had been witnessed. She'd been loaded into one of the vans, looking thunderous, with all her stuff rammed into her backpack and thrown onto the seat beside her.

"Questions about her record," was the official line when anyone asked. Speculation around the camp seemed to vacillate between her being a government stooge or a dust-head. Shan had seemed the last person to cause any trouble, but perhaps that was what a plant was supposed to do. Be quiet, not wander around camp in the night looking for trouble. Phoebe felt sick. She might have been speaking to another operative all along. Or maybe she was innocent. Were they really taking her away or would they disappear her, much the way Apolline had gone? And what had Jerome said to them, anyway? What was he saying about her?

It was clear the little shit was a grass, telling tales about his fellow Us members for some kind of sick power game. Perhaps there were loads of these informants all through the camp. Maybe she should inform on him, concoct something to get him out of her hair for good. But he did seem to be in their good books. Right in Morgaine's yurt.

She sighed at the ceiling. It was time to get the fuck out. Things were too confusing, too dangerous. The handlers had said that she wouldn't be taken out except as a last resort, and if she called them too soon, the whole operation would be blown for good and her status would be 'in question', which had an ominous air about it. So, the only sure way to get out without a bullet in the back of the head or maybe thrown in jail forever was to do the mission.

There was only one place she wanted to access, but it wasn't as if she could snoop through the supervisor's rooms to find a blueprint with 'secret shed plans' written all over it. They locked their doors, just like she did. Besides, she doubted they were the type to keep anything like that, anyway. She'd gone through everything that Mandy had left here, but it had all seemed mundane — some hairbands, a pair of old boots, an empty suitcase jammed under the bed with a disappointing lack of secret pockets. She'd even poked at the ceiling and walls, but no hidden compartments, either.

'Supervisors and above' could get into the secured shed, knew what was in there. So that meant all the people who slept in here, and Milo and Morgaine.

She hadn't even been able to see into the structure when she walked past and saw somebody coming in or out. Something blocked the view through the door, the interior of the building screened. It was the only place she could think of that had a secret worth knowing, so she decided to kick it up the chain of command.

She got out of bed and this time remembered to pull on a fleece. Maybe they would just take her for a person who had night bladder issues.

She turned the door handle and stepped out into the dark, angling for the latrines. There wasn't anyone visible around, no laser dots on the grass this time. All seemed smooth. God, as long as Jerome wasn't hiding in the shadows somewhere, waiting to bust her.

She turned her face up as she walked. The night sky was crystalline overhead, with space traffic overpowered by the brightness of the Milky Way. The splendour of it was still incredible. She felt like she could fall up, and out, into the cosmos.

But she hoped one of those points of light up there was watching. Fuck, Shan's face as she'd been driven away, sunken in on itself in the back of the van, defeated. Was she dead now?

Phoebe stopped for a moment and stretched, head back, as if yawning. "I need to get in there," she mouthed up to the sky and left one arm out, pointing towards the centre of the camp, and the enormous, mysterious shed. If they could see her, they should get what she meant. It was the only thing in that direction big enough to be of interest.

As long as their monitoring systems were sharp enough to see her at night, and she rather suspected they would be, then it was their problem to get her access. All she could do now was wait. And keep looking as innocent as possible.

Selen

Shadows flicker past me, people rendered in black ink. I'm walking the streets of old Glasgow but they're hazy, watercolour sketches. The buildings are so tall and square they make me panicked that they'll fall on me. How do they withstand the storms?

I run down a street that is so hard it hurts my feet. Everything is concrete, a shell over the world. I knew it was supposed to be like this, but the history lessons left out this feeling, this feedback of thump-thump jolting up your heels. Why did they do it? Why any of it?

So many people, it's crazy. They're crowding me, fun-nelled along these hardened streets. I can hear them. My body tunnel's static has tuned, modulated into voices. Too many, too loud. They sound like they're angry at each other, shouting, aggressive. They don't see me, would walk right through me. I dodge and try to get away.

The buildings turn from stacks and blocks to walls. Two walls and no space, no trees, no arcades, no communes in mounds of soft grass. They put people inside these walls, to man the ramparts? They called them tenements. Walls of little boxes with people kept separate, kept paying to live. I see them through windows, windows that are far too big, won't withstand the next Big One from the Atlantic. Or the Deluge. They'll sunder under the waters.

I'm running further, though it hurts so much. How can I breathe? Old Glasgow is drowned, isn't it?

Another shadow looms over the roof of their tenements, a sly finger too big. It writhes along the rooftops, curls down to the ground in front of me. A tentacle. Soon it's joined by another, and another. The skin on them flashes bright red, ultramarine, yellow, brown, flickers fast as thought. They wave gently as an anemone in the water. Then they come together into a point and come straight at me.

The saltwater comes into my nose once more and I fall.

Phoebe

She was in the Pavilion, eating lunch: a shitty ration of badly-cooked millet and beans that stuck to the inside of her throat as it went down. Phoebe avoided sitting with people whenever she could. She was too tired to talk, and if she rushed through her food, she could lock herself in her room until shift started again. They hadn't come for her. Not yet. She needed it to stay that way as long as possible.

A loud bang echoed through the camp like a cannon had gone off, and the ground trembled. Silence as heads turned towards the sound, forks halfway to faces, then Milo half-jumping out of his plastic seat, kicking it back and it tumbling away, and he was running. More chairs scraped back, everyone flocking, pressing to see what was going on.

She got up to follow them, just as worried. Bureau better not have decided to come in guns blazing, shoot first, no questions to answer later. She pictured the bivouacs on fire and tear gas spreading out and as she got out from under the Pavilion. Was that exactly what she was seeing?

Smoke rose over the camp not far from the grow shed. "Should we take cover?" someone asked. A tall figure appeared. Louis. He was waving. Signalling not to panic. He turned and jogged back. They streamed out from the Pavilion to follow him. Yes, it had been coming from the mystery shed, but it wasn't an attack, no gun drones or military. A small crowd had already gathered nearby and there was some shocked laughter.

Phoebe couldn't see over the tall New Aus backs. She tried to tap a shoulder, get them to tell her what was going on, but then Morgaine appeared. She looked gravely on, then spoke in her dry, low voice. "Back off, everyone, give me some room." The bystanders parted and she stalked to the front, by the wreckage of something metallic, crumpled. It had smashed down, almost vertically, through the wall of the shed.

"Looks like a splatellite, boss." Milo was there. The big man was sweating, face pasted with a relieved grin. "Didn't get anything inside. Lucky," he said as she squatted to poke about at the debris.

Inside. There was a curtain of fumes, but the space junk had fallen at such a steep angle that there was a gaping hole in the side of the shed but no other serious damage, not even much shrapnel. Still not quite visible. Phoebe squeezed up her eyes, out here in the harsh midday sun without a hat or sunglasses. She shaded her face with her hand, but the contrast was still too high. No clue what was in there.

Morgaine looked around at the little crowd, her head swivelling. "We need to get this hole covered. You." She pointed at Mandy. "You." Sweetie. "And you." Phoebe. "Get some ag sheeting and get this patched before I lose my fucking temper."

Morgaine shouted at others to get the wreckage cleared. Phoebe could almost see large shapes inside now, but Mandy and Sweetie had already left at a lope to get the things that Morgaine wanted, so she pelted after them.

Morgaine wasn't happy, that was for sure, but as far as she knew it was just another splatellite, just another abandoned relic finally given in to gravity. Surely, she couldn't suspect what Phoebe did: that the Bureau had precisely lobbed it just to give her the chance she had now?

She could hardly think as she jogged after Mandy, helped her pick up sheeting and battens and fixings, just a bright blank inside her mind made worse by the reflections glaring off the plastic. She nearly dropped it all and ended up dragging the roll of stuff beside her like she was trying to dispose of a body, tried not to gawp as Mandy directed the patch job. The guts of the mystery shed were visible. Large vats, industrial sized, covered the concrete pad inside. She still wasn't enlightened. There was a smell, like the inside of a whisky distillery, musty, dusty, malty, and maybe a hint of ethanol. *Was all this secrecy for some goddamn hooch?*

The crowd was dispersing, with some other lower members of Us looking over their shoulders at the gap, but there was Morgaine again. "Agro bacteria," she said loudly. "It's for the land farm, helps with bioremediation. The rest of you get back to it." She turned and walked away. She hadn't met anyone's eyes.

Phoebe held bits of battening still while others drilled it in a frame around the gap. The ground was still hot from the splatellite's landing beneath but some other team had cleared away the mess and filled in the small crater with salty Pans dirt. The funny thing was, Mandy was not relaxing, not yet. "For fuck's sake, hurry it up," she snapped. Despite the fact that the sheeting was nearly in place and Morgaine had calmed down. Why was she so jittery over a hole in a shed wall for some pollutant-eating microbiology?

Unless, of course, it wasn't anything that benign. And they didn't want it getting out.

This thought only got stronger when Jerome swaggered over with a bucket of a clear liquid that didn't move like water, a sprayer attached to a hose, and a smirk. "You girls gonna line up against the shed and strip for me," he said casually. "Decontamination time."

Mandy seethed at him but started to take off her clothes. Sweetie met Phoebe's eye, hesitating as much as she was.

"Just fucking do it," Mandy snarled. "This isn't a game."

10: Hit

Selen

Lying there, arms out, feeling each and every grain of dirt and small, round rock like a princess with so, so many peas. I groaned and looked at the sky. Not mine. The sky above Alba never looked like this. Was this the future? Was this the next apocalypse? I turned my head, looked out along the length of my arm and suddenly I could see myself from above.

I'd been crucified by dirt, a splash of darker red, sea-wet earth around me, lighter, burnt and bleached soil, dirt, dry further out and out. My body had carved a little trench, like a plough furrow. The outlines of my limbs started to bend and blur, get lost in a heat-haze as I got higher and higher above.

"No!" I shouted but it was a wheeze.

It took me back inside myself at least. My mod was making sounds like a piston, like the hydraulics on a dredger. It was slowing, the sound moving down the pitches. Then rumbling. I could feel the earth vibrate beneath me and the world disappear in a cloud of red. Choking me. I coughed and gasped. It wasn't my mod making noises. It was some big-arse vehicle.

The cloud dissipated and a man stood over me. He had brown skin, a sheen of sweat. He wore sunglasses, the type that wrap on to your head. He was looking at me, a question that wasn't getting past his lips.

I wanted to ask when am I, where am I, who? But instead, I just made a noise like *lerrpp*.

A wry smile crinkled up the man's face and he shook his head in wonder.

"G'day," he said. "What you doing out here?"

Phoebe

The Pavilion would be bristling with the arrival of the new spuds, more recruits from Harro's Horde. Another tanker of freshwater to top up their reserves, and some left-over K-Fire to be locked prudently away in stores. Phoebe podded seeds, watered seedlings, transported trays around the grow shed.

There was more of a hubbub than usual, though. People passed, gossiping to each other, eyes all going one direction. And there was a strange edge to the voices, more than the influx normally caused. She frowned at their backs. Was it someone else getting frogmarched out of camp? Was it some kind of setup for her? Maybe they'd brought in word of a Bureau operation in their midst and were setting up her execution squad.

"You might as well go over and pick us up some more tea for smoko, since you're so curious." Mandy was staring at her. Her hand was on the tea caddy which she shook meaning-fully as she raised an eyebrow.

She did not want to go but she couldn't reasonably talk her way out of it. Phoebe jog-trotted along behind others towards the centre of camp and kept her shaking hands in her pockets.

The area of the Pavilion by the ring of chairs for new spuds was a scrum, with people standing around, rubber-necking at something inside the circle. Some were even standing on the dining tables, trying to get a view.

She spotted Sweetie, who was craning her neck to see, and poked her shoulder. "What's going on?" Phoebe stage-whis-pered. There was a hubbub of voices, none of which seemed to be directing things. Phoebe couldn't hear Morgaine. Of course, if Morgaine were speaking no-one else would be.

"The Horde found some girl out at the edge of camp, Harro bought her in with the rest of the new spuds," Sweetie told her from the side of her mouth. "Nobody knows if she's a plant, or what. Said they found her in a huge puddle of water, just sitting there. It's like she just dropped out of the sky."

Was the Bureau up to something? Who was this girl? Phoebe tried standing on her tiptoes.

The voices died down. Morgaine must be there, must have signalled them to shut up. "I'll ask you, one last time. What are you doing here, and who sent you?"

The voice that gave the reply sent shivers down Phoebe's spine. "I don't know, no-one sent me. I swear." *What? No. No, no, no.*

"Get this bitch out of my sight." Morgaine stood up from the chair circle. Phoebe could see her now, and her expression was murderous.

"Let me through." Phoebe started pulling people out of the way. She took a few swinging elbows to her body and face as she desperately tried to push her way forward. "She's my sister!" she blurted before she knew what she was saying.

This brought a new kind of silence and people drew away from her like fat from a soap bubble. She saw the full horror of what waited in the chair circle. Selen, hanging limp between Reggie and Harro, Milo standing by, looking ominous. And she looked so pale, so sick, covered in red dirt with torn trousers. And then, there was that great big hole punched through her middle. She'd seen photos of it but the wrongness of being able to see the background through her was like an optical illusion, a trick, a fake-out.

"What the fuck, Sel?"

"Your sister?" Morgaine looked at her and now the threat seemed to fall on them equally.

"Yes. I didn't ask her to come! I don't know what she's thinking." Would the Bureau have done this? Would Selen have been stupid enough to agree?

"I tried to tell them," Selen said, and her voice was horrific, ragged. "I don't know what's happening to me. I was in Alba. It was night. I was drowning. Something is wrong... with me." At this, she started crying and Phoebe bolted across the space to try to, what? Do something, grab her, take her somewhere safe? If she could huckle her outside, get the open sky above her, mouth the words, 'crash, crash', maybe...

But Milo and Harro fended her off, pushing her back.

"Get out of here, sis," Selen said. Her voice was weird, strained. "Get far away." She looked about ready to faint, her head was rolling, lolling.

"No, I don't think she will," said Morgaine. "Take them both to the shed."

Selen let out a cry like an animal, and Phoebe tried to back away, but the circle had re-formed behind her and there was nowhere to go. Something was pulled over her eyes and there was a thump and a blinding pain. She was suddenly on the ground. Her nose rubbed against coarse hessian texture; they'd put a seed sack over her head. Rough hands lifted her, half-carrying her, dragging her along. The light through the loose woven fabric brightened, she must be out from under the Pavilion's canopy. She started thrashing, struggling, hoping it would make her more visible to the Bureau. Even if they couldn't read her lips, they could see she was in trouble.

If they were watching. Surely the splatellite, that surgical strike on the shed that damaged none of the contents but allowed her a look inside was a sign that they were there, that they had her best interests at heart? Unless the dispatcher of the cavalry was on smoko at this exact moment, she thought. Gallows humour. They were probably about to line her up against a shed and put some holes in her and her stupid sister. "Sel!" she screamed. "Selen?"

Some muffled noise. "Shut the fuck up, or I'll hit you again, last warning." Milo. She believed him, but what was the threat if she was about to die anyway?

It darkened again. There was that odd smell, machine-thrumming. She was hurled onto a hard surface, hit her head and passed out.

Selen

I should never have gone with them, but I had been bleeding in a desert, my throat burning with thirst and the man had given me water. I'd promptly thrown it back up onto the red dirt that was everywhere, everywhere. He'd given me more water, warm, wrong-tasting, metallic, urged me to sip it, and then they'd helped me to get into the tray of a truck. And then that weird woman had me taken in here and tied up.

"Feebs," I croaked. "Wake up. Don't be fucking dead."

That would be the ultimate end to my run of luck. Killing my sister. Because I'd landed here – fuck knows how – and these people seemed to take my presence as some kind of threat. "Shit," I hissed with feeling.

I was in a big dark building with my sister lying beaten on the floor. The people who'd grabbed me and dragged me into this place had me had taped me to a chair, so tight my hands and feet were throbbing. They'd dropped Feebs, hard, and it looked like she'd hit her head. They'd slapped her and shouted at her, but she hadn't responded so they left her lying and went over to there. That airlock entryway thing.

Glass box. To have a little argument. Their words were all muffled, they were waving their arms about.

Feebs wasn't answering. I had to stay alert. God knows what might happen to my sister, to this place if I stopped concentrating.

"Phoebe Remy Muir, I swear to everything, you better wake up before I pass out."

I was on the other side of the world. New Australia. It had to be, because that's where Phoebe was. My mod brought me here because I wanted her. I wanted my sister. I wanted her to make it all better, and now she was here, lying on the floor in a huge, dark building. There was something horrible about this place. I had a horrible sensation all over me. Phoebe was supposed to be on a meditation retreat. What the fuck was all this? These people?

The mod knew what I wanted. Now, I wanted out of here. It had to know that; it knew me. But it was still too dangerous.

If the mod knew me, though, why had it thrown Jayce out of my bed? Did I really want that to happen? Did it know that deep down I knew he was going to be a dick to me? And what about the ferry? God, what did I want? Was I monster?

I'd never really known what I wanted, that was the trouble. It was time to start making decisions. Because my sister was moving, slowly writhing on the floor, and those arseholes were coming back in.

11. Reckon

Phoebe

When she woke, the bag on her head was gone, her face rasped by concrete as she moved. She could see Morgaine, peering at her like an owl, taking up the entire universe. "Good, you've got some questions to answer."

"You'd better not have hurt my sister," Phoebe weakly. Her head throbbed and her eyes stung, her throat was raw. She was lying prone on the floor and couldn't feel her hands, couldn't move her arms. They'd been tied behind her. Sticky, rubbing duct tape, wire-tight, on her wrists, her arms wrenched back.

"What, this brat?" Morgaine moved, pointed angrily, and Phoebe could make out some feet. There was something wrong with them. Her sister's ankles were taped to one of the plastic chairs from the Pavilion. She couldn't see much else. Selen had been wearing long sleeves, long trousers, out of character for her. Had she really been working with the Bureau then? She'd looked bad though, sick.

"You let her go," she heaved out. She was having difficulty getting enough air in her lungs. The atmosphere in this place. In the mystery shed. It was thick, almost sludgy. "What are you doing to us?"

"Me? Nothing. This is all your own doing. You wanted to get in here, didn't you?" Morgaine stood up now, paced about, waving at the huge shapes of the vats. "You happy now?"

"I don't understand."

"You don't, because I haven't told you," Morgaine said. "I don't intend to either, you stupid little fuck. But you? You're going to talk."

Milo came from somewhere back in the shadows and kicked her, hard, in the ribs. Phoebe felt, or rather heard, something go ping in her side. A rib maybe. She grunted with the pain, but Selen was mewling, over there in the chair. Harro must be doing something to her. Fuck, they had to hold out until the Bureau got here. It could be several minutes; it could be hours.

"Wait," she said, "I'll tell you everything you want to know, just give me a chance."

Morgaine spread her hands and then sat near her on the floor in a half-lotus like an indulgent mum about to listen to her child telling her a fairy tale. "Go ahead, I'm all ears."

"I was contacted, while I was backpacking," Phoebe said, coughing. "A guy met me in a bar." She would have to spin this out as long as she could, but the room was spinning too, darkening at the edges of her vision. Selen was taped to the chair, wrists and ankles, Milo holding her head back by the hair. "I was just backpacking. All of that is the truth. But I got in trouble. With the visa. He told me that you were a cult, you were planning something, some terrorist plot. I didn't believe him, but if I didn't do what he said he'd jail me, or deport me, and I wasn't ready to go. Go back." She coughed again, a searing, painful mistake. Was she going to choke up blood? Like a character on a show?

This wasn't happening, it couldn't be.

"Who contacted you? Who sent you, sent her?" Her little sister. There was blood on her. That wasn't right, couldn't be happening either. Taped to a chair, bleeding, crying. Not right. "This little knuck with spacer tech in her, and you, been sent by the space corporations? Huh?" Morgaine leaned

267

in close, her voice menacingly soft. "Little bit of industrial espionage from you, is it?"

"No, she's nothing... to do... It was me, it was the Bureau. Bureau of..." What was it? The name had absconded from her head. "Fucking something security. New Aus Security..."

Morgaine stood bolt upright. She jerked her head at Milo, saying, "Decontaminate later, we got to move," and they exited the shed, the code lock beeping and engaging again as they shut the door. Phoebe wasn't at all sure whether 'decontaminate' referred to the stuff in the vats or her. And Selen. Were they a contamination to eliminate?

"I'm sorry, Feebs," Selen said, crying. "I didn't mean to..."

"No, shut up." Phoebe was angry but not at Selen, she couldn't help being a fuck-up, a liability. It was a savage thought, but no, not now. Now there were more important things. "We get out of this, then we say sorry."

"I can, I think I can get..." Selen stopped and looked at her in the most strange manner, like she was gazing at one of her shows, when you could shout at her and she'd ignore you, locking the world out of her little bubble. There was a loud buzzing, humming noise, something coming from near her, what was she up to? Then she stood up, a shower of coloured sparks fizzing and fading in the darkness.

Phoebe hissed in shock.

"It's the mod, I'll explain later, if there is a later. It feels weird in here, like worms burrowing..." Selen touched the lacuna in her belly. Then she came back to herself and rushed over to rip and tear at the duct tape around Phoebe's wrists, too loud, taking too long. "Can you get up? Did they break anything?"

"Muh..." Phoebe was still numb. What had her sister just done? She looked at the chair. The duct tape restraints were still there, perfect little loops where Sel's limbs had been.

Phoebe got to all fours, shaking the blood back into her hands, then pushed herself up, searing agony from her side. "What did you just do?"

"It's the mod," she said absently, "been acting strange lately. I thought it was the sun, but I fell off the pier when it was nearly night. Nearly sank a ferry from inside the cabin. I guess it must be using sunlight to charge, or something."

"What the hell?"

Sel looked around, at the vats, at the machinery. "It doesn't like it here," she whispered. "What's in these tanks?"

"I dunno, listen," she grabbed for her sister's shoulder, and the movement nearly put her down again as her ribs stretched. She recovered, swallowed the yell that queued up at the back of her throat. "We have to get out of here. Can you, you know, do that? What you just did? But, uh, bigger? Could you get through a wall or something?"

"I don't know. I can't make it do anything. I have to not think and then it does stuff."

"What? What are you on about?"

Sel limped off, looking at the looming shapes around her, rubbing her mod again, ignoring the question. "Is..." she breathed, sounding strained, "...is the stuff in here bad for elagite? It's making my mod feel itchy. What kind of people are they, anyway?"

Phoebe halted, shook her head. No. Couldn't be. But it made a kind of sense. Bioremediation. That's what they were all about. Using bacteria and stuff to cleanse the earth. Elagite, elageum, the miracle materials that made space travel all possible. "Listen, we need to go. Get out of here. The Bureau's coming, but..." She had a bad feeling about the fate of anyone who stood inside this shed. Would they discriminate, would they firebomb the whole place?

Morgaine and Mandy been so panicky when the hole was gouged in the side of the shed. Like they didn't want it getting out. The humiliation as Jerome had laughed when he doused them in that horrible liquid. They didn't want it getting out before they were ready. The Bureau would have noted that, would have drawn their own conclusions. If she was right about it. God, it could be something else. But what else? They'd said it was something big and this was about as big as she could imagine. Maybe it wouldn't be that difficult to escape. The shed was already holed.

"C'mon," Phoebe said, and guided her sister to the patch of plastic sheeting, in the side of the shed, that they still hadn't permanently fixed. She held a finger up and cocked her head. The layers of plastic were too thick to see through, so she listened. Was there a guard outside? Was that commotion in the distance? Were the Bureau attacking?

A gunshot, perhaps the sniper on top of the Pavilion, and Phoebe backpedalled. Maybe taking some early warning shots or... trouble in the camp? Whatever. They wouldn't get very far across the Pans with him about. She pulled her sister away from the flimsy plastic, into a dark corner behind the vats.

"Listen, I don't expect you to understand this, but there's something... Something these people are doing that is crazy, terrible. But..."

How could she say this? If Morgaine was trying to regreen the planet, stop people from going into space by infecting all the elagite and elegeum in the world, wouldn't that force people to make earth a better place? But wouldn't people die if the bacteria started eating space shuttles? On the other hand, if spacers were dying, wouldn't that be a worse harm than doing nothing? And this was all guesswork. The Bureau were coming and would likely flatten the area.

"Fuck," she said, with feeling. "This is too tricky. Look. We need to get out of here." Maybe, if they could get away, they could tell the world about the cancer, the regreening, make everyone do the right thing for a change. The trouble was, she had no idea how to do any of that.

"I think I can do it. But. I might get us hurt. Or we could die, I don't know," Selen said, and her face crumpled. "I don't think I can control it."

"We're going to die anyway," Phoebe said, and her stomach lurched, because it was true. "If Morgaine doesn't kill us, the Bureau might." She coughed again, and this time when she wiped her mouth, there was blood. Milo's boot had done its damage. "Do what you got to do."

"Here, lie next to me." Her sister got down on the floor. Phoebe looked at her. "This is what I 'got to do', so get your rickety old arse down here." Phoebe's knees nearly buckled.

She lay down on the concrete, on the side that wasn't sore, facing her sister. "What now?"

"I have to... I have to not think. Tell me a story."

"I... What the fuck?"

"Like when we were kids. It's to relax me, let the mod take over. Tell me about Old Glasgow."

Oh. Two girls, one little, dangling her feet over the water at the pier, one big, telling her made-up nonsense patched out of half-remembered history, of a city lost beneath the waves...

This was insane. She could picture the Bureau about to send an airstrike in, and this shed becoming a fireball.

"Feebs. Sis!" Selen was begging her, tugging on her sleeve, like she used to when they were kids.

They were going to die, weren't they? Perhaps that was the way to end things right, with a story. Go back to then, back to when things were easier. When the world seemed big enough.

"Once, in Old Glasgow," she began, her voice trembling, "they had a big building where they would play music, and dance, and sing, only it was shaped just like an armadillo..."

Selen closed her eyes. And let go of her sleeve to take her hand.

Selen

I couldn't do it, couldn't switch off. I tried to focus on the words my sister said, but I couldn't do it, I couldn't save her. Why had my mod sent me here? Why couldn't it have let me drown? Let me sleep? Why can I never sleep when I most need to?

...Once upon a time in Old Glasgow there were millions of people on the streets. Everyone drove around in cars that melted icebergs and suffocated babies. Sometimes they drove them faster than they needed to, just for fun, letting out even more of the poisons. Poison for fun. Poison for the world...

Years of studying for exams. Never able to sleep the night before an exam. All those years wasted in filling my head with knowledge that I had never intended to use, all a neat way to refuse the world, refuse getting a real job, refuse to do what they called growing up, what I called slavery.

Yet.

I did know a lot. I knew about elagite. Its chemical formula. Its bonds, its twining, DNA-like structure. I'd learned it and discarded the information. I'd never wanted to be a materials scientist, but my parents had been disappointed in me, urging me to find something respectable to do with my life, but what was the point of doing something respectable when no-one really cared? Like Phoebe, like how she rose to the heady position of fund administrator, doling out money to students like me, whoop-de-doo, unassailable. But who the fuck said her name? Not like they did at Jayce's shibboleths, chanting and bouncing in the impromptu gig's freedom. Being real, though, do any of them care about him, either? Will he be remembered forever? Or flushed down the toilet when the next thing comes along?

You've got to let go.

...Once upon a time in Old Glasgow, there was a metal armadillo. It was an auditorium, a concert hall with metal petals for a roof. People danced and sung inside it, held hands, hugged, kissed, watched enraptured while people did art. In the time before the Deluge when the streets were dry as bone and the straits were shrunk down to a river called the Clyde...

Elagite, space travel, all supposed to be the greatest endeavour of mankind. The second great space race, all centred around Alba, around the port at Killie where my parents work. The lottery to shift the majority of the planet's population into space. The people left behind, like me, like Phoebe, Mum and Dads, a skeleton crew. Skeletons dancing, sharing their art. That's what I wanted art for. To share part of me, to become bigger. To link my Venn diagram with other people's, until we bubbled bigger and bigger all together. Sharing, that is what I wanted. Not art. Yes, art. Art and people are one thing. Human.

Sound of shouting outside. That big gun popping again. They're coming in here again. Time's up.

You've got to let go.

The elagite wired to my subconscious. The exact opposite of what would have been useful. Typical for me, the exact wrong thing. But. It is me. My subconscious self is me. It knows what I want, what I need. It knew to come here, to find Phoebe. Because she needed me. I should trust it. Trust it will do what is best. Why don't I trust myself? Why is my sister trusting me? She shouldn't trust me, I can never—

Shut it off. Sharing. People and art are one. You are one. You are everyone.

...Once upon a time in Old Glasgow. A tentacle beastie lurks in old tenement buildings, deep beneath the crushing black gloom of the Deluge. It's looking for little girls who go swimming in the straits...

Ach! C'mon now. It's time.

Let go.

Little bokeh lights rise in the air above us.

Phoebe

Hauled, light flash, giddy ground movement. A shower of dirt exploding around them, Phoebe throwing up an arm over her face and the air whooshing out of her and a burst of heat on her skin.

She panted, felt hard lumps of the iron-dry Pans' earth beneath her, and choked and coughed up dust and salt. The atmosphere cleared and soon she felt her sister' hand. Still holding on.

Selen sat up beside her, looking towards something, kilometres across the flats. A fireball bloomed up into the sky, like the rocket launches from the space port back home, but instead of white clouds, they were a dark and angry orange.

A gun-drone, a biggie, swooped overhead towards it, only to stop and hover as if perplexed. Phoebe inched her head around to look behind them. A dust plume was heading their way, half-miraged, but she thought maybe it was the Bureau, finally. And it looked like she'd been right about their plans for ending Us.

But she wasn't inside, dying in a fireball. She was here, safe, sitting next to Selen.

"What did...?" she couldn't manage much more.

"Lot of sunshine out here," her sister said. "I think when we appeared over here, the reaction appeared over there. Look, it's hard to explain."

There was the *tink-tink* of cooling metal, coming from somewhere, coming from inside Selen. Phoebe licked her lips, then regretted letting even that little moisture out. It was hot, too hot out here. She hoped the Bureau would see them and stop, and help and give them water, and fix her ribs, deaden the pain.

Selen scooched over to support her sitting up properly, leaned her head into hers. "My big sis, you've always been there for me. It was my turn, let's face it."

"I'm sorry, I think this is trouble," Phoebe said. "The Bureau, they're going to want to know what you did, how you did it. How the fuck did you do it? By the way?"

"Ach," Selen said, rocking her a little, gentle. "It's okay. I've always wanted something real to do." Not really answering the question there, but Phoebe didn't have the energy to fight. "Now, tell me, who was this Spacer who locked us up?"

And Phoebe spent the next few minutes, dry-hacking up dirt between words, trying to explain Morgaine and what she thought was going on, how the cult was going to regreen the earth and stop space travel so that spacers wouldn't die of cancer and techfucks and space corps wouldn't leave the rest of humanity to rot. How they were going to use the stuff in the vats, maybe? To bioremediate, breakdown elagite to prevent space travel? Or something?

Sel laughed, low. "Guess this won't last long then," she said, touching her body mod again. "But, did you agree with them? What they were going to do?"

"I don't know. I got so tired, so stressed, I didn't really have the brain," she waved a hand over her head, "room, space, to think about it properly." Selen grunted with what sounded like a bone-deep understanding of what that meant.

"I think they were going to break a lot of stuff to try to save a lot of people, maybe? I think some folk would have died because of them. But then, so many up in space might die." It was an ethical conundrum, a hypothetical body count game, the type clever people would illustrate with little diagrams and scenarios, all the while ignoring that these were real people being chewed up and spat out. She could only go with her gut because time was running out. It felt wrong to let corporations give people systemic cancer without any pushback. It felt wrong that the Earth wasn't green. And wasn't for people any more, not really.

"What if we told everybody?" Sel said, breaking into her spiralling thoughts.

"Who'd listen?"

"Mum and Dads would listen. They'd be worried about their jobs, about the future of space travel, humans, that sort of thing, but they'd listen. They always listen to me." And Phoebe supposed that must be true. Their little girl, the one they'd let be a perma-student. They'd listen. And they had privilege, the type that were so important they didn't have to be part of the lottery.

And they were home. She started to cry.

The sound of engines and driving was getting louder. Selen tilted her head to look at the approaching vehicles, up at the gun-drone. "Do you think they'll let us talk? Do you think they'll let any of this out?"

Phoebe closed her eyes. The world was going foggy again. She shook her head slowly. "I think the best they'll do is put us in a deep dark hole," she said. "I don't think any governments or corporations want any of this getting out." She eyed her sister, sitting pale in the burning sunlight, her arm around her.

Maybe they shouldn't have stopped Morgaine. Maybe she was right, maybe the ends did justify...

The world went blue at the edges, then she fell through it.

12: Staircase

Selen

I dangle my feet off the end of the pier again and watch ribbons of reflected sky blue scribble and break over the dark green of the Clyde Straits. Buoys crusted with algae bob along in a line out to the deeper channels. I shiver thinking about the things I thought I saw down there, but they weren't real. No dark tentacles are waiting for me. It was all just a dream. Or a memory. Maybe I portalled through time as well as space. Who knows?

Behind me, footsteps make music on the silvery old boards of the pier. Phoebe joins me, sitting down slowly, gingerly. Apart from the injury, though, she looks relaxed. I never realised how much that meant to me until now.

She leans to one side and covers her healing ribs with her hand, grimacing. "We've both got dodgy sides now," she says with a dry laugh.

I got Ken to remove the body tunnel and I look like a whole person again. From the outside, at least. Since the fronds of elagite that grew out of my mod are being eaten up by the cultist's bugs, I guess my time with these superpowers (ha!) are limited.

It's not like it did anything for me that I wanted. And yet, I somehow portalled through to the other side of the planet. I was looking for something useful, a talent. I would never be like Jayce. Not that I would want to, now. It seems ridiculous I was ever attracted to someone that awful. But I did this. That has to be up there as 'impressive', but it wasn't intentional. And intent is everything in art. Or life.

"I wonder what I could have done with it," I say out loud. "Maybe if I'd been any better at being a person, I'd have used it for, you know, good."

"Nah, you can't think like that," she says. She's still got a trace of Aussieness about her accent and it's cute. "Governments would probably just be poking you, trying to figure out how it all works so they can turn it into a weapon or something." Her time working for the Bureau of whatever-it-was has given her a jaundiced view of these things, something I never thought would happen to upright old Feebs. She looks at the scar on my stomach, considering. "And I don't know if it wouldn't have given you what the Spacers had." Cancer. A weird, old-fashioned disease. I shiver and hope the bugs do a good job of clearing it out.

"Do you think she was right?" I say. Phoebe knows who I'm talking about. Morgaine.

She sighs and kicks the soles of her sneakers over the top of the water, just high enough to not get them wet. "I don't know. I'm glad Louis got out though. He was a nice guy. I haven't heard from Shan yet, but I think she's alive."

The explosion at the shed hadn't taken everyone out. A lot of the lower ranked cultist types survived. Were arrested, but alive, according to the splash feeds. But the leader, the one called Morgaine, and the thug who kicked my sister, breaking her ribs... they were gone in the blast. I have feelings about the people that died there, that I killed. I'll have to deal with them, sometime, but there are more immediate things to consider.

"Do you think they'll come for us? The spooks, I mean," I ask her. When we were kids, she acted as if she knew everything, but new Phoebe seems unsure. I guess the experience has changed her, like it or not. Me too. It's not necessarily a bad thing. It's different. We're finding our way.

"I think... I hope they'll find it too difficult to work out what happened. Or prove it, at least." We were there, in New Aus. Then we weren't. "And to be honest, they've got bigger issues."

The blast back in that giant shed destroyed a lot of the smelly bacteria, but not all of it. A lot went into the atmosphere. Some went into the water when we splashed down in the Clyde Straits. We would have drowned if we hadn't been seen by a passing kelp farmer in his boat, but the contamination had already leached out after it had a good feed on my mod.

The bugs were designed to not harm anything except elagite. Just to ride around on skin, in water, in the air, multiplying until they infect their target. I know this because they've put all launches from the Killie Space Port on hold, and similar reports have come from New Aus and some of the Queensland and Pacific Republic. They're looking into metal fatigue, according to the official spiel my parents were given. But we know better. Earth's phasing into quarantine. Any ships that come down are going to stay down. No more one in, one out policy. They'll just have to deal with it, hopefully without anyone starving in the meantime. But they can't keep it a secret any more.

"Did you get enough sleep, yet?" my sister asks.

"Yeah. I had to stop Mum and Dads grilling me about it all, but I think they got the picture when I passed out on the sofa."

"They'll still leak it all out, right?"

"Yup. Daddy A's already reached out to his contacts in China." About Morgaine, Spacer Cancer, elagite. The whole thing. "Thanks for helping. Even after everything, they couldn't really get their heads round it. Can't say I blame them." Once they'd spoken to Phoebe and every single space launch from their place of work got scrubbed, they'd come round, sharpish. Even Mum was on side. A minor miracle.

"I don't think I'd have believed you if I hadn't been there," she says. Then she catches herself. "Sorry, sis. You know what I mean."

"It's okay. I've been..." I scrunch up my face. Everything hits me at once. Jayce, the body tunnel, the lack of any grip on my future. "I've been a little shit."

Phoebe watches one of the seabirds, hovering out over the straits hunting for fish. "A little shit who saved my bacon. And, look, I could have been there for you. You know, helped you a bit more. I buggered off to New Aus because of the breakup with Mikki. I didn't like who it made me. I ran away."

I smile, grimly. "Well, you're human. But no, Sis, this was on me. I refused to do the work. To figure out who I wanted to be. Because I was scared, too."

She takes my hand softly. "And now? What are we now?"

"Maybe we should go back. There." I feel her hand tense up. I turn to her. "What you told me about Morgaine. Do you think that she had a point, at all? Regreening the Earth, getting the Spacers home?"

"She was trying to do something. I don't know. But, one day, I think I'd like to go back to the Pans."

I raise an eyebrow.

"I'd like to, you know, say sorry to her... her ghost or her memory. It sounds stupid." I put my arm around her shoulder and gently pull her close. "I don't agree with what she did, but I think I get it now. And they were doing something. There was a long way to go, but it might have eventually worked. I just don't understand how we aren't all trying to change things."

"I've always wanted to be an artist," I say softly. "To do something real."

She pulls away from me to give me a confused look.

"Green's my favourite colour," I say, and she smiles when she gets it.

Maybe we'll start at home. There must be projects that could help rehabilitate the environment right here. Then maybe, when the dust's settled, we can go over to the Pans, paint a desert with life. It's big. I'm scared. But now I know what I want to do. And Feebs is so damn practical. We'll get things done.

I look out over the straits again, across to BL city. The launches that take off and shuttle people up to the star traffic out of Killie are silent today. Those bugs that came out of me, swimming around in water, in air, eating away a super-power I never wanted.

"Hey," I say. "You remember the staircase to the stars?" Silly little stories, that little girls told each other. About water, about space, about armadillo buildings where people danced and sang. About lights dancing off the water and all the way up into the sky.

"Yeah?"

"We only went and broke it."

THE END

ACKNOWLEDGEMENTS

My sincerest thanks to Joanne Hall and Roz Clarke for championing this book all this long way. You didn't give up and I cannot say how much that means. Thanks also to Cheryl Morgan for rescuing the project and helping it to finally come to fruition.

Many thanks to Premee Mohamed for the info on land reclamation and salt sequestering—you're a star. Scientific errors are my own, or artistic license.

A huge shout out to the people who always support me: the wonderful CL Hellisen for their friendship and solidarity in the word mines, the fabulous members of the Glasgow SF Writers' Circle and British Fantasy Society who continuously inspire me to keep going, and the community of writers, readers, and industry pros that cluster around genre conventions and online. I've made so many friends along the way I can't possibly name you all or thank you enough, but I see you and appreciate everything you've done.

And finally, thanks as always to my rock, my constant source of encouragement, Doug, for putting up with this journey. Honestly, I could not have done it without your love and support.

—*E.M. Faulds*

ABOUT THE AUTHORS AND EDITORS

Juliet Kemp (they/them) is a queer, non-binary, writer. They live in London by the river, with their partners, kid, and dog. The first book of their fantasy series, *The Deep And Shining Dark*, was a Locus 2018 Recommended Read; the fourth and final book, *The City Revealed*, came out in 2023. Their short fiction has appeared in venues including *Uncanny*, *Analog*, and *Cast of Wonders*. They were short-listed for the WSFA Small Press Award in 2020 and 2023, and featured in the 2021 Lambda Awards shortlisted antholoy *Trans-Galactic Bike Ride*.

When not writing or child-wrangling, Juliet knits, indulges their fountain pen habit, and tries to fit an ever-increasing number of plants into a microscopic inner-city back garden. They can be found at https://julietkemp.com, on Bluesky as @julietk.bsky.social, or on Mastodon as @juliet@zirk.us.

E.M. Faulds is an Australian who lives near Glasgow, Scotland, in the oldest house in town. She has short stories published in *Strange Horizons*, *ParSec*, and *Shoreline of Infinity* magazines. Her first novel, *Ada King*, came out in 2015 and *Under the Moon: Collected Speculative Fiction* (Ghost Moth Press) won the 2023 British Fantasy Award for Best Collection.

Find her at emfaulds.com.

Roz Clarke likes to play around with words; her own and other people's. She has short stories in several anthologies, edits novels for Kristell Ink, and is best known for her editing partnership with Joanne Hall, which has produced such anthologies as *Airship Shape & Bristol Fashion* and the BSFA award-nominated *Fight Like A Girl*. You can twt her at @zora_db, or skeet @rozc.bsky.social.

Jo Hall was formerly Acquisitions Editor at Grimbold Books and loves working with authors to help them unleash their visions on the world (for good or ill). Her novels have previously been shortlisted for the Tiptree, Lambda and British Fantasy awards. She can be found on Bluesky @ hierath77.bsky.com.

Roz and Jo have been working together since the Bristol F&SF group started running BristolCon, brainchild of the late Colin Harvey, of which Jo was Chair and Roz held various roles on the concom. Both writers and editors in their own right, they first collaborated on *Colinthology*, a memorial anthology for Colin. They now collaborate regularly on wrangling chickens and digging the vegetable beds on their smallholding in South Wales, with their housemate Heather, Jo's partner Chris, and a motley collection of dogs and paperbacks. You can follow their blog on forest gardening and regenerative living at meddwlcoed.wordpress.com.